PRAISE FOR *SACRED DUTY*

This important work weaves the story of the prodigal son into the fog of war. A gripping account that will leave you on the edge of your seat.

Mark Joseph
Newsweek Columnist

A.M. Peters, (my father-in-law) has reimagined the prodigal son story in a masterful adventure through the hardships of war, that reminds us that there is always hope in our deepest despair.

Joel Smallbone
For KING & COUNTRY
Writer, Director, Producer

World War II history has long been an interest of mine and is the fascinating backdrop of *Sacred Duty*. As a film producer, I appreciated A.M. Peters' cinematic storytelling, in-depth character development, and skillful resolution.

Josh Walsh
Producer, Unsung Hero and Jesus Revolution

A theme of *Sacred Duty* by A.M. Peters is the Latin phrase 'Alea iacta est' that literally means "the die is cast (thrown)"…you have made your move and things are now out of your hands. However, *Sacred Duty* demonstrates that even when the 'die is cast' God is able to bring hope, forgiveness, and redemption.

Helen Smallbone
Author of Behind the Lights and
co-founder of MUMlife Community

Alea iacta est. A taut, military thriller set during World War II, A.M. Peters' *Sacred Duty* asks to whom does a soldier ultimately owe allegiance—country, friends, family, or self? Peters creates rich, visual imagery with his prose, keeping readers engaged and entranced. "The die is cast," indeed.

Thomas D. Parham, III, Ph.D.
Palm Beach Atlantic University Professor of Visual and Media Arts
Author, Hailing Frequencies Open and Screenwriter, JAG

A.M. Peters covers all corners in *Sacred Duty*, from the tragic moral dilemmas of war and the unrelenting pang of guilt to an impossible love story that helps us believe there is still light in the darkest of days.

Louis D'Amato
New York-based Photographer

A.M. Peters writes from the hardships and grit of a vast judicial career eloquently exploring the tension between duty and honor, guilt and grace in a story that is simultaneously riveting and freeing.

Jamie George
Executive Coach, Author and
Co-host of The Thrivalist Podcast

A.M. Peters draws on thirty years of experience in the criminal justice system, and its daily brokenness, heartaches, and hopelessness in recasting an ancient story of hope in a way that feels fresh and relevant for today. From the unrepentant death row inmate to the anesthetized German war hero this story draws us to an inevitable conclusion-no one is beyond redemption.

Kerry Hasenbalg
Author, Counselor and
CEO of the BECOMING Foundation, Inc.

Sacred Duty asks a soldier the age-old question-what is truth? His answer is a suspenseful journey I couldn't put down.

Tom Simes
Writer & Director

A.M. Peters draws on 30 years of working with the hopeless to craft a story that is more than a war story; it is a life story that knocks you down and then lifts you up stronger than before.

Bianca Castillo Peters
FOX News, New York City, News Anchor

My father raised us with storytelling. Now, the lucky souls who open these pages get to finally experience the same magic of teleporting to another world through his words and characters.

MORIAH
Singer, Songwriter, Producer, Actress

In this dramatic story of war, A.M. Peters artfully shows the haunting reality of deciding between good and evil, the lifelong consequences that follow and the hope that remains even for the most broken of us.

Geoffrey Furman
Marine Corps Sergeant, Presidential Security Helicopter Transport (retd.)

Sacred Duty is an internal odyssey of overcoming the oppression of guilt, while juxtaposed with the discovery and meaning of hope and redemption.

Jordan Calloway
Actor & Producer
Black Lightning, Riverdale, & Countdown

Sacred Duty is a life changing sermon you don't see coming and never know you're getting especially for the unchurched.

Yvette Farley
Educator, Administrator (retd.)

SACRED DUTY

THE BATTLE FOR TRUTH

A.M. PETERS

FIRST EDITION

Cover Art by Michael Hari
Dust Jacket Design by Virginia Mathers
Interior Layout by Michael J. Williams

ISBN 9798987269398

The duty of a soldier is to act heroically, within the
bounds of war, doing what one would otherwise never do.
Then there is a Sacred Duty, doing what exceeds every
bound and reason…to inhale the taintless air of Eden.

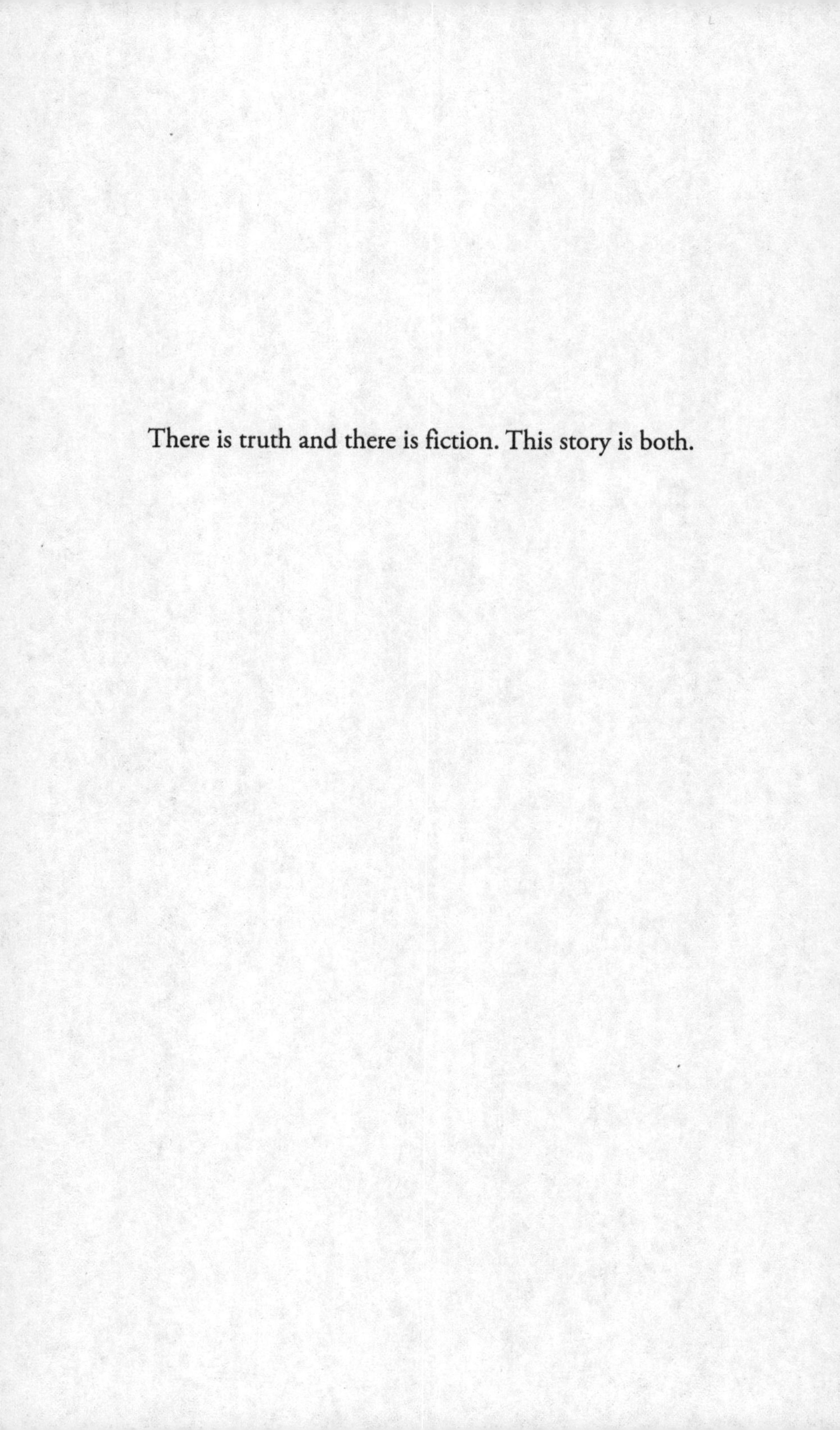

There is truth and there is fiction. This story is both.

To my family
"No one writes alone."

PROLOGUE

Remember those in prison, as if you were
there yourself. –Hebrews 13:3

Texas Correctional Institutions Division,
Mountain View Unit
Gatesville, Texas – Summer of 1977

They say hell hath no fury like a woman scorned. That may be true, but what do they say about a woman of whom hell itself has taken hold and drained of every ounce of humanity? What do they say about a woman made in the burning, sulphuric dens of demons? They say such women are monsters, that they do not deserve to live. That's what they said of Lisa Means—"they" being the Texas Judicial system.

This is her story—and then it isn't. Like all stories, there is what appears at the slippery, slimy surface and then what is just below the mud. Because below the mud is another story, a man's story, from another country, from a different time. But in the end, it is the universal story of humanity. For we are all called to choose between right and wrong.

★ ★ ★

Fifty-five-year-old Peter Engle, a towering six-foot-three and graying at his temples, with a strong handsome face chiseled by pain, and then good fortune, and then by even greater pain, stepped into "the box." This death row visitation module consisted of a line of 3x3 cubicles, each separated by thick security glass. Once-green plastic phones, now faded to their basecoat black, hung on short, coiled one-foot lines. The guard on the free side watched Peter with the kind of curiosity reserved for alien sightings. On the prisoner side, two robust female guards stood shoulder-to-shoulder inspecting the man with similar fascination.

Twenty years. Lisa Means had been in the system for twenty years and never had a visitor. Most of her time served was for a robbery-murder she committed when she was eighteen. But the death sentence came later when her cellmate discovered Lisa had done worse. She would have kept Lisa's secret, but when Lisa shanked her in her sleep over a piece of bread, she was happy to rat her out.

Her execution looming, Lisa believed this visit must be the final visit from her lawyer—the routine farewell—very routine, doing the absolute minimum, her lawyer hating his association with Texas' worst female criminal. A pro forma good luck with eternity spiel.

The prisoner door was unlocked with a big brass key. As the door opened, Lisa shuffled in, her ankles chained and her wrists cuffed tightly at her belly. She looked nothing like Peter had expected. At forty-two, she was an unassuming figure—standing at five-foot-three with brown, shoulder-length hair streaked with thick gray strands and sallow skin framing her brown eyes. No scars or missing teeth—just someone you'd pass on the street without a second glance.

The guards grabbed her slender biceps, steering her roughly to a seat. Peter studied their eyes, recognizing the shared realization:

she was a monster. Not the fictional kind from tales like Mordor, but an actual, flesh-and-bone creature capable of unspeakable acts, deserving of a fate worse than execution. They thrust her into the chair, turned her to face Peter, released one handcuff, and secured the other to a metal pipe that extended along the row of bare desks.

His eyes crinkled a hello.

Her eyes appeared lifeless, except for the tiny pinpricks of hatred that pierced Peter's.

"My name is Peter Engle." He steeled his warm smile, refusing to cower. "And you must be Lisa."

She leaned forward as far as the line would allow, unleashing twenty years of the silence that burned in her belly. Her words were calm yet carried an underlying rage, punctuated by tight breaths resembling an angry bull ready to charge. "Don't you call me by my given name. I ain't her. Ain't been her for twenty years. So, whoever ya are…ya just call me…prisoner."

He nodded. "Whatever you wish."

She snickered with a soft disdain, likening him as some kind of eager mortician eyeing his goods before they qualified. She looked over her shoulder at the guards who stood three feet behind her, listening—one wide-eyed with curiosity, the other squinting in impatience. She looked back at Peter and pressed closer. "You're not from the lawyer?"

Peter shook his head no.

"I knew you was here before they brought me in. I felt ya. I know things, feel things no one else can." She shook her head and muttered something away from the phone. Then she brought the receiver close to her lips. "But I don't know everything. Don't know why…don't know why. Whatcha want, Mr. Peter Engle?"

"I would like to tell you a story, Ms. Means."

She pulled the phone from her ear and started to hang up.

Peter shot his hand up. "Wait. I'm sorry…prisoner. Ms. Prisoner."

"Just prisoner."

He nodded again.

She returned the phone to her ear. "So you got a story? Twenty years and…I ain't had no visitors…lawyer came once, and now… two weeks before they…shoot me up, I get some…" She inspected him from the top of his head to his meaty hand cradling the phone. "…some old man and a…story?" She leaned back in her chair, straining the foot-long cord, and a tiny curve made the corner of her lips. "How old are ya?"

"Fifty-five."

"Got a woman?"

"Had."

"I think you some kinda freak." She leaned forward and spoke just above a whisper. "I know freaks." She sat back and smiled like a child, innocent and hopeful. "What kinda story ya got, mister?"

"It's my story."

"Your story?"

"I tell it everywhere I go, and I've been to many places."

She shrugged her shoulders and shook her head disapprovingly. "Don't know…don't look like ya got much of a story to tell."

"We all have a good story to tell."

She snickered and nodded. "Mine is…they think they know… they don't."

She folded her hands like in prayer, a tease to match her malevolent smile. "Go ahead. Before it's curtains for me. Go ahead, Mr. Peter Engle." She waved her hand at him. "Just go ahead."

Peter closed his eyes and returned to his past, to a time and place Lisa Means could never know. To his story. To what was beneath the mud. To their story.

38 years earlier…

WAR'S ENDURING PRESENCE

Ostbrandenburg, Germany
1938 – Twenty Years After World War I

Peter Engle walked into the barn to begin his chores and found his father sitting in a dark corner on a milking stool. His eyes darted away with concern over the melancholy he often saw in him.

Max swiveled on his stool to face him, his look blank and distant.

"Are you okay, Father?"

Max studied his son's face for a moment, taking in his concern. A smile appeared, wiping away some of the sadness from his eyes. "I'm fine, son…just fine."

Peter attempted a faint smile in response, then recognized the sadness that haunted his father, when he remembered the Great War. The auspicious black patch over his father's missing right eye forever captured the horrible memories.

Peter hid his sigh with his hand; the words in his father's head so loud he could feel the condemnation of hundreds of young soldiers unearthing themselves. *You took away our best years. You showed no mercy. Widowmaker. Killer. You are damned forever.*

Max stood and dusted off his pants. Despite his deep bouts of anguish and guilt, Pastor Max Engle, the Great War hero, still found joy in serving his congregants. Everyone had a story of Max's kindness and sacrifice. Peter was a witness to a boundless commitment that sought to oppose the perpetual war in Max's mind—the hungry were fed, the despised and rejected befriended, and the few who wanted nothing to do with God were loved without condition.

Peter wanted to be like his father in every possible way. And while other Germans were bitter over the shattered promises of the Great War, his father had a better message emanating from deep within his soul—one greater than the ravages of discontent that animated the Nazis and the new German ethos.

"Are you sure you're okay, Father?" Peter asked hesitantly.

"I can't hide it from you, can I?"

"You don't need to."

Max shook his head darkly. "If only I could not see their faces or hear their charges."

Peter put his hand on his father's shoulder and spoke with a rasp tinged with pride. "It was war, Father. You had no choice."

"We all have a choice."

Peter nodded hesitantly knowing his words would fail again. "It was many years ago. What you have chosen since…no one deserves God's forgiveness more than you."

One corner of Max's mouth turned up in a broken smile. He pulled him into a deep embrace. "I have you. What more do I need to know that I am forgiven?"

Peter playfully shoved his elbow into his father's ribs and pulled away. "Let me do all the chores. Please. Go work on your sermon." He picked up a broken stack of hay and tossed it into a trough. He handled a second with similar ease.

Max watched in wonder. Peter was only seventeen and already the strongest man in the village. Peter was six-foot-two and growing. He was gifted with a rugged handsomeness, the desire of every young woman in the village. But it mattered nothing to him. His heart was still in America, with a Texas farm girl named Julia. He cared for little more.

"I am sorry about your letters to Julia," said Max. "The Nazis think they can control everything. But they cannot control the truth. She knows you love her, and when this stupidity ends, you'll see her again."

"Yes…yes. But please, Father. Go work on your sermon. Your congregation, including me, needs to be emboldened to resist them."

He nodded in agreement.

"And your friend, Martin. Will he be there?"

"You know Martin…maybe, maybe not."

★ ★ ★

Texas Correctional Institutions Division,
Mountain View Unit
Gatesville, Texas – Summer of 1977

Lisa pulled the phone from her ear and let it dangle in her hand like she was about to drop it and walk away. She looked past Peter at a wall clock. She touched the phone back to her ear. "Ya kiddin' right? Ya wanna tell me a story about krauts in Germany, about stupid farmers, church people, stuff before I was even born? Out of all the stories I could get before they snuff me out…" She shook her head.

"Dear Prisoner, I don't believe you have a nail appointment scheduled today."

"Oh, so the old man's funny, huh?" Her eyes tightened, searching him, wondering who he was, what he wanted. She'd get her answers. "Who are ya, Mister?"

"Like I said, just one with a story."

She pulled a strand of her hair and twisted it in her fingers. "Feel like I know ya…like I been close to ya. In my spirit…feelin' it. Ever been at Fanny's on 9th, in Prairie View, second floor? Did a lot of business there."

He shook his head slowly.

"Well, go ahead. But hurry up and get to something I might like." She shot him an evil smile.

"Get to the killin' part, huh. Ya got killin' parts…in that story of yours?"

His face was blank, unaffected by her wickedness. He picked back up where he left off.

ALEA IACTA EST— THE DIE IS CAST

Ostbrandenburg, Germany, 1938

Martin kissed her passionately, too passionately. She pulled his strong frame closer, locked in his passion wanting to stay there forever. But she knew it was too much. She would lose control again. She peeled herself away and set her palms against his strong chest. "No, Martin."

"I'm sorry, Elise," he said. "When I kiss you…really, when I'm just near you, I can't control myself. I don't know what to do."

She looked at him with an ease in her eyes. His words were intoxicating to her. He was tall and handsome, with deep, dark eyes that hid something mysterious that she both desired and feared. His hair matched his eyes, lurid, always falling across his face like a mask. And his voice was deep and rugged, delivered with confident pauses so as to maximize the impact and allure of each word.

Elise was in love with him, but that was not enough. She looked away and hesitated with what she knew must be said. "There's something I need to tell you." Tears filled her eyes.

Martin touched her chin gently. "What is it, Elise? Is it bad?"

She nodded affirmatively as thick tears broke from her eyes, like clear marbles rolling down her cheeks.

"You're leaving?" Martin removed his hand from her face and stepped back in disbelief. "But you said they'd let you stay."

"It's become too dangerous. My father is certain war is coming. Belgium is safer, he says."

Martin interlaced his fingers tightly on top of his head like he was keeping his emotions from exploding through. "But you can't go. I…I love you." He embraced her again and held her tightly. He stroked her hair and kissed her again once on her lips with a sadness that cooled all his passion.

She unpeeled her face from his chest and looked up at him like he was her hiding tower.

"You can come too, Martin. You can start a new life there."

"Who will I stay with? I can't stay with you. Your family hates me."

"They don't hate you, Martin. They just don't understand you… like I do."

Martin dropped his embrace and his hands balled into stone, his eyes shooting at the ground with an acrimony he did not want her to see. "I know hate Elise. I know it well." He sighed long and deeply against the part of him he never wanted her to know. He freed his eyes so he could gaze at the only face that had ever tamed his rage. "I can't come with you," he said hoarsely and without a trace of doubt.

He held her and kissed her again with an unrestrained passion that knew its brevity. His hands pulled her tightly against his chest so that she could hardly breathe, and their emotions escaped in heavy moaning that would soon take them across to the forbidden point they had passed the night before.

***

Martin smelled his familiar alcohol-drenched breath before he heard his hateful spits and slurs, like the buzz of a bee before it stings.

He gently released Elise but would not turn around to see his father.

Elise scurried away, frightened by the man's presence.

He watched her leave with disapproving eyes, then quickly turned around to face his son. He felt his unsteady legs struggle under his whiskey-filled body. He spoke in his characteristic gravel. Disgust like vomit in his throat. "You make me sick. You're just like your mother. A whore, a selfish whore."

Martin kept his wide back against him hoping he'd walk away.

"Martin!" he yelled. "I'm talking to you."

Martin dropped his view to his feet doing all he could to restrain himself. "Yes, you are. But I'm not listening anymore. I'm finished listening to you."

"Turn around and face me now," he commanded as he grabbed his son, pulling hard against his shoulder until Martin willingly turned to face him.

Martin's hands exploded from his sides in concrete fists.

His father's eyes widened in disbelief. He stepped closer and raised his hand. "You dare defy me." His hand came down and across Martin's face.

Martin took the blows, repeatedly, until the man tired. "You bastard. I should've left you when your whore mother left," he said with a final strike to his face that dropped him to the ground in drunken exhaustion.

He lay there, too drunk to get up, still mumbling angrily, weakly fading into unconsciousness.

Martin looked down at him—his only family, all he had ever known—wanting to stomp on his neck, to put the miserable man to death, and to finally end his own suffering. He listened to his whispers, lined with the dirt he lay in. "I hate you. I hate you."

He sighed against a cry that he would never give life to. He stooped down, picked him off the ground, and hefted him over his shoulder like a sack of grain.

He laid him in his bed and covered him.

It was noon.

★ ★ ★

Later that evening Peter walked to Martin's home at the edge of the village. He carried a bundle of butchered deer meat on his shoulder. Martin's house was nothing like his. It was a similar structure—a simple little house made from ancient river rocks built one hundred years before. But the door and window frames hadn't been painted in as many years. Unlike Peter's home, there were no flowers, no garden, just numerous, untidy stacks of chopped wood all around the front of the house.

He made his way past a row of spruce trees that lined the village graveyard, then a hundred paces south he cut through the overgrown hibiscus shrubs that covered a small, fractured stone fence that abutted Martin's house. He was about to knock on the door when he heard an angry groan and a crushing chop from behind the house.

★ ★ ★

Martin raised his long arms high above his head, bringing them down with tremendous force onto the defenseless wood chunks and splitting the logs into splintered pieces that flew around him. He took one more decisive whack, then set down his ax and pulled his shirt on. He turned around and forced a hello with a weak nod.

Peter handed him his portion of the deer meat, which Martin gladly accepted.

Martin shook Peter's hand before grabbing his ax again to split another log.

"Are you going to tell me?" Peter asked.

"Nothing. There's nothing to tell."

"Well, you're supposed to cut the logs in half, not pulverize them to dust."

Martin forced a grin and sat down next to his best friend.

Peter looked closer and could see his lip quiver. "I know. Your father again? How many times have I offered? Come live with us away from him," Peter said as he gestured with the swing of his chin toward the front door of the house.

Martin studied him for a moment, a smile wiping away the puffy sadness around his eyes.

"You still don't understand. Here, there, all I am to him is a reminder of what my mother did. I don't know why he kept me." He shook his head. "Maybe just to torment me."

Peter's anger gave way to compassion. He felt his eyes well up with tears. "I'm sorry, Martin."

"It's worse than that."

"What can be worse?"

"Elise is leaving…to Belgium."

Peter's eyebrows raised in curiosity. "You like her, but you barely know her. It's only been a couple of months, Martin."

Martin shook his head in disagreement. "I love her, Peter."

Peter's brows furrowed in surprise. "Love, Martin? You hardly know her."

Martin's quiver left as his lip tightened in anger. "How do you know I don't love her? Who says?" He shot a challenging look into Peter's eyes. "Just like you said with Julia. You said you knew right away." He stood to his feet and grabbed his ax. "Got things to do."

Peter stood and stepped closer. "So, what will you do?"

"She leaves in two days. I've thought of everything. I'll join the *Wehrmacht*—that's always been my plan anyway—and then I'll find her in Belgium…and…" He looked at Peter searching for reassurance. "…and I'll marry her."

"That's what she wants?"

"I haven't told her."

Peter sat down again quietly hoping for wisdom that would dissuade Martin from making what he saw as his biggest mistake. But nothing came. Martin had never said such things. And who was he to doubt his feelings for Elise? Many had doubted his love for Julia. He would not do the same. He stood to his feet again and faced him directly. "Okay, Martin." He put his hands on his shoulders. "You're my best friend. I'm with you...always with you."

Martin threw down his ax and grabbed Peter's hand with an elation that instantly crushed his sadness. "You'll join me then?"

Peter pulled his hand away. "I have to go. Come by tomorrow."

★ ★ ★

Later that evening Martin lay in his bed thinking about what he would say to Elise. And it was time to tell her parents. They would understand. He was a good man, a strong man, and he would be a brave soldier they would all be proud of. His eyes were peeled back with all the excitement tomorrow would bring. He forced them shut and tried to exhale all the elation that filled his heart. Tomorrow would be the greatest day of his life.

But while he set his heart to dream of Elise, she boarded a train with her family to Belgium. No note. No goodbye.

★ ★ ★

Months passed since Elise's abrupt departure. Peter tried his best to spend as much time as he could with Martin before he left for battle. They sat in the barn drinking a bottle of *Wickuhler*. "To the *Wehrmacht*," Martin toasted. They drank their beer and let their minds wander. "What will it be like, Peter? We'll find adventure...see the world. We'll be the greatest soldiers Germany's ever known."

26

Max walked in with a plate of bread and butter. "To the strongest boys in the village, perhaps in all of Germany." He laid down the plate and fought the pride in his smile. He put his arm around Peter's shoulder. "I am a proud father." He stepped toward Martin and put his arm around him. "And a proud pastor."

Martin felt the bolts of his steely disposition turning, loosening. How he wished he had this from his father. It had never been, and he knew it would never be. And that reality, just an elephant's tail, crushed the enormity of love he knew Pastor Engle had for him. He felt Max's hug now as nothing but a reminder of what he would always be denied. He tightened his shoulder prompting Max's release.

"You boys enjoy. I'd love to sit and talk, but I have a certain beauty holding a dance for me." He shot them a playful wink and left.

Peter studied his friend, as he always did. It was hard for Martin to accept love. Perhaps Elise had found a way. But he doubted it. He even wondered at times if their friendship was as close as he believed. He loved him like his own brother, but he had the advantage of love from those that mattered most. Martin did not. Peter lost himself in his thoughts. *What will the war do to us, Martin? What will it do to you?*

"Peter, Peter…"

Peter rattled his head of his thoughts. "What? I'm sorry, what?"

"This is important, Peter. Pay attention."

"Sorry. What were you saying?"

Martin shook his head in disappointment. "You and I are going to be great soldiers, Peter. The greatest."

"Martin, you know I can't go."

"You have no excuse. You can't get to America, to Julia. Whether you join or not, you still can't get to her."

Peter's eyes painted around his friend coloring the barn walls with a searching pause. "Alea Iacta Est."

"What?"

"Something my father told me once. Something great Roman soldiers understood. It means, 'the die is cast.' You can't take back what's already meant to be. No need to worry over what we might be or do. It's been decided. You'll be a soldier. I won't. That's it. The die's already been cast."

Martin looked down at his bottle and spoke sadly, nodding affirmatively. "I know. Your father, the great agitator, the great pacifist would have it no other way."

Peter looked away, not trusting his voice. He waited until he felt his face relax away his tension. "I'm my own man. I'll do what I'm called to do, when I'm called to do it. My father has nothing to do with it…it just is."

Martin took another swig. "Yes, but your father's a great man, maybe the greatest I've ever known." He placed his beer on the ground and shot him a critical eye. "Loyalty…I admire that in you. If he was my father, I'd do the same."

Peter swiveled his half empty beer between his legs looking at the amber swirl in contemplation. He took a long drink, nearly emptying it. "It just is, Martin," he said again, but with a certitude as empty as the bottle in his hand.

"I wish it was different. How can I be a good soldier without you? You're my brother. I fall, you pick me up. You fall, I pick you up."

"You'll be a great soldier. I know you, brother. You'll be Germany's greatest soldier." He raised his bottle in a toast.

Martin raised his bottle to meet Peter's toast and forced a half smile.

"And your father will be proud of you."

Martin's gaze fell to the floor. He took another swig then chuckled sardonically. "Maybe… if I was the greatest soldier Germany has ever known, with lots of shiny medals on my chest.

Maybe if the Fuhrer himself ordered my father to be proud of me," he said teasingly.

Peter stood, his chest pushed out, his lips tight. "You will be. And we will all be proud of you."

Martin stood and placed his hand on Peter's shoulder. "You always have too much hope," he said through a contemptuous smile.

Martin's words troubled Peter. He tried to encourage him, but now, for the first time, he could see that perhaps he was right. Perhaps there was too much distance between their hearts—his beating with a shiny optimism, Martin's shrouded with too much despair. He tried again, desperate to keep his friend close. "Things will change. I believe it deep in my soul, brother. The die is cast for a better tomorrow."

Martin finished his beer and laid it down on a haystack. He shook his head slowly. "Keep all the hope for yourself, Peter. Doesn't work for me." He forced a smile. "Better to be surprised by good fortune."

Peter drilled his eyes into Martin's and grabbed his shoulders. "Friendship…how about our friendship? I'll be your friend until the day I die. Nothing can change that."

Martin nodded slowly and stepped back out of his grip. Peter took one last look into his eyes knowing his words failed to penetrate Martin's defenses. He let out a deep sigh and walked out of the barn.

Martin watched him leave then picked up his empty bottle in a useless toast. He shook his head with a sad certainty whispering to himself, "Alea Iacta Est."

★ ★ ★

Ostbrandenburg First Congregational Church was a little church set a quarter kilometer from the river Spree, near the

German-Polish border, only one kilometer from Peter's farm. It was an old church built a hundred years earlier. It was small, seating no more than fifty congregants. It had large, thin-paned windows that drew in the natural sunlight, and two entry doors that swung out, often left open whenever Max was there, weather permitting. And he was almost always there, either preaching or sitting quietly, listening, always listening to the cries and fears of his congregants. And lately those fears filled the hearts of many. They knew he had been warned. Some began to stay away. The Gestapo was everywhere, even in little villages like Ostbranden-burg. They noted who attended the insurrectionist's sermons, as they called them. Yet many stayed, convinced he was on the side of God, and they were willing to suffer the consequences.

It was Sunday morning, and the pews were half-filled. Max led his congregation in a hymn by the great reformer Martin Luther. Max loved all of Luther's hymns. When concluded, he smiled broadly and asked them to sit.

In the front row sat Peter and his mother. They looked upon Max with the greatest respect and admiration knowing his sermon would bring them comfort and strength.

Three strangers entered the church, each wearing dark suits, long coats and hats—the thin disguise of infiltrators who wanted their identities and disruptive purpose clearly known. They removed their hats in hollow respect to the institution, their eyes set on Max in a languid, disdainful stare.

Max quickly painted his eyes over his congregation, then fixed on the strangers. The older one gave him a weak nod that he did not return. It wasn't the first time the Gestapo paid him a visit.

He looked down at his notes and breathed in deeply. He prayed silently and then lifted his eyes slowly taking in all the faces of those who still found that there was truth in their pastor's words—and believed that truth was worth dying for.

"Jesus standing before Pilate said the following, 'I am king. For this reason I was born, and for this I came into the world, to testify to the truth. Everyone on the side of truth listens to me.'

And Pilate responded, as many have throughout the ages, as men do today…" He stared at the men seated in the rear with an intensity that made them angry. "'What is truth?' What is truth? It was Pilate's way of saying there was no truth. Each man does what he believes is right in his own heart, never submitted to a greater authority, the ultimate authority that exists in God."

He closed his Bible and pounded his fist on his lectern. "And these are the kinds of men that do the most terrible things. Their thoughts, their hateful ideas, unbridled…these men will kill and destroy without hesitation…they will destroy entire nations and peoples under a banner of pride that is straight from the devil himself." He paused, taking in a deep breath, exhaling his anger. He tried to speak calmly, softly. "I will not shut my mouth. I know the truth, and I alone am ready to suffer the consequences."

The men in the back stood to their feet, each one filing out of the pew with threatening stares that told Max that the volley of intentions was over.

When he finished his sermon, he prayed and walked to the back of the church to say goodbye and give his blessings. When all the congregants had gone, he walked back in and closed the church door.

Peter remained outside talking with friends. As he walked back to the entry doors, one of the Gestapo men, the taller one with graying hair, called him. "You are his son?"

Peter nodded.

"Please ask the good Pastor to come outside. We'd like to speak to him."

Peter approached them without fear and nodded a hello. "You're the fifth group sent. How many will they send? You know my father by now. He's not going to change what he says."

The man smiled with a kind crinkle in his eyes that surprised Peter. "I understand. Your father is dogmatic about his beliefs, his pacifism."

"He has seen enough bloodshed."

"He was one of our greatest heroes in the first war. He still has much influence. It could be wielded for good."

"What he says, what he has always said, is for the good."

"He is a pacifist. He objects to us taking up arms even to defend ourselves. Is that what you believe?"

"I am not the one with the influence."

"I understand," he said warmly. "Then please give him this." He handed him a letter. Peter noticed it came from Minister Miller, the Minister of Religion. "Please tell him to read the letter. Minister Miller can do nothing else to protect him."

The man shook Peter's hand, tipped his hat, and walked away.

* * *

Three weeks later, Martin boarded a train for Berlin. Peter and Max were there to see him off. They waved goodbye with a dis-ingenuous enthusiasm.

Martin took a window seat, searching the platform beyond them but saw no one else. His mind pretended to say goodbye to a crying Elise, and to a proud father. His jaw tightened, and as the train left the station, he drilled his eyes shut and whispered to himself, "Alea Iacta Est."

As the train picked up speed and left his village behind, Martin opened his eyes and saw his hard, confident stare reflected in the window that belied the tear etching his face like a long, deep cut that leaves a permanent scar.

He wiped his sadness away feigning strength behind his up-turned collar.

★ ★ ★

Peter sat next to his father on a small, horse-pulled wagon. He could still see a faint plume of steam that trailed from the escaping train carrying his friend.

Max held the reins in his hands loosely. He strained to his right to see his son with his good left eye, wanting to give him assurances, but nothing came.

Peter's eyes filled with tears. "He has no one now." He tightened his trembling lip. "God seems cruel sometimes."

Max sat quietly, resisting the urge to give understanding as he had done all Peter's life. Ever since Peter had returned from America, Max sensed a growing resistance in his spirit that chilled his words.

"Do you think my calling has always been to love and protect Martin?"

Max pulled on the reins stopping the horse in her tracks. His spirit unrestrained, he looked straight ahead forcing a pleasant smile. "You've been a brother to him. A great brother." He sighed, then looked at Peter directly. "Never give up on anyone, son. But know that many will disappoint you. Some will break your heart terribly."

"Is he my calling?"

"You mean, should you follow him?"

Peter looked away not wanting to see disappointment in his father's face. "Father, I know who sent the letter. There are no more reprieves, only consequences."

"Yes." He paused, fighting the army of tears sieging his resistance. His head sunk under the heft of his sadness. "I killed many men. Their faces haunt me daily." A tear fell from his eye.

"I would do anything. I'd give my life gladly to take back all I've done, but I can't. All I can do is speak the truth…I know it doesn't erase what I've done, but maybe it will change what others do." He put his hand on Peter's shoulder. "I'm just a man, son…a very flawed man at best. You…you must find your way and do whatever God calls you to do. Not man, not even me." He lifted the reins. "And I must do what I am called to do." He snapped them hard against the horse's rear.

Peter heard his father's words stirring in his mind. *Find my way.* He had never doubted his father's position, but he had never chosen it.

It was time to choose.

★ ★ ★

Peter's mother hurried herself cleaning the kitchen as a popular American song spilled from the family phonograph. She sang to herself, her thick German accent smothering the lyrics, "I got rhythm, I've got music, I've got my man, who can ask for anything more."

Peter walked into the kitchen and watched in wonder. He clapped his hands and startled her.

She turned and faced him, laughing in embarrassment. She grabbed his hands and pressed them around her waist. "I've got rhythm….come on Peter… I've got music."

He moved awkwardly, side-to-side trying to keep step but failing. He didn't care. He just loved being near her. She was the most exuberant woman he had ever known. He had never seen her downcast, hopeless, or troubled. When Father's depression overcame him, she held him, sometimes for days, covering him with songs of hope. She was his best medicine. And her laugh was big and boisterous. She was tall and strong. She had flawless, smooth skin and rosy, high cheekbones that cupped her deep green sparkling eyes. Her hair was like the color of weathered hay, light brown with whisks of bright blonde. She worked the farm with Father and Peter; she made the meals, and lovingly embraced the role of pastor's wife. All the women in their village and beyond sought her advice and comfort. She was a perfect woman, a constant reminder of Julia for Peter.

Father walked in with a gentlemanly bow pleading for his turn.

Peter relented and watched. They were the best people he knew, and theirs was the most wonderful love he had ever seen. They danced cheek-to-cheek like young lovers oblivious to their son's watchful eyes.

Mother's eyes widened. "The Gaisburger!" She leapt toward the stove moving the pot from the fire. She fanned herself with a towel and smiled. "No problem."

"Shall we continue?" asked Father, his hand outstretched for hers.

"You still enjoy dancing with me after all these years?"

"More than ever." He pulled her close and kissed her neck. "You have taught me well my dear."

She giggled like a schoolgirl. "Father, please, Peter is here."

Father smiled with a sly grin and winked at his son.

Peter smiled and his lips stretched wide across his face as he thought of their love. Someday he would dance with Julia. Someday he would have a son, a son as fortunate as he. Someday…

* * *

When the dancing and dinner ended, Peter excused himself to do what he did every night. After an hour, he found the words to end another letter:

> *So my dearest, Julia. As long as I breathe, I love.*
> *And all my love is yours. I'm already making ar-*
> *rangements to come to you. No one else knows. No*

one can. And even though you can't receive this letter, my faith says you know my heart, even the very words I write, for my spirit is with you. I can feel it. Take care, my dearest Julia. I close my eyes and kiss you a hundred times. Each kiss as precious as the first that set our lives together forever. Take care, my dearest Julia.

His mother entered and reached over his broad shoulders, embracing him. "I have something for you." She stepped back and presented a small box.

He placed the box on his desk next to his letter to Julia.

"Open it."

"Now?"

She nodded encouragingly.

Peter opened the box and found a bright purple scarf made of a material he'd never felt.

Mother took it from his hands and tied it around his neck. "It was made by a Jewish woman I know. Like that of the kingly priests of old."

"It's beautiful, Mother. But I don't see much use for it, here on the farm."

She cradled his face in her hands. "You're always in a hurry to know. You'll know. You'll see." She kissed him on the cheek and said goodnight.

He returned to Julia's letter, signing it, and folding it gently in half, laying it on a stack of a hundred or more already neatly set on the corner of his desk.

"Someday, my love," he whispered. "Someday…I'll come to you."

★ ★ ★

Schumannsville, Texas

In the Blackland Prairie, a sprawling 17,600 square miles of Southeast Texas, sits Guadalupe County named after the Guadalupe River that runs through it. The river fed a farming town called Schumannsville established by German immigrants in 1848, named after its founder August Wilhelm Schumann who immigrated from Kothen, West Prussia, with his wife and eight children.

Julia was a descendant of Shumann's, like many in her town. Tonight, she ran her fingertips across Peter's last letter. It was nearly a year old. She sat on her bed looking out the window at the endless rows of corn that stemmed from her humble farmhouse. She closed her eyes mouthing the embodied words of his letter that had become like Peter's spirit, present and palpable. She held the letter against her bosom and cried. It had been too long. She wrote every day, with no response. She wondered if he was even alive. Even worse, if that were possible, what if Peter's love was merely a juvenile infatuation, something never really rooted in the earth that bound her heart?

She removed a cypress ring he made for her and placed it on her nightstand. She walked over to close the window and returned to her bed letting her weakening body fall into its soft embrace and pretending he held her once again. But she was not very good at imagining. She trusted wholeheartedly in her unseen God, but everything else was or wasn't. And right now, it seemed that their love wasn't. She cried for hours, then rolled over on her bed and saw a thin ray of moonlight crawl across her bed onto her nightstand illuminating her cypress ring. She closed her eyes softly and remembered the serendipitous meeting of their lips, the pure exchange of their breath, the origin of their love. She picked up the ring knowing it represented a hope that was stronger than all the stifling uncertainty.

She slipped the ring back on her finger. "Someday, my love… Someday."

A CHOICE MAKES A CHOICE

Evil is not in the business of creating but destroying. When it does…it begets more evil.

A mile from Peter's farm, a German sergeant inspected his men quickly as he fastened the collar of a Polish uniform around his thick neck. His pock-marked face and full mustache made the sergeant a standout from his bare-faced, youthful men.

They struggled to put on the uniforms of Polish soldiers killed minutes before. The uniforms were cut from a harsh wool that scratched their skin and were still wet with Polish blood. The sergeant ordered them brusquely. "Ready yourselves. Today you will be the pride of Germany."

His men stood with their chests out, arms stiff at their sides beaming with eagerness to do his bidding.

The sun would rise in an hour.

★ ★ ★

Max forced the ax head down splitting a chunk of wood in two. Peter milked a cow nearby. Mother kneeled in prayer beside her bed. She squeezed her interlaced fingers tightly in response to an ominous chill spreading through her body. She stopped

38

suddenly and opened her eyes wide with concern. "Dear Lord… dear Lord," she whispered.

★ ★ ★

The soldiers cut through the woods toward the farm, the sergeant atop his gallant, black horse, directing them with crisp hand gestures.

Some went around the south end of the farm and the others went north toward the rear door that led to the Engle kitchen.

Max saw them first. When the soldiers parted north and south, they revealed the sergeant upon his black horse, his eyes fixed angrily on Max. "Mercy. Mercy, dear Lord," mouthed Max. He dropped his ax and yelled, "Peter…your mother…go to your mother."

Peter had never heard an urgency in his father's voice. He jumped from behind the cow and ran out of the barn.

"Hurry, Peter," commanded Max as Peter paused by him unaware of their approach.

But the soldiers—incognito, brusque, hungry to finally be soldiers—met Peter at the back door, their rifles pointing him away. As instructed, they yelled in Polish, "Back, back to the barn."

Peter stepped backwards toward the barn, then stopped suddenly. *Mother.* He charged back toward the house and was met with the butt of a rifle that drove a deep gash into the side of his head.

"Peter, no! Do as they say. It will be alright," yelled Max.

Three more encircled Peter, their rifles fixed on his head. He rose from the ground, his hand pressing tightly against his wound, blood trickling from between his fingers. He staggered toward the barn until he found himself on his knees, his hands tied behind his back like his father.

The sergeant looked down upon them, his head tilted, judgmentally speaking in perfect Polish. "You are the great German war hero, Max Engle?" both a question and a condemnation.

His mighty horse's strong legs shifted dangerously close to Max, blowing a wet, angry cloud of air through its nostrils across Max's face. "Even my horse expected more," he said with an evil disdain. His men chuckled in chorus.

He dismounted and stood next to the kneeling pastor. "The great Max Engle, now the pastor who preaches weakness." He shook his head in disgust. He grabbed him by the hair and pulled him up off the ground. "This day, let it be known that Poland strikes first blood." He grabbed Max's face and squeezed it so that he could stare into his eye. "And the coward does nothing," he said gruffly.

This was Minister Miller's plan, the Fuhrer's plan. Those believers across Germany that followed the pacifism preached by Max would now see that war was inevitable. And more than that, war was simply an act of self-defense against a Polish evil that sought to destroy the Deutschland.

Max saw through the ruse. His eyes fell on the crucifix hanging from his captor's neck. He spoke calmly but authoritatively. "You're being used to open the gates of hell. It's not too late. God forgives."

He grabbed Max by the throat. "Forgiveness? I don't need forgiveness. When I'm done here, you'll be begging for forgiveness." He threw him to the ground, ripped his handgun out and pressed it against his temple.

Max caught his breath then turned to meet his executioner's eyes. "I am ready to die. You…my friend. Are you?"

The burly sergeant reeled back and struck his face with the iron butt of his gun. Max fell to the ground, his blood quickly covering his face.

Peter cried out, fighting his impulse to jump to his feet. "No, please. Please. He's done nothing. He's not your enemy. Please."

A gross, hoarse chuckle spewed from the sergeant's throat as he straddled Max. "Ready to die, Great War hero?"

Max forced his aching head in a nod. "I've been ready for a long time…do it."

"Of course…but your end isn't why we're here," said the sergeant. He marched over to Peter and stood over him with his head tilted in a curious inspection. He put his gun against Peter's temple and looked at Max. "This is the end, Engle. A bullet for your son, and then one for your wife."

Max shot up from his knees, his eye straining to see past his blood. "No, wait…please," he begged. "I'm the one you want… no one else. The Minister, the Minister of Religion…he's my friend. Please speak to him."

The sergeant shot Max a sick smile. "You stand to your feet? So you'll fight to defend your family?" He laughed. "Ah good… the Great War hero comes to life. He pulled his gun from Peter's temple and stood upright, confident. "Cut the man loose and give him your handgun," he ordered.

"Sir?" questioned his soldier.

"Do as I say," he barked with an anger that made the soldier snap to it. He placed his gun into Max's free hand.

"Save your son, Engle." He stepped away from Peter with his arms wide open, a clear target. "That's what God would want…isn't that right?" He hissed like the questioning snake before the Fall.

Max raised his head for one last look at Peter. "I love you, Peter. Don't let anything deceive you. I love you." He dropped the gun and shut his eyes in prayer.

Peter nodded slowly, setting his last look on his father as he mouthed a desperate prayer. "I'm not afraid, Father. I made my choice. I'll be waiting for you on the other side."

The brute returned to Peter releasing a short, scornful laugh that splattered into Peter's face. "Just like him? You won't fight?" He beheld his young soldiers with instruction in his eyes. "The old man…at least he fought for his country, but this boy is worse.

He's young and able to fight, but he won't. He won't even lift a finger to defend his own father." He grabbed Peter by the collar and lifted him off the ground. "Am I right? You will not fight?"

Peter looked in his eyes with a burning hate and shook his head.

He shoved Peter's face into his hot, contemptuous words. "And your mother? You won't even defend her, you coward?" He tossed him violently to the ground then motioned to his men with a shot of his chin toward the farmhouse.

Two soldiers ran into the house and within seconds the screaming began. Peter heard his mother's pleas for mercy. He heard her call out to Jesus. He heard the tearing of clothes, the breaking of glass and thuds against her bedroom walls.

The sergeant kicked him in his gut with the point of his boot. But Peter's muscled core reflected the hit with little damage.

His eyes tightened in inspection. "You are strong. You could have been a good soldier. Instead, you're a worthless coward like your father."

Peter begged. "Please, I'll do anything. I'll join. I'll fight for Germany…please don't hurt them."

The sergeant shoved his filthy boot onto Peter's neck, then pulled his handgun from his side. "Cut him loose," he ordered. He stepped back letting Peter kneel again.

Peter's hands were now loose at his side shaking in anger. He heard his mother's screams weakening. "Please, sir, have mercy on her. You can kill me but have mercy on her."

He bent over, now eye-to-eye. "I take great pleasure in killing you. There's no place in this world for weakness like yours. Look at you, free to defend those you love and still…nothing." He stood erect and placed his handgun at Peter's temple and yelled to the men in his mother's room. "Finish her."

Peter looked at his father whose head lay low against his chest in silent prayer. He heard his mother's screams weakening, her body giving way to death. And he looked for a last hope, where he had always looked, and he saw his father, his lips moving silently in surrender. "Father, Father. We can't just…what do I do?"

And he heard nothing but the slow, dull click of the sergeant's trigger pulling next to his temple.

His head lifted to the sky; his eyes widened, all white, his eyeballs rolled back and hidden from his father's moral moorings which, just days before, had become fully his. He screamed like a cornered animal with a sudden power reminiscent of his father's deadly wartime efficiency.

"Nooo…" His hands shot from his side snapping over the sergeant's gun like a steel bear trap. He turned the gun and put a bullet between the evil man's eyes.

The young soldier next to him widened his eyes in fear. Before he could lift his rifle in defense he was already on the ground in a pool of his own blood.

Father's face contorted in a familiar, sick agony. His eye was screwed shut, his mouth agape trying to take in air that escaped him. He knew what men feel when they kill. It was a powerful hate that possessed the mind and body and now it possessed his son. He screamed. "Stop, Peter. Stop!"

Peter pointed the handgun at the next soldier and pulled the trigger. The gun jammed and the soldier threw down his rifle and ran off.

Peter grabbed his rifle and ran into the farmhouse and within seconds several shots were fired.

★ ★ ★

Peter cradled his mother's lifeless body. His eyes fell into a fixed gaze, and though they were her familiar, beautiful eyes, gone was the sparkle that animated her wondrous compassion, joy, love, and life.

Blood spilled from Peter's chest and stomach. His face grew colorless and his grip around his mother's cold hand weakened. But he smiled. "I'm here, Mother. I won't let go. We'll dance forever now mother." He gently closed her eyes with his trembling finger.

He sat still, weakly stroking his mother's tautening face. He looked at the soldiers, and their bodies stiff with the death he delivered unhesitatingly, and then back at his mother's pale, cold face, and he knew he would soon join them in judgment.

He closed his eyes and caught the long gaps between his breaths. He felt no guilt or shame in what he had done. He had chosen. He released a last weak sigh, unhinging his soul.

★ ★ ★

Max peeled his hands from his face to see the death Peter had so competently dispatched. He reached over and shut the eyes of the youngest soldier, his hands, already stiff, extended up toward empty, useless clouds, as if pleading for one final warm embrace that would never come. With his hand resting on the young man's face, he prayed softly.

When he was done, he heard no weeping, no cries for help. His family was gone. And all his sacrifice, every good work, the years of dying to self, and his uncompromising commitment to truth—all of it, none of it could curtail the cruel judgment that patiently waited for this moment. He had no reply but to seize the gun that lay nearby. He placed its nozzle firmly against his temple. His finger wrapped the trigger. "Click, click." In that moment he saw God's judgment as it was, as it had to be—righteous and enduring, for all of Max's evil in the Great War, all the men he killed in an unbridled hate, all their scorned cries for mercy...their blood demanded what Max was finally given.

He tossed the impotent gun to the ground and wept bitterly.

★ ★ ★

Minister Miller watched through a set of binoculars. First the dead soldiers were removed from the house and thrown into the back of a military truck. Then Mother was brought out. The German soldiers stopped near Max as ordered.

Her body lay covered by a white sheet on a gurney held in the air by the soldiers.

Max fell to his knees and wept uncontrollably. He pulled the sheet away to see her face for the last time. He kissed her cheek gently and stroked her hair whispering a cry, "My dearest love... my angel."

The soldiers pulled away with an indifference forcing the sheet from his hand. They marched to the truck and callously dumped her body into the bed with her executioners.

The Minister pulled his binoculars away from his eyes. The muscles in his jaw rippled as he resolved to not let his heart overcome his reason. He had done all he could to stop it. Max was to blame, only Max. He grit his teeth in anger.

"Sir," came from behind him.

He turned to face a soldier. "The boy is still alive. He's lost a lot of blood. He won't make it."

The Minister considered his words carefully.

"Sir, the mission..."

The Minister interrupted with an urgency. "Save the boy."

"But sir..."

"Save the boy." He pulled the soldier forcefully toward him. "Save him or you will pay with your life."

The soldier saluted and ran off.

★ ★ ★

**Texas Correctional Institutions Division,
Mountain View Unit
Gatesville, Texas – Summer of 1977**

Lisa frowned and smiled, her face slightly twisted, like she doubted the story. "So, this story…ain't made up?"

"No…it's my story."

"So, you live, your mom dies…hoping they kill yo' father."

"Death isn't always the worst punishment."

"You think killin' me ain't the worst thing?"

"It doesn't matter what I think. What do you think?"

She looked away at nothing, her eyes scanning the room. She fixed on the wall clock for a minute then glanced at the guards flanking her and saw they had inched closer, close enough to hear Peter's voice spill out of the receiver. She nodded at Peter. "I don't think about nothin'. Never have. No memories, no dreams… nothin'." One side of her face raised in a smile, the other hard as concrete. "I'll be a seed in the ground soon, that's about all I think about."

The guard to her left slapped the back of her head. "Shut up and let 'em tell his story."

The guard next to Peter agreed. "Keep going."

DEATH COOPERATES WITH NO ONE

Tegal Penitentiary
Reincikendorf, Germany
Two weeks after the killings

Max sat in the corner of a damp, windowless cell in the Tegel Penitentiary, Reincikendorf, Germany, near Berlin. This was not a place for the common criminal. The war effort made no provision for crime, criminal process, or incarceration. If one was foolish enough to commit a crime, he or she was summarily executed by local police. Nor was this a place for political agitators; they were sent to internment camps without a trial. The inmates here were a select few. Most had secret information that would be extracted in one horrific day of torture or over long periods of slow, deliberate suffering.

But Max was different. He had no vital information. He had no trial, no visits from friends or relatives and he would soon know why.

The cement floor was ice cold. His knees pressed against his chest and his arms embraced them tightly in a vain effort to restrain his shivering. He wore the same clothes, still blood-stained from the worst day of his life. A guard gave him a filthy, tattered blanket to cover his head and shoulders. Most of his time was spent walking in place in this 3x3-foot space hoping to warm his body. His legs were too cold and stiff now and his feet seemed disconnected, like two slabs of discarded, spoiled meat. He knew it was just a matter of time before he'd freeze to death. And he wanted death desperately, but his instincts had cruelly overcome his will. His body would not sit long enough to allow cold's grip to freeze around his heart. He sat anyway under a stingy shard of light that spilled from a thick crack in the ceiling, hoping his desperate will to die would soon overcome his despicable drive to live.

The guard, a portly man in his fifties, wore a knit cap tight around his ears and wide face. He looked into Max's eyes and saw nothing. He expected a deep sadness, a tearful response to words that had destroyed him forever. And then he realized that Max did not completely understand his predicament. *He should know.* So he folded his newspaper in half and gently pushed it through the rusty bars near the shard of light that lit the headline:

PASTOR MAX ENGLE DOES NOTHING TO SAVE WIFE AND SON FROM POLISH INVASION

Max saw it and then looked away from the light and into the darkness of the cell slowly dropping his head into his hands.

The guard exited having done what he was ordered to do. He shut the iron barred door behind him. He took a few steps toward the warmth of a fire and then stopped. He looked around and found the quarters empty. He returned to Max and coughed loudly to get his attention.

Max looked up.

The guard opened his coat to display a wooden cross that hung from his neck. He smiled compassionately, closed his coat, and walked away.

Max's eyes filled with tears. He closed them as hard as he could, wishing to wipe away what he had just seen. He asked for only one thing from his God, and in all the boundless mercy of God, the finality of his suffering was still forbidden. The guards who tortured and killed the other prisoners would not hang him, nor put a bullet in his head. They were ordered to keep him alive, without alleviating his suffering.

Every moment he lived was consumed by the deepest yearning for death. And he would find it…with or without God's permission.

★ ★ ★

Beelitz-Heilstatten Hospital, Berlin

The nurse moved her hands with a gentle certitude tucking sheets against Peter's side without waking him from his desperately needed sleep. She wore a white dress, fit firmly about her long torso. Her hair was pinned up under a small white hat trimmed with red edges. She finished and stood back examining her patient. Her lips tightened in concern. She shook her head releasing her despondency. She touched his forearm and walked out.

Peter lay in a deep coma, now fourteen days. His protruding collar bones no longer hidden beneath layers of muscle tissue, his cheeks red and high like mountains over a desolate valley that were his thin, colorless lips, all told that death still lingered.

Martin stood outside Peter's room anxiously smoking a cigarette. He snuffed it out and entered hesitantly. He sat next to him dressed in his formal Wehrmacht uniform. He rested his hand on his best friend's shoulder and fought the tears that belied his crisp, sanguine uniform. Peter had nothing now but an association with Germany's greatest coward. Martin suddenly felt guilty. All those years of envy wanting what Peter had, and now he wanted none of it. He squeezed his shoulder and whispered, "All we have is each other now."

"They say they can hear us," someone said from behind.

Martin turned and jumped to his feet with a stiff salute. "Heir Minister."

Minister Miller returned the salute with the same respect. "Sit, son. You look tired. Have you been here from the beginning?"

"Yes, sir."

"No one expected he'd still be alive. So much blood lost."

"But if he survives, will he be the same, sir?"

The Minister smiled softly as his eyes scanned Martin in inspection. He stepped on the other side of Peter and nodded cautiously; still not certain Martin could be trusted. "He will never be the same. And because of that, Germany will never be the same." He looked directly into Martin's eyes with an intensity that made Martin uncomfortable. "His father and I were the best of friends. Did you know that?"

"No, sir."

"I could have saved them from all this." He shook his head. "Max is a stubborn man," he said through clenched teeth that sought to defray his guilt.

"Is it true what they say in the papers?"

He nodded slowly. "None of that matters now." He placed his hand on Peter's hand. "I see that you are close to him."

"He's my best friend, the greatest friend anyone would ever want." His lips trembled. "My heart…my heart breaks for him."

The Minister cleared his throat of emotion. "The greatest heroes always come from the ashes of life." A weak, unexpected smile broke the Minister's terse lips. "Not as I expected." His smile fell. "But his greatness comes…it will come."

Martin pulled his hand from his friend's shoulder and set his gaze on the Minister; his eyes still tight with questions. "I don't know how, sir. Everything was taken. Everything he loved. He'll never be the same."

"Yes. Never the same. Now he can be who he truly is."

The corner of Martin's lips turned up slightly. "He was always destined to be a hero." He looked down at his friend compassionately. "I ask just one thing, Minister."

The Minister lifted his obstinate, straight chin in curiosity.

"If he lives…whatever he's called to do, let me be by his side."

"You're his best friend you say?"

Martin nodded.

The Minister looked back at Peter and touched his forearm, then returned his gaze to Martin. "Pray he lives, and you will be his Jonathan."

Martin saluted proudly and walked out.

The Minister stood over Peter with tear swollen eyes. "Live, my son. You must live."

He turned to walk away and noticed Martin's military cap on a stand next to a window. He reached for it but stopped when he heard a tapping at the window. There he saw a large black crow tapping on the window so vigorously that its beak bled.

He left the cap and walked out.

TO RENOUNCE TOO LATE

Tegal Penitentiary, Six Months Later

Max stopped grinding notches into the thick cell wall that was now his home. Counting the days no longer brought a sense of order, or a quieting of the voices in his head accusing him day and night.

Guards came at different times avoiding any kind of routine that his mind desperately desired, and tonight was no different.

Two guards grabbed his frail body and drug him to the same place again. A firing squad of six soldiers, all suffering from some infirmity or disability, unfit for noble duty, lined up with their rifles aimed at his heart.

He stopped resisting long ago. A handkerchief was neatly folded nearby. It was never requested, as he wanted to see their pathetic faces. But now his eye lay shut. He knew what was coming. It had been done many times, a psychological game that had taken its toll.

Their captain gave the orders, and the shots rang out.

The executioners long stopped laughing. It became rote to them too. But they had their orders—shoot blanks until they had none left.

The captain said what he always said. "That which you want most, we will not give. You are a traitor and a coward. You are not worthy of our bullets. Every day you live, you will remember that." He motioned for his return.

Max stood there in his filthy clothes numb to everything but the terrible awareness that he was still alive. His head lay low on his chest. He raised it slowly and looked at the captain. "Please sir, I will renounce my beliefs," he said weakly. "I will renounce it all if you will put a bullet in my head. I will renounce."

The captain grinned wickedly and unholstered his gun. He placed it gently against Max's temple. "Renounce, Pastor."

Max's eye looked up to the heavens and he spoke with quivering lips. "I was wrong. The Fuhrer is right. We must fight. It is God's will."

The captain lowered his head that he might see directly into Max's eye. "And Jesus, Pastor? Is Jesus for us?"

Max closed his eye and tears fell down his cold face. He nodded yes.

"Say it, Pastor. Jesus is for the Fuhrer. Say it."

He responded weakly; his eyes closed. "Jesus is for the Fuhrer."

He grabbed him by the nape of his neck. "Again Pastor. Louder," he yelled.

"Jesus is for the Fuhrer."

"Louder, so all of Germany can hear you," he commanded again.

Max yelled with the little strength he had left. "Jesus is for the Fuhrer. Jesus is for the Fuhrer!" He opened his eye and set it hard against his captor speaking with a raspy importunity. "Now kill me damnit. Kill me now," he insisted.

He pulled his gun away and re-holstered. His wicked grin growing wider. "Oh, our dear Jesus wouldn't want that. Would he, Pastor?" His pale, stern face came close. "My orders are to keep you alive. Barely alive. Though I'd really enjoy putting a bullet in your cowardly head." He shoved him to the ground. "Get him out of my sight."

Max was thrown back into his cell where he tucked himself into a dark corner. For the next three days he took nothing of the moldy bread offered and denied himself even a sip of water. On the eve of the third night his filthy fingers fell from covering his face onto his chest where his silver cross medallion lay. It was a gift from his wife given on the day of his ordination. The tips of his fingers caressed it gently, then suddenly he gripped it hard in his shaking hand, ripping it off his neck and tossing it through the prison cell bars where he could never reach it again.

OUT OF THE ASHES

Heroes are not born heroes; they are made through hellfire.

Early 1940, outside Paris, France
One year after Peter's hospitalization.

Lieutenant Peter Engle stood at the peak of a hill, alone. He lowered his binoculars and breathed in heavily. Stubble covered his face, and his thick, blond hair found a curl in its uncommonly long and unkempt manner. The purple scarf given to him by his mother draped around his neck—all that was left of his past. He was taller now, a clear six-foot-four, and his long muscles had solidified into a power that no man could rival. He brushed his hair from his face with a thick, robust hand that had taken many lives now without a trace of remorse or guilt. He was stronger than his father, reformed, reborn by his father's moral ineptitude, baptized as a warrior, nothing but a warrior, his heart not split in two like his father's, but cold, metallic, able to destroy even innocence, as it had been destroyed in him. He had his calling now, and Germany praised him for it.

His tired eyes scanned a tattered letter penned years earlier by the only person life and hate could not fully destroy. But like everything else, Julia's words were quickly fading into the black abyss that had invaded much of his heart. He released his breath in a long sigh, folded the letter gently and placed it in his shirt pocket. He walked down the hill to ready his men.

Always moving, never resting, they lay exhausted at the bottom of the hill. Each one handpicked, talented, unquestionably loyal to their leader. But unlike the rest of Germany's finest, these soldiers fought, not for the Fuhrer, not for Germany, but for their fearless Lieutenant. They were a special unit called The Knifepoint—sharp, concise, the first to enter the battle and the first to strike. Developed by Minister Miller, now the Minister of Special Forces, The Knifepoint had proven to be one of Germany's most important weapons. And although they were at times rogue, the Minister wished he had more men like them, especially men like Lieutenant Peter Engle.

✳ ✳ ✳

His men were already in formation, their weariness pushed away for another battle. He joined them, all in a circle, their arms interlocked and on their knees.

He nodded at his best friend.

Martin returned a nod and started, "Our Father who art in heaven, hallowed be thy name..."

The rest joined in a chorus that brought them the courage and strength they needed for what was next.

✳ ✳ ✳

They marched toward a French farmhouse, a temporary headquarters for the enemy. Their objective was clear, though with great controversy, as was always the case. That was the word used by his superiors, "controversy." But Peter didn't care about controversy. He didn't care about anything, and that was his greatest power. No longer restrained by God, or higher things, nor anchored by convictions, his mind and deadly hands were free to do whatever was required to fulfill any mission and to protect his men. And his men knew they were a distant second to the objective.

He gave them their instructions. General Shultz was to be rescued. He was a few kilometers away, a prisoner of the French Army, along with sixty of his men. The best intelligence put the General in a large, comfortable parlor on the first floor of the farmhouse. He was well taken care of, laughing and sipping wine with his French counterparts.

The General's officers and enlisted men were huddled en masse, prisoners in a barn, with no food or water, too weak to revolt and too cold to care.

The farmhouse was well fortified. The French set up two perimeters and more troops would soon arrive to establish the house as a proper headquarters.

The Knifepoint was out-manned twenty-to-one.

General Shultz, a personal friend of the Fuhrer, had vital information that would compromise the Wehrmacht plans. It was expected that he had already gladly talked to spare his life.

The Knifepoint's orders were clear. Exterminate all enemy combatants, bring the General back, and if possible, free the remaining captives.

★ ★ ★

Peter looked at his watch again; it was 4:00 a.m. He tossed his MP 40 machine gun over his shoulder and stepped into the darkness followed closely by his men in a tight, disciplined line. He grabbed the "Vampire," a night vision device that often gave The Knifepoint an upper hand. He watched a set of French soldiers hunkered down in a nearby mortar crater one hundred meters out. One wore radio headphones, the other was fast asleep. He directed his men to hold their positions. They relaxed, unstrapping their rifles with a cockiness that he acknowledged with a raised brow.

He slid his body, like a deadly snake in the night, closing the distance in seconds. He pulled the purple scarf just below his eyes like an executioner hiding his identity, and then a "snap" that sent the French radio operator limp onto the other's feet.

Peter squeezed the second soldier's mouth shut. He whispered in his ear, "Make your peace."

The soldier squirmed, kicked and clawed, but Peter's overwhelming power subdued his body and spirit, and he quietly whimpered his final prayer. Peter dropped his stilled body and signaled his men to move forward.

He sent them out by twos, each pair doing as they were trained—as they had observed their leader do many times over. Each encounter a quiet, quick death until the rendezvous at the final line of resistance that surrounded the northern edge of the farmhouse. The other half of his men, saboteurs clothed in French uniforms, circled toward the southern perimeter. They entered the compound with French wine bottles in hand, in a feigned drunken stupor, singing with perfect French accents, "La Java Bleue."

A French lieutenant, already angry that he had not been allowed inside with his general, turned from the warmth of a fire with his handgun unstrapped and at the ready. "Damn fools, I should kill you farm rats." He ordered his sergeant. "Get those fools to shut up or I'll put a bullet in their heads."

The five dropped their bottles and unleashed a hail of bullets, one that ended the French lieutenant's cold anger instantly.

The French soldiers ran in different directions, in panic as the squeezing intensified. Peter and his men tightened in, and the French were hit from the north and south. Many dropped their rifles in the chaos, their hands lifted in a quick surrender. In minutes the few had corralled a hundred enemy soldiers.

Peter motioned to Martin. They left their men and headed toward their objective.

Inside the farmhouse a panicked French general and his officers took cover hoping to forestall Peter's attack. They pushed General Shultz out the front door. He wobbled in his sleepiness and the persistent sway of too much wine. He steadied his back against the door. He was a large man, with an obtrusive gut that forced his coat open at the waist. He pushed away from the door addressing Peter and Martin with a commanding tone that failed to conceal his drunken slur. "Well done, men. Now get me the hell out of here. I need a bath."

The French leaders listened intently.

General Shultz waved his hand at the captured French. "Kill the French bastards, but I made a promise to the general and his officers, they will be spared," he commanded proudly. "I always keep my word," he said with less bravado. He stepped forward never bothering to look at his rescuers directly and threw his hand on Peter's shoulder like he was just railing to steady himself.

Peter pushed his hand off.

He looked into Peter's eyes not finding the fearful submission he was used to. He tightened his lips in anger and caught Peter's rank. "How dare you. Do you know who I am? I will have your head, you petty nobody," he growled. He chuckled sardonically. "The Fuhrer will have all your heads," he shouted pointing at Peter's men.

Peter grabbed the General's hand and squeezed it until bones began to break.

The General screamed in agony and fell to his knees. "Lieutenant, please, I am a loyal soldier, committed to the Fuhrer, to the *Deutschland*. What are you doing?" His desperation intensified as he grabbed Peter's pant leg. "I can give you anything you want. I have money. I am a rich man. Anything, anything you want."

Peter breathed in deeply, releasing a slow, calm breath. "Are you prepared to meet your maker, General?" he asked calmly.

The General wiped his tears as he fought to control his fear. "What? Please, young man. I am an old man…" He struggled to stand, but Martin pushed him back down to his knees.

Martin looked at Peter with tight, questioning eyes. "Our orders."

The General looked around for help, yelling for decorum. "This man is not following orders. I am a General."

Peter ordered his men to turn away. He pulled his purple scarf to his face and screwed his handgun against the General's swollen face.

"Are you prepared, General?" repeated Peter.

Martin looked at the General with disgust. "Let the dog live, Peter. We don't need the scrutiny."

Peter shot Martin a look that stilled his suggestion.

The General looked up past his scarf into Peter's cold eyes and his resilience evaporated. "I was once a lion…once a warrior like you." His eyes fell onto Peter's gun, and he shook his head dismissively. He looked back into Peter's eyes with defiance and certainty. "You think you're invincible. Your day will come." He nodded agreeing with himself. Then he looked back at Peter's handgun. He whispered in surrender loud enough for Peter to hear. "Son, please…there is no dignity in being taken by one's own…no dignity."

Peter looked into the General's eyes and saw a pride that once was. He knew what was coming and made no effort to avert it.

The General grabbed Peter's hand and forced the trigger down, directing a bullet into his own head.

Peter pulled his hand back, the smoke slowly floating from the hot barrel.

Martin's eyes fell from their astonishment and tightened as he looked into Peter's vapid eyes and finally knew his old friend was gone.

★ ★ ★

Ten miles from the French farmhouse, the following day

It was 2:00 a.m. Peter's men were asleep in the Church of Sainte-Mere-Eglise and would sleep for the next 24 hours. But not Peter.

Peter had not followed orders. The unlisted French were let go and General Shultz was dead. There was little consolation in freeing the German enlisted men. That didn't seem to matter to his superiors.

He sat in a chair, a bright light on his face. The voice of a superior officer came from behind a desk. He was cast in shadow, his identity always hidden.

"We didn't really care about the General. He's better off dead." He leaned back in his squeaky chair and waited for tension to fill their space. But it never did.

Peter sat there calmly, a coolness that felt like defiance.

His superior leaned forward with a long squeak from his chair. "Is there something you want to say, Lieutenant...about that?"

"I believe he was right."

"Right?"

"The General gave the enemy vital information. Death was the only recourse to right his wrong."

"You were going to kill him and defy orders?"

"I don't operate in intentions." He cleared his throat. "What is done, is done."

He lit a cigarette, momentarily exposing his face from the shadows, long enough for Peter to see his repulsion. "You'll be contacted in a few days."

Peter stood and saluted. And turned to leave.

"Lieutenant."

Peter stopped and spun around to look into the shadows again.

"Do you believe, Lieutenant?

"Believe?"

"Yes. Do you believe in the cause?" He extinguished his cigarette and stood. "You're a brave man, Lieutenant. And you're a vital asset. But I don't know if…"

Peter's face tightened as he interrupted. "Believe? If you want me to believe, stick me in the shadows where I can't see the eyes of the men that I kill…or hear their desperate cries to something… something they believe." His lips quivered in anger and he nodded defiantly. "Believing…is for the weak…for you in the shadows."

He saluted and walked out.

***

Peter sat in the first pew of Sainte-Mere-Eglise. His eyes were red with sleeplessness. He looked around finding his men still in a deep slumber. He stood and moved as quietly as he could, stepping over and around them. Half the roof was gone from a recent bombing, allowing the morning light to brighten a large crucifix that lay on its side against the northern church wall. He paused for a moment and gazed at the life-sized figure of Christ, his body and face pock marked by shrapnel. He had never been in a Catholic Church and had never seen such a portrayal of Jesus. Though he was bothered by its disgraceful display, he was more upset that it mattered to him at all.

He didn't need God now. The war was his gospel, and his orders his Bible. That was working, as long as God didn't get in the way. But an occasional dream, a childhood memory, a beaten-down statue of Jesus brought the Divine back to life.

He looked back at the figure, inert, on its back, cracked, disfigured. He smiled mockingly and breathed in the silence of a thing that has no life. He stepped outside waiting for further instructions.

***

Martin splashed water onto his face. He could smell bacon fat burning. He smiled knowing Peter had already started on breakfast. He watched the men sleep, so calm and peaceful. Only one had been lost. Like many of his men, the soldier had no next of kin to notify. They were misfits, forgotten, rejected men who had found family and purpose in The Knifepoint. He was buried in an unmarked grave, like the others before. They were good men, the best he knew, but there was no time to remember, to mourn. That was not their way, and everyone accepted it.

He saw the giant crucifix on the floor. He stood before it in reverent silence. When he was done, he stepped back and breathed in deeply. "Please watch over us and receive our dead."

He turned around and lovingly kicked one of his men who was lying on the floor. "Wake up and smell the spoils of your victory."

The soldier sat up, inhaling the scent of bacon, and broke into a drowsy smile.

ELISE IS LOVE

Peter opened the envelope. Always a gray envelope, plain, with no identifying information or markings. The courier left fresh supplies, saluted, and drove off. Always a different courier, someone who had no idea what The Knifepoint meant for Germany, and no idea who Peter was. Peter tore open the envelope and read. When he was done, he struck a match and burned the instructions.

Martin sat next to him. "Where next?"

Peter hesitated and scratched his chin. "Belgium."

"Belgium?" he said with wide eyes. "Finally, Peter. Finally, I can find Elise. He looked back at the statue. "Thank you, God."

"That won't happen, Martin."

Martin stood abruptly, his eyes in an intense squint. "You said that someday we would find her, Peter."

"When the war is over, Martin. Not now. We have our orders. I can't waste time trying to find her."

"Waste time? But she's all I have, Peter."

"It's been too long, Martin. She's probably dead."

Martin felt his muscles tense like they did just before battle. "Probably dead? Look at you. You read that letter every day like there's some hope of seeing Julia, thousands of miles away. That's hopeless, Peter. Not my Elise. And I'll find her. You won't stop me."

Peter stood, ready to meet Martin's challenge, but then he softened. He scanned the church and his eyes fell on the crucifix. "If finding her doesn't jeopardize our mission, or our men…" He paused and looked into his friend's eyes and nodded. "The mission. Our men first, Martin."

Martin's anger dissolved. He smiled and glanced back at the downed crucifix. "I asked God to give her back to me, Peter."

Peter nodded and smiled weakly, clearing the fatigue from his eyes.

* * *

Fort Eben-Emael fell to the swift power of the German forces. The Belgium army surrendered within days. But one man had eluded them. He was Hebert Pierlot, Prime Minister of Belgium who was planning an evacuation to London. He had information that the Wehrmacht viewed as highly sensitive. He was hiding amongst the civilians and could not be found. Peter briefed his men.

They were dropped just outside Brussels, near the Zenne River. They searched night and day, interrogating civilians in ways only they employed. After three days, they had nothing. The Belgium leader was a needle in a haystack and his people would rather die than reveal his whereabouts.

It was evening. They walked along a simple cobblestone road doubling back to the leader's last known address. Along the way they saw bodies stacked on filthy sidewalks, hundreds of uncooperative civilians and their surviving families sitting next to their dead, still weeping over their decaying corpses, their eyes filled with a scared hatred that longed for revenge.

Peter inspected their glares sifting through their hate for a clue that could lead him to their man.

Martin watched a group of young Belgians that seemed to hurry away as Knifepoint approached. One stood behind, a young woman, her face covered with a scarf. As he walked past her, her scarf fell, and her eyes widened. She stepped toward him and then stopped suddenly.

"Martin?"

Martin felt a rush of hot blood hit his temples.

She stepped onto the road under a light pole, and he saw her face clearly.

His grip around his rifle loosened. "Elise. Elise?"

She took another step toward him.

Peter pointed his gun at her.

"Martin," she cried. She ran and fell into his arms.

Peter ordered his men to stand down. They lowered their weapons and watched with curiosity.

Elise sobbed, forcing a few words from her thin, pale lips. "It's terrible, Martin. The world is falling apart."

He took her away from his men and into the shadows. He held her hand gently. "Elise, I always knew I'd find you."

She embraced him tightly, and she could feel his muscles soften. "So much has happened." Her body shook in fear.

Martin held her close, but she shook all the more. "You're okay now. I'll make sure you're taken care of."

"My family is dead. I have no one, Martin."

"You have me. I'll protect you. I promise."

Peter approached; his rifle slung peacefully over his shoulder.

"Peter, this is Elise. Remember Elise?"

Peter forced a smile. "Oh yes, of course."

He extended his hand. "I wish we could have met again on better terms."

She shook his hand, and he felt her fear. "You're out here alone?" he said with suspicion.

"Yes. I have no one else."

"Why are you out here alone?" Peter asked.

Martin shot him an angry stare.

Elise looked at Martin with hopeless eyes. "I have nothing. I have nowhere to go."

Peter looked over his shoulder. "It's not safe for us here. We must keep moving."

"Where are you going?" she asked desperately. "I can guide you. Please. I have no one. And the others, they left…" She paused, not wanting to explain further.

Martin took her hand again. "I won't let anyone hurt you."

"Martin," Peter gestured with a swipe of his chin.

They stepped away. "What are you doing? We have our orders. Say your goodbyes, quickly. We'll come back for her when our mission is done."

"I'm not leaving here."

"And do what? Stay with her? Leave us?"

"No, my brother. I would never do that. But we can find a way to protect her."

Peter lit a cigarette. He had no options for Martin.

"There's nothing we can do, Martin. Not now. There are eyes all around us. We're vulnerable here." He released a plume of smoke filled with tension. "Say your goodbyes, Martin. Now. Set a rendezvous in a few days. Now," he commanded.

Martin looked at Peter with an anger that melted quickly into a sadness that understood. He ambled back to Elise under the heaviness of his cold orders.

She smiled with hopefulness. But as he came close, she knew he was no longer her friend, her lover, but a soldier with a duty like all the others. Her eyes fell and she began to cry.

He held her in his arms and stroked her matted hair. Tears filled his eyes. "I'm sorry, Elise. I'm so sorry."

"Please, Martin. Please. I can help you. I know things."

"I'm sorry, Elise. Not here. I'll come back. We'll meet up in a few days."

"Who do you look for?"

"I can't tell you."

"I know. We all know. The Germans have killed us looking for him. You want Pierlot."

Martin looked at her with suspicious eyes.

"I know where he is."

"You're desperate. I understand."

"No. I know where he is. I have an uncle who is a high ranking official. They left with him. They left me behind in their haste. I have no loyalty to them." She looked longingly into his eyes. "I have only loyalty to love. I have always loved you, Martin. You know that."

"You left me."

"My parents, the war took me from you, but not my heart. Can't you see? It must be our destiny. Please Martin, let me live, let our love have a chance. Don't let this war separate us again."

"You know where he is? Are you sure?"

"I know where my uncle went. He will be with him."

★ ★ ★

Elise led the men without a word as instructed. They approached a small town called Dinant. A row of apartments, three stories high on the east and west side of a narrow road led to the hideout. She showed Peter a crudely drawn map she made after Peter had hesitantly agreed with Martin. The only way to their home was through this narrow road. It was poorly lit, both an advantage and disadvantage for his men.

Peter stopped his men as he peered down the narrow road to the house at the end, about 300 meters on the east side. The only light came from a second story window where he hoped his target slept. It was just past midnight. He looked at Elise, directly into her eyes, finding a desperation that made him regret his decision. "Tell me again…you are certain this is the place?"

"My uncle fled but left this address with his secretary. She was killed, but her son found me, on her orders, to give me this address. He found me a week ago, but the Germans…" she said with wholehearted disdain, "…would never let me through."

Peter examined Martin's eyes and he saw uncertainty, insecurity, neediness—all the things that marked Martin before the war. "Something's wrong, Martin. We've got to get the hell out of here."

Martin grabbed his shoulder. "Wait. We've crossed worse. This is nothing. If he's there, we take him. If he's not, we leave."

"And her?"

Martin looked at Elise with abandonment. "She understands."

Elise nodded.

They followed Peter in two lines, one on the east, the other on the west side of the narrow road, pushing tightly against the cold, dark brick that dripped with an earlier rain. They advanced slowly, quietly, Peter in front of one column, Martin in front of the other. Martin placed Elise in the rear, fifty meters back.

Elise followed but her steps slowed.

As they came closer to their target, they passed an alley on the eastside when a sudden crash came from within.

Peter swung his gun around turning it back into the alley.

A cat ran out the alley and across the road into the west alley.

Martin turned around to check on Elise. She was gone.

Peter looked up at the target apartment, at the solitary, lit room and saw a little girl in the window who was abruptly pulled away. He looked over his shoulder at his men, his eyes wide with a guilt that already knew their end. And before he could release his command for retreat, it began.

Rifles, handguns—forty in all—broke through the apartment windows above and a hail of bullets cut through their lines hitting many of Peter's men. Several were killed instantly, and several were wounded.

Peter shouted his orders, and his men did all they could to return fire. But they were trapped, the tight quarters giving no cover. When it was over, half of his men were dead.

ELISE IS DEATH

Elise's hands were blue and numb, a rope tight around her wrists. Daylight had broken and her face was covered in a soft, orange light that accentuated the gauntness of her once beautiful face. Gone was her desperation. She wore a cold countenance that defied her impending execution. A frigid, weak breath escaped from her mouth, taking the last of her pleas to live.

All that was left was the choice of her executioner.

Peter walked away from her and stood next to Martin who smoked a cigarette with a vigor and anxiousness bound in anger for what she had done, and a love too strong for the justice that awaited her. He stomped the cold from his stiff legs onto his last cigarette. His words choked in his throat. "I prayed. Why would God bring me to her…for this?"

Peter grabbed him by his shoulders and slammed him against a near brick wall. "Praying? You should have prayed before you led our men to their death!" he shouted.

Martin gave no resistance. "I'm sorry," he cried. "You're right." He pulled at Peter's holster. "Kill me, Peter. Kill me, please," he pleaded.

Peter pulled him away from the wall only to slam him against it again. He reached down and pulled out his gun, shoving it into Martin's stomach. "I do this for our men. They were my brothers too." He put his finger tightly against the trigger.

Martin looked into Peter's eyes. "Kill me, brother. Better you than my enemy."

Peter lifted his gun at Martin's chest. His tears broke in heavy streams down his face, icicles etched in the cold. And he saw Martin's eyes and all the sadness of his childhood, none of it ever redeemed, just greater sadness heaped on a mountain of sadness.

Martin nodded him forward, but Peter felt his finger weaken from the trigger. He shook his head and released him.

Martin fell limp onto the ground. He spoke weakly, crying. "I'm sorry. Sorry."

Peter dropped to a knee and gently placed his gun into Martin's hand. "Kill this weakness, Martin, before it kills us all."

He shook his head. "How can you ask me to kill the only person I've ever loved." He held Peter's gun weakly.

"Love? Don't you see now, Martin? Love is our greatest enemy. It killed our brothers. It will kill us." He squeezed Martin's hand around the gun. "Put a bullet in its head."

"I can't. I can't. Please don't make me, Peter."

"Then I'll do it, and the last thing she'll see is hate in my eyes."

★ ★ ★

Martin stumbled toward Elise, his gun dangling weakly at his side. Her eyes fell slowly down his arm to the gun in his hand.

He stood next to her on weak legs swaying under a cold, bitter wind. His eyes fought to avoid what his heart wanted—one last, eternal look that could find love in her eyes, enough to forgive him for what he had to do.

But she looked away at nothing. "I'm glad it's you," she said with a calm finality. She looked back at him, her eyes ablaze with enmity. "…not some filthy, heartless German soldier."

He touched her chin with a trembling finger. "Elise, I still love you. You're all I have."

"If you love me, then give me what I need most."

He looked down with heavy eyes. "I can't let you go, Elise."

She pressed against the cold wind that swept her hair across her face. "Martin, I want it all to end. I want to…I want to…" She fought the words that had no place now. "I want to see my daughter." Her head fell low, dangling weakly from her neck as if she were already dead. "I want to hold her again," she said with a gasp.

Martin felt his eyes widen with a hopefulness that chewed at the outer edges of his despair. "A daughter?"

Elise lifted her head animated by the power of fond memories. "Yes. She's beautiful, the most precious thing that ever lived." Her boldness quickly evaporated, and her eyes dropped in surrender. "But the war took her. And all I've wanted is death and vengeance."

"Vengeance…that you were willing to have me killed?"

She looked away; her hate tinged by a morsel of guilt.

Martin wiped his tears and nodded slowly in agreement. "Maybe you will see your daughter again."

She looked past him toward the horizon, an emptiness in her eyes.

He lifted his hand, the gun shaking uncontrollably, squeezing the cold metal and pressing it tightly against her temple. He forced the words out that caught in his throat. "Today you see your child."

Her eyes fought closure, and rest. "Send me to our daughter."

Martin's eyes blinked uncontrollably, spilling all the moisture left. "What?"

"Send me to her. Please."

"She was ours? My child?" He said in an evaporating disbelief. He lowered his gun and embraced her cold, wet body kissing the top of her head. "Our child?"

"No, Martin." She grabbed the tip of his barrel and forced it against her heart. "No. End this for me. I beg you," she answered forcibly.

Martin shook his head and marched away.

* * *

"I can't kill her, Peter." He grabbed his friend by the shoulders and shook him with an exuberance that he knew would change Peter's heart. "We have a child."

Peter burned a pathetic gaze into Martin's eyes. "And some of our brothers had children. You've forgotten that, Martin? What will I tell their children?" He yanked Martin's handgun from him and set toward her.

"No, Peter. Please," begged Martin as he followed close behind. "She doesn't have to die." Martin grabbed Peter's shoulder.

Peter turned and his eyes burned Martin's protestation into an insipid, frosty ash.

Martin fell to his knees and wept under the familiar, steely certainty of his Lieutenant's command.

Peter lifted his purple scarf abruptly over his face and turned, quickly shooting Elise twice in the head. Her body fell hard to the icy ground. He returned and towered over Martin like a cold, concrete edifice impervious to the warm pleas of the wind. "Don't ever make me do what is yours to do again." He lowered his scarf and walked away.

* * *

Martin buried Elise in a shallow, icy grave. He walked back to Peter and handed him his gun, looking at him from head to toe, examining him as if he were a stranger. His eyes flowed with tears and his body convulsed in a silent cry.

Peter grabbed him by the back of the neck and pulled him into his strong embrace.

Martin's sobs echoed loudly as he buried his face into Peter's neck. Abruptly, he pulled back and composed himself. He looked down at his chest and ripped off his Knifepoint patch. He presented it to Peter with a quivering hand. He looked over his shoulder toward Elise's grave, then to the muddy ground that enveloped his boots.

Peter nodded in understanding.

Martin looked up one last time at his friend's face. All that he had ever known of him, all that he had envied, was gone. "If I stay…" His head shook in a burning acceptance of what would come.

And Peter knew he was right. A line had been crossed. Friends were now enemies, brothers now adversaries. Death was certain.

Martin swung his rifle over his shoulder gripping the icy, leather strap in his hand fighting a powerful urge to deliver a death blow to Peter's throat. Instead, his hand slid from its wavering grip and fell loosely at his side. His eyes settled there with a vestige of love that wanted to shake Peter's hand one last time. But his hate commanded his love into a shrinking childhood memory not fit for war…not fit for anything else. He lifted his gaze past Peter to a steady transport truck and walked wearily down the road.

Peter watched Martin walk away with his familiar heavy amble until he was out of sight. He looked down at Martin's muddy boot impressions and sighed. He rubbed his cold hands together, tucked his gloves on, stepped over his prints and left.

★ ★ ★

**Texas Correctional Institutions Division,
Mountain View Unit
Gatesville, Texas – Summer of 1977**

Lisa chuckled and slapped the metal table with her left hand. "Ya killed her. Ya killed your best friend's girl." She nodded, her eyes wide like she was seeing Peter for the first time. "Ya ain't that different from me. No sir…ain't that different." She pushed her chair in closer. "Now I like ya story, Mister. A good killing… nothin' like a good killin'. The other war stuff, that's kill or be killed. But this one's different."

She saw the tears in his eyes and stopped her blabbing. She felt the hot breath of her guards against her head. "Shut the hell up and let him tell his story, you damn witch."

She nodded and pushed a smile across her face that told Peter to continue.

HIDDEN DEEP INSIDE

Innocence can never be killed, only maimed.

A fleet of Messerschmitt Bf 109s cut through the air above Essen, North-Westphalia, Germany, east of Berlin. The ceiling shook and a fragment of plaster fell onto Heinz's bed. It was cold and he wanted nothing more than to stay under his blanket for as long as he could. Six boys—the eldest fifteen years old and the youngest ten—slept in one small room in beds stacked to three levels, two boys per bed.

Heinz was the smallest, the youngest, a five-year resident at the home, since his mother's passing. He never knew his father, but he could never forget his mother. He kept a lock of her hair with him wherever he went. His hand caressed it under his pillow as he drifted into a better time…

He felt the gentle touch of her hand sweeping across his golden hair and her kind prodding. "My dearest, time to wake up. Mother loves you. Wake up now. Breakfast is ready."

And the dream drifted away as he rolled over in his bed, uncovering his bed mate.

Ralph, twice his size, awoke to the cold, finding his covers confiscated. "Heinz, you idiot." He tossed him out of bed onto the frigid plank floor.

"I'm sorry, so sorry." He stood to his feet and quickly made sure Ralph was covered and tucked in. "There you go, Ralph. Nice and tucked in. You stay there now. I'll get a fire going."

"You're not getting back in. You sleep on the floor and freeze to death. I don't care," barked Ralph.

It was how all the boys responded to Heinz. He was tiny, and easy to push around. And they were not only orphaned boys, but the progeny of undesirables, the criminal, the insane, the sick. Like their deceased mothers and fathers, they too were already deemed unfit for the great new society. Their suffering gripped them; their pain animated them toward hate. But Heinz was different.

Heinz started on the fire, a quiet, happy hum escaping from his nostrils. He smiled, despite his circumstances, because death could not separate him from his mother. And that made him the happiest boy in the orphanage, perhaps the happiest in all of Germany. He slowed his eyes and breathed in the warmth of the fire.

"Heinz, Heinz…" Fraulein Emma awoke to the sound of a crackling fire. Heinz sat asleep next to the warmth. His head lay low with his little chin resting on his chest. She shook his shoulder. "Heinz, Heinz, what are you doing up? It's too early."

He opened one eye, glassy and red. "Mother?" His eye closed and he breathed deeply back into his stupor.

Fraulein Emma was a large woman, with arms as strong as any man. She scooped his little frame off the floor and placed him back into his bed. She returned with her heavy overcoat and laid it over his sleeping body.

★ ★ ★

Fraulein Emma stirred a pot of *Hafemehl* as the boys readied themselves for breakfast. She was a sullen woman who lost her husband in the first Great War before bearing any children. She opened her home to orphan boys soon thereafter. She took in those that could not be placed elsewhere. And with the rise of Hitler's evils, the list of orphanages for boys like hers was short.

The boys sat at a small table with their elbows pressed against each other's sides anxiously awaiting the same breakfast meal they ate every day, except on Christmas when Fraulein Emma added two drops of honey.

Heinz sat at one end, at the edge of a seat dominated by another.

She served them in steamy wood bowls as they each bowed their heads, waiting, Pavlovian, until the "Amen." They had fifteen minutes to eat and wash their faces and then off to the mine. All worked from sunup to sundown, even little Heinz. In fact, he was the most valuable worker in their bunch, often called upon to place dynamite in caverns too small for the others.

Fraulein Emma required them to line up for a boiled egg and a half toast for lunch, and then a hug. They all complied robotically, except Heinz. He loved her and always waited at the end of the line to have his moment. He wrapped his little arms around her wide waist and pressed his face against her firm belly. And she always held him longer than the rest. "Off you go now. I pray His angels protect you." And she did pray for them, every day, every hour. And sometimes the angels kept charge and other times they did not.

★ ★ ★

They walked in a straight line—Ralph, the tallest leading, Heinz the smallest in the rear. Ralph was the leader because he was the oldest, the strongest, and as he often said, his father was a lieutenant in the Wehrmacht, so he should naturally lead. No one believed his story, but no one dared to question him. He had bright orange, curly hair that encircled his round, chubby cheeks. The miners called him "clown face." He was always the brunt of their jokes from the moment he stepped into the mine until the final whistle of the day. But away from the mine, he was in charge.

They were headed to the Zollverein Coal Mine. The precious iron ore was desperately needed for all the weapons that fed the Wehrmacht. Since all the young and able bodied filled its ranks, those too old or young or disabled to fight were left behind to do this backbreaking, dangerous work.

Ralph dreamed of joining the Wehrmacht. He loved the *Hitler-Jugend*. He found purpose and significance and pride there. But those days were gone.

His father never recovered from his mother's death. In his first battle he snapped and killed five of his own men. That was a year ago. And that was when Ralph was stripped of membership with the Hitler Youth and forced into what he called "this hell hole." He barked his orders and the boys did as he commanded. "Straight line. One more mile. No slowing down." He turned around to see Heinz slipping away. "Heinz, if I go back there, I will kick you in the behind so hard, I'll put you in Poland."

The others laughed, but Heinz pushed himself even harder knowing his little legs and lungs wouldn't deliver. The gap widened and he prepared himself for what he knew was coming.

Ralph ordered the boys ahead and then ran back in angry strides until his screaming, hot breath covered Heinz's face. "Why don't you just stay with Fraulein Emma, wash dishes, and sweep floors. That's all you're good for, you idiot," he screamed. He shoved him onto the ground and kicked him several times. When Ralph was done, he shook his head in disapproval. "You should kill yourself, like your whore mother did."

Heinz sprang to his feet, his fists in little balls. His lips quivering in anger. "She wasn't a whore. She was a good woman."

Ralph laughed. "You're as stupid as you are weak." He shoved him again and walked away.

Heinz sat on his rear and put his hands around his closely cropped hair, once golden, now dark from mine dust that could not wash out. He squeezed his head wanting to erase Ralph's words and all the words of many others who had maligned his mother.

She came to him again and spoke softly into his ear.

"Yes, Mother," he said to himself. "I know. I'm sorry." He wiped his tears and stood up. He looked down the road in the direction of the mine and saw a dark curtain of black smoke and dust moving toward him. He lowered his head and walked toward it.

They reached the mine's mouth, dark and cold, dust so thick their spit turned a charcoal gray. Ralph marched them to the shift manager, someone different every day.

Ralph saluted. "My team is ready, sir."

He chuckled. "Good. Very good," he said as he inspected the line of boys, their eyes set straight ahead. He turned his attention back to Ralph. "Well done, young man. You will make a great soldier."

Ralph beamed with pride as he constrained an inappropriate smile.

"What is your name?"

"Sir," shouted Ralph. "My name is Becker, Ralph Becker. My father is Lieutenant Becker, same name sir," he said proudly.

The shift manager's eyes narrowed. "Lieutenant Becker?" he answered with stiff, angry lips. He looked Ralph squarely in the eyes. "He's a disgrace to Germany. Don't you ever mention his name again. And one more thing." He grabbed Ralph by the shoulder. "That coward isn't your father; he *was* your father. He's dead. Long dead, as he should be." He pushed Ralph away. "Get them in now," shouted the man.

Ralph's eyes filled with tears. He turned to the boys and screamed his orders pushing each one in until he came to Heinz.

Heinz heard what was said. His heart hurt for Ralph. He was incapable of withholding compassion, powerless to ebb the tide of sorrow that often filled his heart for the suffering of others.

"It's okay, Ralph."

Ralph's eyes widened in hate. He threw Heinz's little frame across the rocky ground and kicked him until the shift manager pulled him away.

Ralph ran into the mine.

Heinz stood and wiped the black dust from his already filthy pants and stepped slowly into the darkness, wiping his eyes of the sadness he felt for Ralph.

★ ★ ★

Heinz exited the mine, wiped his black face and found a place to sit. It was lunch time. He sat alone and waited. Always waiting until moved. He watched Mr. Klein sitting by himself smoking a cigarette.

He walked to him and sat. "Hello, sir."

He puffed his cigarette and took his time to respond. "Hello, young man," he said with a sadness that pulled Heinz closer.

"Would you like an egg?" asked Heinz, as he handed it to the man.

"No, thank you." He looked away and spoke softly, almost to himself. "Not hungry."

Heinz put away his lunch and considered his words. He spoke with a sigh. "All this digging and clawing in the dark to find something good hidden deep inside."

Mr. Klein looked at him as if noticing him for the first time. "There's no good here. No good. No good anywhere," he responded with tears in his eyes.

The sad tinge in Heinz's heart deepened. He smiled softly and turned his chin upward. "Except memories."

Mr. Klein gazed into the boy's eyes and for a moment his pain was suspended. "What's your name?"

He extended his hand. "Heinz, sir."

"You are the boy they put in the small spaces for the dynamite." He nodded negatively. "Dangerous. So dangerous. So wrong."

"I don't mind. I'm never alone."

"I've seen you do it. You are always alone. Those cowards…"

"Well, sir, I have my mother with me always." He chuckled to himself. "I know what you're thinking. But she's with me always, all my memories of her."

"Memories." The word unearthed itself from the deep darkness of his heart.

"Yes, sir," he said proudly. "Beautiful ones. I see her in my dreams and sometimes when I'm in the darkest corner of the mine, I see…I see her smiling and I hear her gentle words." His smile stretched and his eyes crinkled. "I thank God for my memories. I get to go back…" He looked back at the mine, "…before all this. And no one can take that away from me. Not even the darkness in the mine, not the war, nothing."

Tears fell from Mr. Klein's eyes. His words stuck in his throat. "I buried him yesterday. My boy, my only boy." He quickly wiped the tears from his face and flexed his jaw muscles as hard as he could. He forced a chuckle against his agony. "So many memories." He took his final drag and tossed his cigarette down. "He was such a bright boy. Would have been a doctor, I think." He pushed the beginning of a smile across his face. "So many memories."

Heinz nodded, tapped Mr. Klein's shoulder, and walked away.

Mr. Klein looked to where the boy was sitting and noticed. "Heinz, Heinz," he called out.

"Yes, sir."

"Your lunch. You forgot your lunch."

Heinz smiled broadly. "No, sir, that's for you." He waved and walked back into the mine.

★ ★ ★

Weeks passed since his first conversation with Mr. Klein. Heinz could see the change in him. He always smiled in the morning when Heinz walked by. He talked about his son with a sparkle in his eye. He was alive again because his son was alive in him. It was time.

★ ★ ★

They sat next to each other, as they often did at noon. Heinz finished his toast and drank a cup of cold water. "Mr. Klein."

"Yes, Heinz."

"I'm going to ask something that I've wanted to ask for some time, but it's a hard thing."

Mr. Klein's eyes narrowed as he leaned in closer to the boy. "What is it? Ask."

"Well, I have a friend who has no memories, no dreams, none like we have."

"Oh, but everyone has them, Heinz."

"Yes, sir, but for some, too much sadness makes them hide far away."

He smiled and gently rested his hand on the boy's shoulder. "That's right." He nodded.

"My friend, Mr. Klein, has one dream. He wants to be a soldier."

"Well, I understand. Like my son," he responded as his smile dropped.

"But my friend can never be one. He's like me."

Mr. Klein shook his head. "If the boy wants to fight for his country, he should be allowed to fight," he said curtly.

"I wish he had a different dream, but that's all he ever thinks about. And I don't think he'll ever find his memories without it." Heinz paused, wanting better words. "The army won't accept him, unless he becomes someone else."

Mr. Klein slowly placed his lunch down on his lap and looked away. "Someone else?"

"Yes, sir."

"This friend, you must really care for him."

"I can feel his pain. It's so bad, Mr. Klein. Like yours the day we first talked."

"The day you gave me back my son." He nodded in appreciation. "My son…yes, my son. I understand." He carefully wrapped his lunch in a stained cloth napkin, looked into Heinz's eyes and nodded approvingly.

★ ★ ★

Three weeks later the boys marched their way toward the mine as a military transport truck came their way. It rumbled slowly through the mud, full of fresh soldiers headed off for battle. The bed was uncovered exposing them in their proud, clean uniforms and Stahlhelm, steel helmets. They were wet and cold but cheerfully singing a chorus of "Teufelshund," a battle song preparing them for victory.

The boys stopped, stiffened and saluted in respect as they were required to do. Those in the truck ignored them, as they were required to do. But one seated at the end nearest the gate with red curly hair escaping from under his helmet, stood to his feet. He planted his hand firmly on his heart, and he thanked Heinz with a rhapsodic nod that was immediately quashed by another soldier.

OPERATION GREIF

On the other side of the fog is the way. But first, the fog.

Reichstag Building, Berlin

Peter walked up a beautiful marble staircase that led to the third level of the Reichstag building. Once the German parliamentary building, it was now a center for Nazi special operations. There he stepped onto a lush, violet carpet splattered with a gold floral design. The walls were also marble, decorated with Germany's finest paintings. Above him, every twenty feet, hung massive chandeliers that brightened everywhere his eye could see. He was so removed from the filth and loudness of battle that the silence and beauty moved him to a calm he had forgotten ever existed.

He stopped to examine a painting that intrigued him. He studied a man, well dressed, his back to the observer, standing atop a dangerous rough rock formation, overlooking a sea of fog. He seemed to have met his end, his next step uncertain and dangerous. He felt like that man. Knifepoint had been dissolved, half of his men were dead, Martin was gone forever, and his love for Julia had long receded into a dark hopelessness. For the first time in his life, he was uncertain of who he was, and unsure of why he was still alive. He took a step back wanting to run from the pull the painting had on him.

"Wanderer Above the Sea of Fog."

He turned toward the voice.

He spoke as he absorbed the painting with fond eyes. "One of my favorites. It has spoken to me many times."

Peter pulled his shoulders back and saluted. "Sir."

He saluted back. "So, what do you feel when you see this painting?"

Peter looked back at the painting and did his best to conceal his thoughts. "Nothing, sir. I'm not accustomed to such things. I grew up on a farm. I've not seen many paintings." He turned away from it and studied the Iron Cross that lay around the thick neck of Lieutenant Colonel Otto Shmitt. He stood two inches above Peter's six-foot-four frame smiling at him with a penetrating cleverness that seemed to read Peter's thoughts. Peter returned his gaze to the painting.

"Nothing?" chuckled Shmitt. "This portrait has inspired many great Germans, young and old, for generations. And you feel nothing, Lieutenant?"

Peter's eyebrows lifted uncomfortably with his prodding.

"The man in the painting is all of us. Live long enough, and we all find ourselves here…in a fog of uncertainty." His eyes set back on Peter as he spoke with a deftly precision. "I can see it in your eyes, Lieutenant. It speaks to you, even now." He put his hand on Peter's shoulder. "Come with me."

★ ★ ★

Peter sat across from his large mahogany desk uncomfortable with Shmitt's long, penetrating stare. He felt his heart pulsating against his tight collar.

Shmitt sat stiff in his chair with a faint, unreadable smile that broke wide and reassuring. "I'm amazed at how much you remind me of the younger me…much younger."

Peter forced a blank, courteous grin.

"I was about your age when it happened." His elbow sat firmly on his desk; his hand clasped at his face carrying his chin. The right side of his lips curved up in a sarcastic grin. "We all lose our way; even the great Lieutenant Peter Engle can lose his way."

Peter intruded, lurching forward in his chair until his hands rested on his desk.

"Sir, I don't mean to disrespect you, but I don't need this."

Shmitt's smile dropped and his eyes, unblinking and black, tossed his disappointed response back.

Peter's lips tightened in a defiance he felt played into Shmitt's hands, but he didn't care. "I don't need to be set right. I don't need to be reminded of our great, noble purpose, or of the greatness of Germany." A frustrated sigh broke his resolve. He spoke slowly. "I'm sorry, sir. I don't need any of that."

Shmitt's fingers slid slowly down his long scar, resting comfortably around his chin like a wise counselor who possesses the insight he hopes his patient will also discover. "Why do you fight? Why do you fight so bravely, so gallantly, Lieutenant?"

Peter looked away at nothing, wanting to say nothing. "I give it no thought, sir. None at all. No heart, no purpose. That was taken long ago." He looked back at him, his eyes thin with frustration. "I just do my duty."

Shmitt pushed his chair away from his desk. "Duty, Lieutenant?"

He nodded.

"Yes. But duty always flows from something deeper, especially with men like you. Fearless men who never question their orders. Men who succeed against all odds. Men like you find something that drives them, something bigger, deeper than themselves. For some, it's love of country, for others, the ache of revenge. What really is it for you, Engle?"

Peter felt his head pushed down by the weight of his questions. He wanted to walk out, to salute curtly and leave no matter the consequences. Shmitt was right—he was the man in the portrait— lost, no way forward but into a fog of uncertainty. And that could never be because Peter existed apart from his soul, animated by a bundle of cold impulses, like a barefoot man who steps on a nail, reacting to a terrible pain he could not see—a pain deep within that could not be faced as it would rip him to shreds. And Shmitt wanted him to look at it, to handle it, to measure the pain into small doses that could be taken by others, by soldiers infected with Peter's DNA.

Peter's hands crushed the elegant mahogany handles that curled around his chair, fighting his urge to run. He swallowed hard, pushing his fears into the well that once was his soul and choked out his words. "What makes the ocean waves rise and fall? Is it something deep below? Or is it just the simple surface wind?"

Peter willed his eyes into his superior's enigmatic stare. "It is just what we see. There is nothing…nothing below, but a cold, dark, meaninglessness. That's all, sir."

Shmitts's lips loosened and separated, a retort about to escape, but then they closed firmly against what he knew were now useless words. He nodded with a languid consent. "I've made it my mission to stir the deep waters, but it's become so murky, I don't know. I'm old now. I should know. But perhaps you're right, Engle. I make too much of it." He reached into his desk drawer and pulled out the familiar gray envelope tossing it onto his desk. He tapped his finger on the envelope in a final deliberation, then spoke in English with a strained American accent. "You miss all those summers in Texas?"

Peter responded in kind with no hint of a German accent. "Been a while, sir. Haven't been back since…"

Shmitt returned a smile. "Perfect, as I had hoped."

"Yes, sir, every summer since I was a boy." Peter's mind wandered for a moment and then he smiled. "I do miss…I do miss it."

"Ah, I can tell by the look on your face." He pulled the orders back and held them weakly in his hands. "You found love there."

Peter shook his head. "I found something there, sir. Love?" He paused, his eyes bouncing about looking for his words. "Whatever I found was lost long ago," he said with a pushed temerity.

Shmitt's eyes narrowed. "I'm sorry to hear that. One should be in love at least once in one's life." He inspected Peter's reaction carefully, seeing nothing. "So you have no connection to the States anymore?"

Peter's eyes floated lazily. "I have no connection…no connection to anything, sir."

His brow fell strongly. *No connection to anything…Engle you are a dangerous choice. But you might be the best choice.* He tossed the orders within Peter's reach. Peter's eyes fell on the cover: OPERATION GREIF.

"I have a team. A small, very specialized group. All have lived in the States at some point in their lives. They're ready, well trained. I want you to lead them."

"The objective?"

"The American generals are prideful men. They hold too much information and are unwilling to share it with those they lord over. You come in the front door as American G.I.s, separated from their platoons, eliminate generals and other leaders in their sleep, confiscate their orders, and disappear out the back door like ghosts in the night." He nodded confidently. "They'll fall into chaos."

Peter remembered the painting and thought to himself, *The fog clears.* He sheltered a wearisome sigh deep in his lungs, held the orders in his hand, stood abruptly and saluted, his eyes clamped down hard and into Shmitt's like a sniper's stare. He turned around and left with his orders.

"Peter."

Peter stopped.

"It was an honor to meet you." His smile returned. "Though you remain a mystery to me."

Shmitt extended his hand.

Peter stepped toward him and shook.

Shmitt wrapped both of his hands around his. "If we survive this war, I hope we can build a friendship someday."

Peter forced a respectful nod, saluted again, and walked out.

MY SECRETS DIE WITH ME

Tegal Penitentiary – Two years in captivity

The next morning Max was moved to another cell, deeper within the prison. It was larger than the last one, but it had no window. He fell onto a thin mat on the floor.

The portly guard whispered to him. "This is better. You'll see." He shut the iron door and walked away.

Max heard a stir in the darkest corner, then a deep, pneumonic cough muffled by a hand. He slid back against the nearest wall and prepared for the worst. The man cleared his throat and inched forward into a tiny circle of light that broke through a hole in the ceiling. The light widened as it dropped toward his face. He was an old man, eighty or so, with curly gray hair that turned in on itself over and over, forming a crown of sorts. He wore thin, wire rimmed glasses on top of high, red-cold cheekbones. His nostrils were wet with his sickness. He spoke in a tired, gravelly tone. "Greenberg, Franz Greenberg. That is my name." He smiled broadly and then looked over his shoulder toward the guards stationed nearby. "Come, dear sir, come into the light."

Max leaned onto his hands that pressed against the cold floor and his face dipped into a thin line of light left unoccupied by the stranger. His eye patch, filthy and loose, caught all the light.

Greenberg nodded. "Let me get a good look at you."

Max felt the intensity of his inspection, though he felt no alarm, no threat from the old man.

"Please turn your face to your left, that I may see you completely," said the old man.

Max obliged and then glanced up toward the hole in the ceiling.

"Yes, yes, yes," said the old man, nodding. He broke the space between them, close enough to feel the warmth of Max's breath. He put his hands on Max's shoulders. "We will be friends," he said with a smile. He pulled back into the darkness. "What is your name, friend?"

"Max, Max Engle."

"So, Max. Who are you?"

Max didn't want to answer and was glad to find it was rhetorical.

"You are important enough not to kill, not to send to the camps." He moved back into the light. "Though I see you have not been tortured," he said with his eyes squinting. He rubbed his wrinkled chin. "All the others are dead or transferred. But you are spared, kept alive, like me." He struggled to stand, permanently bent over at the waist, his chin resting near his heart. His arms were twisted from many torturous breaks never properly mended. He stepped fully into the light and exposed his long nose that slid down his face to the left and then the right, also broken in many beatings. Greenberg felt Max's inspection. "Yes, yes, the beatings and breaks all meant to bring me to death's door, but never to cross the threshold." He hobbled in a circle within the cell. "I will never cooperate." He stopped and peered intensely at Max. "My secrets die with me." He wagged his finger in front of Max's face. "They think they can break me, but I will never give them what they want." He continued in his circle. "But why do they keep you alive, Max?"

Max cleared his throat to answer, but Greenberg interrupted again. "You have no secrets?"

Max shook his head slowly.

"What do they want from you?"

"I have nothing. Nothing," said Max sadly.

"Who are you, Engle? What sort of man are you?"

"I was a pastor. A pacifist," he replied, hating the words that dug up what he wished remained buried forever.

Greenberg stopped his pacing and rested his hands on his hips as his body swayed precariously. And then he stiffened. His weakened muscles strengthened around his brittle bones, and for a moment he could raise his head up to look directly at Max. His eyes widened with a pleasant surprise. "A pastor? Yes, yes, of course," he said to himself. He closed his eyes and spoke softly to himself, then opened them and looked up to the heavens. "Yes, yes," he whispered as he sighed pleasantly. He picked up his tiny circular pace mumbling to himself.

TO KINGDOM COME

Shumannsville, Texas

Noah was Julia's younger brother. The boy had a list of maladies that made his existence a bit of a miracle. Today he took his stance in a batter's box, his slender frame almost as thin as the bat he held. He pulled his cap down tightly, forcing his ears to jut out low and wide. He stared down the pitcher through his thick oversized glasses with a confidence that made little sense. He pulled a handkerchief from his rear pocket and wiped the perpetual pus that wet the corners of his eyes, and then he refined his gaze. He ran his fingers through his sweaty hair and adjusted his cap back down to his eyebrows. He squeezed his bat and dug in.

The pitch came fast and right down the middle. "Strike three. You're out," yelled the umpire.

Noah's audacious eyes widened in disbelief. "But that was…" He caught himself, and as was his way, he bowed his head in respect and whispered to himself. "Ain't no strike."

"What'd ya say, boy?" barked the ump.

"Nothin', sir. No disrespect, sir." He spun on his heel and turned toward his team's dugout.

"Boy," said the ump.

Noah spun around like a top undone.

"Ya oughta get those glasses checked," added the ump.

"I oughta get my glasses checked?"

The ump nodded and spat a wad of well-chewed tobacco onto the dirt.

Noah felt his anger rising and he gripped his bat harder. "Well, I just might do that. Thank you, sir." He ran off to his dugout and plopped down onto the bench. "I just got 'em checked," he said to himself. "That ain't very nice."

"Whatcha blabbin' 'bout Noah?" asked a teammate.

"Nothin'." Noah stood to his feet and began to cheer for his teammate in the batter's box as he swung, crushing the ball a hundred feet over the homerun fence. Noah watched the ball soar until it was out of his sight. He whispered to himself, "Someday I'm gonna hit one. Gonna hit one to kingdom come."

★ ★ ★

It was a hot summer day in Shumannsville. Noah walked home with Julia at his side. She was always at his side. She was five years older and more like a second mother to him. Noah was born premature, and as a result, he suffered with a heart condition, terrible bouts of asthma, and a mysterious condition that rendered him completely blind for weeks at a time. He always worked his hardest on the family farm, and no one gave more effort to baseball than he did. But in both cases, his passions always failed under the heavy weight of his limitations.

"Someday I'm gonna hit one over that fence, Julia."

She smiled at him and handed him a soda pop.

He took it and drank too much, too fast, releasing a roaring burp. He looked at Julia with wide, embarrassed eyes. "I'm sorry, Julia."

"Nothin' to be sorry about. But try not to drink so fast."

"Yup. I have that problem. Always in a hurry."

She chuckled. "You are. Don't know why."

"That's easy. Ain't as fast as the rest. Always catching up. That's it."

They walked down Highway 239 toward the farm, six boys trailing close behind. Noah looked over his shoulder at them. "I wish they wouldn't do that."

"What?"

"They always follow. Always wanna see ya. Every boy in town is in love with ya. It's sickening."

She smiled and shook her head disapprovingly. "Boys, Noah. They're just boys."

"Yeah, I know. No one will ever measure up to that Peter Engle. I wish you'd forget about him. He's long gone. Probably fightin' for the Nazis."

"You don't know what you're talkin' about Noah," she said with a restrained annoyance. "And I don't measure others to him. Don't need to. Just made a promise, that's all. Somethin' you know nothin' about. And let's keep it that way."

"Well, someday I'll find a girl. And I'll stick to my promise. I'll be there through thick and thin."

She laughed in agreement. "Oh, that I am absolutely certain of."

"Ya know I'm a man of my word. Never told a fib."

"Yes, sir. And I love that about you."

Noah beamed with confidence. Julia's constant attention and encouragement made him the young man he was. He took his cap off and ran his fingers through his hair as he often did when he felt strong. He put it back on, squaring his brim to shade the midday sun from his eyes.

But Noah was right. Every boy in town was in love with Julia. No one ever teased him. He had plenty of friends, even the most popular boys liked him. But he knew it was all because of Julia.

And that was alright by him because Julia was the most amazing person he had ever known. She was kind and giving, especially to those who needed it most. She taught Sunday School since she was twelve, always looking for the weakest lamb in the flock. He often reminded her of the time she walked ten miles each way to visit one of her Sunday School students in the hospital. Her reputation for caring for others even spread beyond Shumannsville.

And of course, she was beautiful. He once heard a boy describe her beauty. Noah would have punched him in the nose except he was right. The boy said Julia was something God made to just do a little showin' off. But she was no pushover. She worked the farm and the crops all her life and could run as fast as any boy, except Jake Wilson. No human could run as fast as Jake. And that's why the boys were all scared of her. Her beauty drew them, her kindness hooked them, and her power scared them. And he also knew there was no one in town worthy of her. Perhaps Peter was the only one for her. He hoped not. He was a German, and Noah figured he had American blood on his hands by now.

They walked side-by-side, their arms slung around each other's shoulders. They were dripping with sweat but that didn't matter. Noah looked at her and smiled. "Thanks for coming to my game."

She tugged down on his hat until it covered his eyes. She took a short swig of the soda and offered it to him. "Slowly," she ordered.

He guzzled it and burped loudly again. They both laughed as they turned left off the highway onto the long dirt road that led to their farm.

★ ★ ★

It was Saturday. Noah quickly removed his uniform and jumped into his coveralls. He stepped into the afternoon heat, tugged his baseball cap low over his face and joined his father in the cornfields. Father, drenched in sweat, skillfully wielded a husking hook in his right hand. With a swift motion, he used it to strip the corn ear of its husks, then grasped the ear to snap it from the stalk. He was so adept at this that he could do the work of two men.

Noah watched him in motion and shook his head in disbelief. "You're like a machine, Father. A regular corn huskin' machine."

Father stopped and turned to see him, offering his beaming, characteristic smile. "No machine, son, just us Fischer's giving our all. Come now, tell me 'bout the game."

Mother sat behind Emily, the family horse that pulled the corn cart down each row. She smiled at Noah and pulled the reins to steady Emily who was always too anxious to get to the next row. "Tell us, son. How was it?"

"Won again. Johnny homered…again."

"Wish we could be there but can't spare a moment right now," said Mother with a half-smile.

"That's okay. Julia was there. Anyway, ain't goin' back. That's gonna be my last game."

Father stopped and turned around again. "Seasons not over yet, is it?"

"No, sir, but ain't important. This is."

"Baseball is your favorite thing, son. We'll manage here. Might be getting some Mexicans to help finish out the season."

"Thank you. But I gotta be done with childish things."

Father looked at Mother and saw what he expected. She jumped off the bang board wagon and stared at him with concern. "No, son, finish the season. You're only seventeen once."

"Most of the boys are doin' the same. Ain't a problem. Three of them joined already. Ain't a season to go back to."

"Who joined?" questioned Mother with concern in her eyes.

"Billy, Jack and John, the twins. They're headed to basic in three weeks."

Mother put her hand to her mouth. "Oh dear."

Father put his hand on her shoulder and tapped it compassionately. "I knew about it."

"Why didn't you tell me?"

He nodded as he slipped his husking hook back onto his hand. "Was said in confidence, dear."

He swung at the stalk again and ripped another ear off throwing it into the wagon.

Mother jumped back onto the wagon and snapped Emily forward.

"Ain't that somethin'. They're soldiers now," said Noah with a proud smile that caught Julia's eye.

A WISH TO MATTER

Noah walked for thirty minutes without saying a word. When they reached their turn off, Julia looked at Noah and nodded like she was stepping into a field of landmines.

He looked back toward town and shielded his eyes from the sun. "You think the Lord can do miracles, right?"

"Yes," she answered with squinted, curious eyes.

He nodded with an upturned corner of his lip. "I'd like to see one."

Julia tilted her head at him wanting to correct him like the Sunday School teacher she was. "Come on, Noah. You're a miracle."

He looked away trying to hide the frustration in his eyes. "Heard it a hundred times. I'm alive. I know." He reached into his pocket and unwrapped a stick of gum, chewing it with an aggression that told Julia all she needed to know.

Julia's eyes filled with tears. She grabbed his hand and squeezed it. "You're the greatest joy I've ever had. Nothin' gonna bring me more joy ever." She let go of his hand. "If I ever lose you, I lose everything. You understand?"

He forced a smile and held her hand again. "I know, Julia. But there's gotta be more for me."

She looked down at his hand—his long, skinny fingers—and for a moment remembered his little baby hands, how they gripped hers with a certainty that he would always be protected by her. Her gaze returned, catching a determination in his eyes that scared her. "Noah. Please, think about it. The military can't take someone with your condition. Ya know that."

He grinned and his eyelids fluttered as they did when he got excited. "Whatcha always say when I talk 'bout hitting one out the park? There's room for a miracle, Julia. Always room for a miracle." He tugged her hand. "Come on," he said with a tricky half-smile.

"Not today. Not in the mood, thanks to you."

He pulled harder. "Come on," he insisted.

She forced a smile and reluctantly followed.

★ ★ ★

Noah pulled back his arm and let it go. He couldn't see well enough to hit a ball, but he could sure throw one. The rock flew into the air like it had wings escaping from his view.

Julia pressed her rifle against her cheek and pointed in its direction. She pulled the trigger and split the rock in two before its descent. "Again," she ordered.

Noah obliged, throwing this one even higher and farther.

They did this for an hour, as was their custom. He always felt the strength in his arm was made for something special.

"Last one, Julia."

"Okay. But this time let's do a double."

He smiled at the challenge, picked up two chunky rocks and gave her a wry smile. "Ain't gonna do it this time." He pointed in two directions. "Different directions. Ain't possible."

Julia raised her rifle and wrapped herself around it, letting one eyebrow escape in a perfect arch.

Noah rubbed the jagged edges away from the two rocks and prepared for the throw. He reeled back, heaving one east toward the river, the other west across and above the cornfield that captured their home.

Julia attacked the first, splitting it in two, and snapped west, devastating the second before it reached its safety. She lowered the rifle to her side and glanced over at her brother whose mouth was agape.

"Julia," he said in disbelief. "Thought for sure you'd miss on purpose."

She tucked her rifle under her armpit. "Ain't a sign, Noah. Just skill."

His chin raised knowingly. "Maybe a little of both." He pulled his cap from his back pocket and tugged it down onto his head. And one of those smiles that already lives in good fortune to come, invaded his face.

★ ★ ★

That evening, Julia looked out her second-floor window watching Noah as he walked between the unpicked rows of corn that stretched as far as the banks of the river. He walked down one row and turned back along another. His hands were outstretched on either side gently touching the stalks with his fingertips. She watched him for hours, into the night. She could feel something hunting him. Whatever it was, it was already chaining itself around his thin ankles forming him, instructing him, directing him in ways she wished not to discern. Julia knew this because she had this gift; from his birth she could discern Noah's thoughts. And now she wished this deep channel that fed her his ideas, his worries, his dreams, was gone.

She tried to look away hoping her intuition would falter, but her eyes were strongly set against her will. He stopped in the middle of a long row illuminated by the moonlight and sat down. He was speaking now, his voice too far to hear. But she knew what he was saying. God had given her entrance into their conversation. She shook her head in disbelief. "No," she said to God. "No. Please, no."

★ ★ ★

Two months later Noah was saying his goodbyes at the train station. Julia held him tightly, her hand caressing the back of his head like she did when he was a baby. She cried so hard she couldn't speak. Mother and Father finished their goodbyes, but she could not utter hers.

He pulled himself away from her and wiped the tears from his face. He squeezed her shoulders. "It's my miracle. Look at me," he said as he gazed at his uniform. "It's the greatest miracle I have ever known." He laughed and cried at the same time.

The army doctor detected nothing unusual in Noah's heart. He was deemed as fit as any other recruit. Julia promised she wouldn't tell. It was a miracle. And it was skill. Noah always had a great ability to memorize baseball statistics. So he stood before the eye chart without his glasses having previously memorized each line from the largest to the smallest letter.

Julia watched him leave with the train's sudden heave. She still couldn't believe it was happening. She tried to fight her thoughts. *He shouldn't be on that train. Why did you let him go?* She prayed for a greater miracle as she waved and yelled, "Come back to us. Come back to us, Noah."

He stuck his head out the window into the darkness and waved back, veiled by a thick curtain of steam.

Julia saw only his translucent outline behind the steam as if he had passed into another world. She pinched her eyes shut and knew in her heart that she would never see her brother again.

1,241 MILES

Noah got through basic training. He wasn't the worst trainee, and he certainly wasn't the best. He met young men from all over America. He liked them all, and they all seemed to like him, but one in particular—one so different from him—seemed destined to be his closest friend. Close enough to give him his new name.

"Tex, what the hell you doing?"

"I'm gonna hit the damn bullseye, Franco."

Franco, a tough Italian kid from Chicago who only stood five-foot-four grabbed the tip of Noah's rifle and pulled it away. "Tex, look," he said pointing.

Noah peered to his left and saw their drill instructor walking out into the range to get their targets. "Oh."

"Shooting your drill instructor, Tex…I can't even think of what they'd do to you."

"Franco, ya saved my hide again."

Franco shoved the rifle into Noah's chest. "You're a good shot. Better than me, but you're gonna need me to point out the krauts. They're the ones with the spiky helmets and the funny mustaches. Got that, buddy?"

He laughed nervously. "Ya sure got my back, Franco."

"I got your back. You know why?"

"Sure, because we're buddies."

"Yeah, of course," he answered with a weak sincerity. "But gotta tell you, my mama Luisa told me I'd be alright if I stick close to the angels. Mama Luisa's never wrong. Never." He poked his stiff finger into Noah's chest. "You ain't no angel, but you're as close as I'll ever find." He patted his chest gently where he poked a little too hard. "You're a good man, Noah. Best I ever met. I'm gonna make it…as long as you don't shoot me."

Noah blinked a couple of times brushing away his uncertainty. Then he shot a hopeful look up at Franco. "But we're buddies, right? Buddies for life?"

Franco grabbed him by the waist and lifted him off the ground in a strong bear-hug that squeezed the air from his lungs. He dropped him onto his long, skinny feet. "Franco and Tex, brothers for life…capiche?"

Noah heaved in a breath of air and nodded enthusiastically.

They were from different worlds—their homes 1,241 miles apart, Noah tall and skinny, Franco short and stout. And yet they were bound by a brotherhood that many blood brothers never experience.

"We gonna get Hitler himself, Franco. You and me. We gonna be the most famous soldiers ever known. Right, Franco?"

Franco smiled and then pushed his buddy along to the next target. "Yeah, sure, Tex. You and me…famous. No doubt about it."

★ ★ ★

June 6, 1944, D-day, Omaha Beach.

The USS Bayfield Attack Transport ship carried Noah and Franco and 2,452 other soldiers from the U.S. 1st Infantry Division. They were known as The Big Red One based on their shoulder patch depicting a large red number one. The ship was sleek and swift, part of the largest military armada of ships in history and over 156,115 troops headed straight for the beaches of France set to change the course of the war.

The landings started in the early morning hours. It was now two o'clock in the afternoon and Noah's Higgins boat, a small watercraft, ferried Noah and thirty others from their ship to shore. Franco had been sent ahead in another Higgins boat loaded to its maximum. They said their goodbyes with a nod. There was no time for words. They locked eyes until Franco turned to face the shore. Noah fixed on Franco's boat until it was a speck among a thousand specks in the shallow waves. He heard a whistle blow cuing him to climb in. He stood, crouched low, his hand gripping the thin, plywood sides of the Higgins, fighting for balance against the crashing waves that both repelled them and drew them closer to what he knew might be his end. His boat hit its mark and the front wall dropped exposing the men to machinegun fire. Noah jumped into the cold water and instantly thought of the beach in Galveston, Texas. Unlike Galveston, where the water smelled of salt and seaweed, Noah immediately inhaled an acrid, mechanical exhaust-like smell that made his nostrils sting. He heard the roar of his Higgins unit as it pulled away for the last time.

He pushed the water apart as he made his way toward the shore. At first, he went around the floating bodies that covered his path. Then he began to push them away, seeing the leaking of their blood into the salty water. He lifted his hand to block a bright, intrusive ray of sun that slipped in between a lingering morning fog. He watched the bloody ocean water creep down his arm into the watery grave he had disturbed.

There was a bump against his back, and then another. He turned to see two bodies pushed against him by the relentless waves. Beyond that, the fog was too thick to see anything else.

Then the fog split suddenly like a curtain opened to reveal the beginning of a tragic opera. There between the shore and the transport ships floated hundreds of dead GIs. The currents were shifting, bringing them closer to shore, closer to him. Their lifelessness was unmistakable; they floated face down, the backs of their heads gently bobbing in the water. *Could one of these guys be Franco?* he thought. He began to search through the bodies frantically, one-by-one. "Franco! Franco!" he yelled, his words lost in the endless mortar and machinegun fire. He turned to another, and he heard coughing and gasping for air.

"Help me." The soldier coughed, spilling blood and sea water from his mouth. "Help me," he said with a flattening urgency.

Noah grabbed him by the collar and pulled him to shore. He rolled him over and tried to reassure him. "Gotcha, buddy. I gotcha. Hey, partner. Hey," he yelled, pulling him closer. He squeezed his face and then slapped it. "Come on. Come on." But the soldier's eyes glared back at him with a wide, permanent stare that sent fear through him. He rolled away from him and watched the waves claim the soldier back into the ocean.

He took one last look around him and saw thousands of soldiers, some moving, most already concreted in by machine-gun fire. He watched men's mouths moving, felt concussions against his chest, but heard nothing. His knees gave up their strength and he fell face-first back into the gritty sand.

The smothered sounds of war erupted all at once—mortars exploding all around him, the whiz of thousands of bullets narrowly off their mark, desperate screams from countless soldiers pleading with God for mercy, and death—to the full dread of war. And it was too much.

He began to dig frantically into the sand like a sun-scorched crab desperately burrowing for the cool of its den. He dug until the ground was too hard and his fingertips bled profusely. He tore off his bayonet, lifted it over his shoulder and stabbed the ground repeatedly like a passionate killer. After several minutes, the foxhole was still too small to save him. He lifted his hand for another stab when he felt someone grab his wrist.

★ ★ ★

The next day Noah climbed a bluff on Utah Beach. The shore below was littered with rows of tangled barbed wire and olive drab helmets too numerous to count. Shredded life belts discarded from the thousands of bodies moved hours earlier lined the beach. Landing craft stuck in the shallows—parts of things he couldn't and didn't want to identify.

He couldn't remember where he was when Franco found him. The entire landing had been wiped away from his memory, though his body seemed to hold every minute of what happened. His stomach returned all he tried to eat, and his bones shook continuously despite the warmer weather. He smoked a cigarette from his fifth pack, now an expert, his fingers forced inward and elegant.

Captured German soldiers, thousands of prisoners of war, were busy carrying the last of the large plastic bags from the beach up a long, narrow trail that led over the bluff. Noah and many of the survivors of his platoon were assigned to Mortuary Affairs.

He heard a whistle call and jumped to his feet following a line of American soldiers up the path previously climbed by the German POWs. On the other side of the bluff, he looked down into a temporary grave as long and wide as all the cornfields in Shumannsville. He felt his eyes stretch beyond his control—thousands upon thousands of dead soldiers arranged symmetrically, orderly, row after row; the last body was far beyond his view. He gasped for air and was ravaged by the stench of rotting flesh and blood. *Oh God, oh God, too many…too many.* He wanted to run away but there was nowhere to go. He felt a nudge from behind and quickly followed the soldier in front of him. He was handed a pick, a stick, a marker, and a bag for personal effects. He was to quickly identify the soldier, mark the stick with his name, shove it into the ground like an unfinished cross, collect any belongings, and bury the body where it lay.

He worked through the night with generated light. Much of the time it was hard to see the names on the dog tags and, when needed, a desperate and eager German prisoner would run over and shine a single flashlight on the tag. At first, Noah hated working next to the enemy. He longed to shoot all of them, but they were necessary. Four thousand and four hundred allied soldiers died on that day. Nine thousand were wounded or missing.

Noah worked until daylight. A whistle blew and he fell in line, his feet heavy, shuffling through the sand with a sadness he knew he would carry for as long as he lived. He dropped his gear at his station and followed the rest to a meal and a few hours of sleep before they would start again.

Noah picked at his meal then lay where he was told. He covered himself with a blanket from head to toe trying to hide the uncontrollable shaking of his body.

Franco sat up in his cot and tugged at Noah's blanket. "Hey, Tex, you awake?"

Noah peeked over his blanket trying to hide his tears. "Hey, buddy."

Franco saw his tears and did his best to ignore them. "You okay? You okay, Tex?"

"Sure, Franco, just tired. Goodnight."

Franco looked out the open tent flap. "It's morning, Tex. You get some sleep, buddy. We'll talk…later."

★ ★ ★

A few hours later Noah woke and stumbled over for a cup of coffee. He sat next to Franco who scooped up the last of his watery eggs and spoke in between chews. "Nothin' like a cup o' joe in the mornin', huh?"

Noah broke a smile toasting his cup in agreement. He felt his hand begin to shake. He took a deep breath and tried to relax his grip around his jittery cup.

Franco watched. He placed his plate on the ground and smiled at his friend. "You haven't done it yet."

Noah's eyebrows raised curiously. "Done what?"

Franco tossed his look behind him. "Yesterday, I took a short walk, away from here, from everyone. Stood toward the ocean, could smell…it just happened. Just broke. A big one, Tex. I mean crap coming out my nose kinda cry."

Noah's eyes narrowed. "And that's it?"

"Don't know, Tex. Gotta happen." He smiled again, picked up his bowl and stood. "Better now." He nodded assuredly and walked away.

"Hey, buddy, hold on."

Franco stopped and returned. "Yeah, Tex?"

"I owe you my…"

Franco interrupted, his palm in Noah's face. "No." His lips tightened. "All them boys dead. You and me still here." His gaze fell onto the sand beneath him looking for words that mattered. A tear broke as he smiled what he wanted to communicate. "We got another day, Tex." He shook his head. "One more day."

★ ★ ★

And another day was given. Noah, Franco, and a handful of other GIs were set as an advance guard to escort a Colonel Weiss headed to Cherbourg, a French seaport.

Colonel Weiss held long, cylinder containers tight against his chest, as if they possessed the secrets of the world. His surveys and photographs were essential for the Allied offensive. The military, in many cases, operated on old maps that failed to reflect the rapidly changing landscape. Bridges were down, buildings obliterated, and roads annihilated. He had already helped the Brits and the French. Now he sat before them, a short, bald man with two heavy cameras strapped around his neck that caused him to slump like one way beyond his years.

Another soldier dressed in French civilian clothes, unknown to anyone, joined. A dangerous guy on a special mission was all they were told, but quite the opposite in appearance. He was hard to miss. He stood head and shoulders above the rest and looked more like a Hollywood actor. He slept in a single man tent and kept to himself. He never saluted the officers, nor attended briefings. It seemed he was under no one's command. Noah watched him and was fascinated. The sun was setting when he approached him.

Noah stood cautiously, a few feet from him. The mysterious soldier looked at him, nodded, and returned to the study of his map. Noah stepped closer and reached out for a shake. "Noah. My name's Noah Fischer."

He took his time folding his map and stuffing it into his jacket pocket. His head lifted and he gave Noah a stare that made him uncomfortable.

"Sorry. Am I bothering you?" Noah asked.

He looked at his extended hand and grabbed it with a strong shake. "Jimmy. Jimmy Williams."

Noah released and took a quick glance over his shoulder where his platoon was encamped. "We all got a bet 'bout ya."

Jimmy nodded. "Is that right?"

"Yup."

"You know I can't talk about my mission."

"Of course. Ain't that," he answered with a quick assurance. "So, have you been in the movies? Some guys say they recognize ya."

Jimmy chuckled. "Nope. I've never even seen one."

"Never seen a movie?"

"Where I'm from…well, let's just say those sorts of things don't exist."

"But you're American, right? You're on our side."

Jimmy stood, now a tower of steel. "Noah, right?"

Noah nodded.

"I grew up on the reservation. Navajo nation. We don't have such things."

"You're a Red?" he asked surprisingly.

Jimmy's eyes narrowed with a challenge that made Noah uneasy.

"Oh, sorry. Did I say something wrong?"

"I'm Indian," he replied, "on my mother's side. Father's a white man. Got a problem with that?"

Noah shook his head defensively. "No, sir. Not at all. You're an American," he said as he patted his forehead of nervous sweat. "An American Red. And I'm an American uh, uh, well my family comes from Germany. So I guess I'm an American Kraut, though I don't want that well known. Anyway, I'm proud to know ya."

Jimmy's face softened and a small smile took hold. "Texas, huh? What part?"

Noah beamed with pride. "Shumannsville. Ever heard of it?"

"Not Shumannsville. But Red Rock Reservation, that's my place, it's in Arizona, not too far from Texas."

Noah smiled broadly exposing his big front teeth. "Hey, we're neighbors."

"Yup, that's right." Jimmy considered the boy's innocence. He reminded him of his brother Joseph. And like Joseph, this boy was not made for war. He felt his heart ache. *This boy don't have a chance. Not a chance in the world.*

Noah reached his hand out for a parting shake and Jimmy took it with a kinder squeeze. "Sure was a pleasure meeting you, Jimmy. When this is all over, bet you'll have a story we'd all love to read."

"We all will…every one of us."

Noah walked away looking over his shoulder to give another unnecessary wave goodbye.

Jimmy returned a soft wave that floated in the air as one does when saying goodbye for the last time.

★ ★ ★

The Colonel sat in the rear of the transport vehicle keeping to himself until Franco broke the silence.

"Hey, Colonel, I know you can't tell us anything, but I was wondering if you could take a picture of me and my buddy here."

"Franco, come on, he's got important things to do," said Noah.

Colonel Weiss stroked his cameras like they were his precious children. "Maybe some other time," he said dismissively. He returned to stare out the back of the truck.

"Gotcha, Colonel. Sorry 'bout that," responded Franco. He shot a glance at the mysterious Jimmy Williams who sat apart from the rest, his hands comfortably around his M1941 Johnson Light machinegun, returned a slow nod backed by eyes that looked through Franco like he wasn't there.

Hours later the truck came to a slow, squeaky stop. Lieutenant Murphy, the commanding officer, the elder in the group, mid-thirties, gray stubble on his chin, aging him by ten years took a long nervous drag of his cigarette, jumped out of the truck, ordering the men out, then spoke secretly with the Colonel.

When he was done, he lit up another cigarette. "Okay, boys," he said between puffs. "Rest of the way on foot." He tried to study a crinkled map spotted with coffee stains.

Jimmy watched intently, noticing Murphy's struggle.

Murphy squinted and drew the map within inches of his face, and then took an eraser to it. He wiped the residue and looked again. "Oh, hell. Damn coffee stains looked like a mountain range," he murmured to himself.

Jimmy nodded at Franco who saw the same thing.

Once he had his bearing, Murphy folded the map and addressed his men confidently. "We got a few villages to go through. Krauts been bombed to hell. Not expecting any resistance. Our mission is simple…get the Colonel to a safe place where he can take his nice pictures and, uh, Williams…" he said with a wry smile, "…just along for the ride."

Jimmy looked past him at the horizon, eager to move on.

Murphy took another long drag, expelled, and tossed the stale cigarette to the ground. "Any questions?" He crushed the cigarette with his boot and answered before anyone could make a sound.

"Good. Let's go. Keep alert. Franco, Fischer, point. The rest, twenty paces back with me and the Colonel." He motioned them ahead. "Move out."

★★★

Franco and Noah walked together about five meters from each other, both still trying to walk out the anxiousness that had settled in their bodies. Franco looked over his shoulder at the rest of the escort who seemed too far off now. "We get some action, they're too far."

Noah looked back at them. "Yup. Let's slow our pace a bit."

Franco looked at Noah and nodded. "How ya doing?"

Noah searched as far as his eye could see down the dirt road they walked on. "Ya think we'll get some action?"

"Gonna happen sometime."

Noah grabbed his helmet strap and stuck it in his mouth chewing on it like a wad of tobacco. "Yup."

Two hours into their march, Franco looked through his binoculars, then lifted his hand abruptly. "Got movement three clicks north."

Lieutenant Murphy trotted to his point men. "Let me see." He took the binoculars and then quickly returned them with frustration. He let out a puff of smoke into Franco's face. "Oh, sorry 'bout that, Franco," he said with ridicule. "It's a damn dog." He waved the others over.

Colonel Weiss brought up the rear and spoke for the first time in their presence. "We got to get there in the next two hours. I need daylight," he said with a faint demand.

"Yes, sir, understand that." Murphy pointed forward. "That's Caen up ahead. What's left of it." He pulled out his crinkled map and pointed at it. "We get through there and we can get to this ridge and you can do what you do."

The Colonel nodded and looked at his watch. "Two hours. That's it."

Murphy grabbed Franco's binoculars again and barked orders. "We got two burnt out Panzers at the mouth of the city, and the rest, on the east, nothing but rubble. On the west, two buildings, damaged, but still intact. Enemies on the run, boys. Come across any locals, just say 'American'. That's it. Do not engage, no matter how beautiful…Franco," he said with a frown.

The others gave the usual cat calls.

Franco stuck his chest out. "You got it Sarge. But nothin' I can do 'bout them French dames wanting a little touch of this," he said teasingly as he squeezed his flexed bicep.

Murphy looked at him with a hollow stare. "Yeah, yeah, Mr. Atlas. Just ignore 'em."

Jimmy smelled the scent of burning rubber and diesel fuel that breached his breath. War was close. He was ready to engage the enemy though his orders were strict—no engagement until he reached the rendezvous point with the underground French resistance. He fought the urge to kill and to protect these men. He watched Noah and Franco—separated, vulnerable—and turned to all his O.S.S. Training. Improvisation and flexibility, these ideas made sense in battle, certainly more than strict adherence to generalized orders. He felt the strength of his hands around his machinegun readying it for its purpose.

★ ★ ★

Franco and Noah approached first. They could feel the heat emanating from the first tank. Franco held his M1 carbine tightly at his side, his trigger-finger eager and stiff. He motioned with a quick nod at Noah who already knew to step cautiously.

A German soldier hung from the tank's opening. He smelled of burnt flesh and rot. The hungry dog seen earlier had his way with most of what was left of him.

"That's nasty," said Franco.

The rest of the men stood back safely about two hundred meters waiting for them to clear the way.

Noah headed toward the second tank. It had a large hole in its midsection but was otherwise intact. He motioned Franco over as he stepped closer. Then he saw her.

A young woman, in her late teens, burst from the top of the tank.

Both immediately trained their rifles on her, their triggers nearly pulled.

She began to scream something in French.

"Hold your fire," yelled Noah.

She cried hysterically, her eyes wide with fear. She moved her head frantically side-to-side, her words grumbled and panicked.

They lowered their rifles and lifted their hands to calm her down. "It's okay. American! American!" yelled Noah.

Lieutenant Murphy looked on with suspicion but ordered the rest to stand their ground, a safe distance away.

Jimmy walked past him disregarding orders that everyone knew were never for him.

Noah came closer and tried to calm the girl. "It's okay," he said, patting his chest repeatedly in reassurance. "American, American." He could see her face. Her skin was smooth like Julia's, but colored with the faintest tan and a natural red that painted her cheeks like two roses. Her eyes were a bright blue green, a color he had never seen in all the women in Texas. Her hair was dark and wavy and fell on her shoulders like the collar of a royal cape. She was the most beautiful girl he had ever seen, the princess of every fairytale he had ever read.

Though her screams persisted, she stopped looking at Franco and only focused on Noah. Noah lifted his hands, palms exposed. "American, it's okay, it's okay," he said softly. He wanted to take her in his arms, to calm her, to hold her until she understood he was good, that America was good. He moved close enough to touch the tank speaking in a gentle whisper "American, American. Good, good."

She seemed to tire with each passing second, her screams quickly falling to a whimper. She looked at Franco then back at Noah. And then her screams began again.

Noah put his rifle down and began his ascent to the top of the enormous tank.

"No, no, buddy. Wait a minute," yelled Franco with urgency.

"She's just scared. Gotta show her we ain't the enemy."

The Colonel turned his head, his ear straining to hear the girl. His eyes widened in understanding. He dropped his cameras and broke from the rest.

"Get back here, Colonel. They haven't cleared it," ordered Murphy.

"She's saying…" He came closer straining to hear.

"Colonel. Damnit. Wait," he yelled. He ran after him.

Close enough to hear it all, the Colonel spoke to himself. "She's saying get back." He stopped and yelled at Noah. "Get back." But he was too far to be heard. "Get back," he repeated.

The girl continued her warnings now all directed at Noah who was only a few feet away. As he climbed closer, he noticed her arms were tied at her waist. Then he felt a presence that chilled his soul. He stopped and waved Franco away.

"Get the hell back, Tex!" yelled Franco.

Noah moved closer. He would save her. That's what he believed she was saying. "Save me. Please save me."

The Colonel sprinted toward them. "Get back. Get back!" he yelled.

A presence moved within the tank. Noah could feel it. And then there was a stillness, and the girl closed her eyes. Her screams ended in a final defeated breath.

A German tank commander suddenly jumped out from the tank's innards and yelled in words Noah immediately knew. He held a gun against the young girl's head.

"He says to get away. Keep going or she's dead," yelled Noah.

Franco already fixed his shot on the German's head. "I got a good shot at 'em, Noah."

The German commander continued to yell, his face bloody, his voice desperate and tired.

"No, Franco. Don't shoot. Wait." Noah put his hands out in surrender and slipped down the tank. He spoke in German. "Okay. No problem. We leave, you let her go?"

The commander nodded eagerly then jerked his head west away from the village. His eyes grew wider as the rest of the men surrounded.

"What the hell's he saying, Tex?" asked Murphy.

"Wants us to leave. He'll let her go when we leave."

"He's a lying bastard. I got 'em, Lieutenant," yelled Franco.

Lieutenant Murphy shook his head. "Hold, Franco. Hold."

"Got a clear shot, Lieutenant. Gotta take it!"

"Wait, Franco," urged Noah. "Wait. He's moving too much. Wait, please." He climbed back onto the tank unarmed.

"Tex, what the hell. Get away," ordered Murphy.

Noah blocked Franco's shot. "I got this." He spoke to the tank commander calmly in his language. "You give me your word, you'll let her go? You promise?"

He shook his head again looking at Noah with wide, panicked eyes and spoke to the others in his best English. "I promise. I promise."

"Get the hell down, Tex. Now!" ordered Murphy.

"Yes, Lieutenant." He jumped off finding his footing next to him.

Lieutenant Murphy grabbed him forcefully by the arm. "You do that again and I'll put a bullet in your head." He let him go briskly and turned his attention to Franco. "Drop your aim, Franco. Let's get the hell out of here."

Jimmy looked at Lieutenant Murphy and shook his head. "I got 'em."

The Lieutenant grabbed his forearm. "I'm still ranking officer. I call the shots 'til I get you to your drop-off."

Noah looked at Jimmy and knew what he would do.

Jimmy pulled his arm away and circled behind the tank.

The tank commander continued to scream his orders in broken English, "Go, go away. Promise…I promise you." His hand trembled around his gun that still pressed hard against the girl's temple.

She seemed to understand that her salvation would not come. She dropped her face, closed her eyes softly, and murmured a prayer. When she was done, her eyes stretched wide with certainty. She snapped her head back hard into the German's nose.

Before the German could tighten his finger around the trigger, he felt a sudden squeeze around his wrist so tight his bones cracked. He dropped his gun and released a scream that was immediately silenced with the snap of his neck. His body fell lifeless into the tank's innards.

The French girl turned to see Jimmy, her eyes blinded by the sun. She turned her gaze into the tank and spotted the handgun. Before Jimmy could jump off the tank, she filled the dead German's body with holes.

Jimmy jumped from the tank and shot a look at Lieutenant Murphy, and the flash of his eyes shut down his response. Murphy lit another cigarette with a shaky hand. He took two quick puffs and shouted his smoky orders. "Let's get the hell out of here. Daylight's burning."

Noah stayed behind, catatonic, both impressed and shocked by Jimmy's mechanized killing.

The French girl popped her head out of the tank catching a glimpse of the tall stranger that saved her.

Her eyes now clear and hopeful looked on him longingly. She uttered something unknown in French, its sentiment clearly understood.

Noah snapped back, his eyes returning to a normal size. "Who the hell is this guy?"

★ ★ ★

Two days later the squad met its objectives. Colonel Weiss had his pictures and Jimmy was close enough to his meeting point to leave. It was clear to everyone that Jimmy was never being escorted anyway. He was there to protect the Colonel. He packed his gear and strapped his machinegun over his shoulder. He stopped to say goodbye to Noah, who sat in his tent alone.

He entered. "Good to know ya, Noah." He extended his hand.

Noah snapped to his feet and shook eagerly. "You off?"

"Yup."

"Well, wish ya the best. I'll be praying for ya, Jimmy."

Jimmy smiled. "Take care of yourself," he said as he took a step out.

"Hey, Jimmy…"

He stopped and poked his head back in.

"Wish you weren't leaving. We could really use ya here." His smile stretched in exuberance. "You're like something out of a movie, or one of my comic books," he said with a chuckle.

Jimmy's eyebrows climbed and fell quickly into a compassionate frown. "Just a soldier like you."

Noah's posture slumped, his chin trembled, and his large blue eyes narrowed to abate his tears. "Just wanna matter, ya know? Wanna make a difference."

Jimmy nodded a yes. "You will." He shot a lazy salute and was never seen again.

TO SEE AND BE SEEN

A few days later Franco wiped pus from Noah's eyes. "We gotta get you to a doctor, buddy."

Noah grabbed Franco's wrist and squeezed it. "No, Franco. It'll pass. Always does."

Franco pulled his wrist away angrily. "You can't see a damn thing?"

"It'll go away. I've had it since I was a kid." In one seamless motion he lifted himself upright and certain and punched his fist into his open hand. "Can't be happenin' now. My time's comin'." His eyes searched the interior of his tent looking for something to say. A nervous, fragile smile pushed his plea. "I ain't going home 'cause of this. Please, Franco."

"I'm not your problem. Lieutenant's gonna send you away. He's gotta."

★★★

Lieutenant Murphy waved his fingers in front of his face. "Can't see a thing?"

Murphy shook his head hesitantly. "You say you've had this condition for years? How the hell they let you in? A blind soldier. Well, I'll be…"

Noah sat up and pleaded. "Please, Lieutenant. It always goes away. Just a few days is all."

Murphy raised his voice. "What the hell do you want me to do? You want me to hold your hand in the meantime?"

Noah dropped his head and gave up. He shrugged his shoulders acceptingly.

"0700. I'll have transport here. You're on that truck." He took a few brisk steps away, stopped and pivoted into the compassion his soldier needed. "Look, Tex. You're a good soldier. Proud to have ya. But I can't take any chances. Sorry."

★ ★ ★

Franco sat in a foxhole two kilometers from their temporary camp. Colonel Weiss had one more set of pictures, some modifications, and then they'd return to base camp. Although base camp was nothing special, they all longed for a shower and rest. For now, Lieutenant Murphy had Franco watching the perimeter. There was nothing to see but an ugly patchwork of burned trees, limbs forced down as if in surrender, adjacent to singed foliage still partially green, in a proud resistance, their days numbered. The sun began its fall behind the perimeter like a closing curtain ushering the show's end. Franco rubbed his exhausted eyes with the back of his dirty sleeve.

An hour later, he crushed his sleepiness with a set of push-ups and popped to his feet when he saw movement in the distance. He grabbed his binoculars and zeroed in. "Ain't no dog this time," he said to himself, as he cranked his radio. "This is foxhole one. Foxhole one. I got eight headed my way. Repeat…eight headed my way."

He tensed his eyes through his binoculars again. "Oh, hell no. Can't be."

"Sarge, they're friendly. Repeat, they're our guys."

★ ★ ★

Franco crawled out of his foxhole and began a cautious march toward them. He held his rifle across his chest with a restrained suspicion. "What the hell they doing out here?" he asked himself. "Identify yourself!" he shouted.

The men lifted their hands above their heads and stopped. It was Lieutenant Peter Engle and his new men, Operation Greif, in full force, Germany's special force dressed in U.S. 101st uniforms, taken from the bodies of paratroopers freshly removed from their tree lined grave. The plan was simple. They would take out the Colonel, take his maps and photos, and then wipe out his advance guard.

Peter yelled a response, "U.S. 101st Airborne." He gave his new assumed identity. "Sergeant John Jenkins, U.S. 101st Airborne."

Franco strapped his rifle casually around his shoulder and motioned them over.

"Sergeant John Jenkins," repeated Peter. He shook his head. "It's a damn mess. Got us spread all over the damn place. We're the lucky ones. Some of our boys dropped right into the damn krauts' kitchen. Poor bastards."

Franco shook his head again. "What the hell."

"Mind if we put our hands down?" cracked Peter with a smile. "You ain't gonna shoot us, right?"

Peter's men laughed.

Franco nodded. "So. Tell me again. What the hell happened?"

Peter watched Franco's hands still gripping his rifle. He wiped his face with a handkerchief and responded coolly, "Well, best I can tell, it's a whole lot of things. Coordinates are wrong, the air ships took a hell of a beating and some of us had to jump early. We just made it out in time. How many made it…I have no idea."

Franco looked past them toward the forest from which they came. "How long you been out here?"

"Been two days. Could use some water," answered Peter.

"I didn't ask you. I asked him," said Franco pointing to another soldier.

Peter's hand drifted toward his handgun set at his waist. "Yeah, no problem."

"Well, it's like Sarge said, about two days," responded the saboteur private.

Franco nodded and pulled a pack of cigarettes from his pocket. "Smoke?"

They talked for a few minutes, smoked, and drained Franco's canteen.

"You boys hungry?" asked Franco.

"Hell, yes," said Peter.

"How 'bout a beer?" asked Franco.

"Beer? You got beer?" said Peter with a feigned glee.

"Got a few in the truck. What kind ya want?" asked Franco.

"You mean American beer?" questioned Peter. He felt his heart beat faster and his muscles squeezed as they did just before he killed his enemies. In all his training they never covered American beer. He felt sweat bead up on his forehead. His hand shifted onto the butt of his gun again.

Franco's eyes narrowed a beam into Peter's focused stare that moved from his hands to his gaze. *Who the hell is this guy? Somethin's wrong.* He took a deep breath and cleared his hesitation. *Damn it. These guy's been through hell.* "Only the best for the best. What kind ya want?"

Peter felt his hand stiffen then suddenly loosen. It wasn't the right time to fulfill their mission. "Ya kiddin? Hell, right now I'm so damn thirsty I'd drink a glass of warm piss."

Everyone laughed.

Franco smiled, shot his arm around Peter, and tugged him toward the camp.

★ ★ ★

Peter leaned against a large boulder, sipping his beer. His men sat with the other GIs talking and laughing. Franco approached and handed him another beer.

Peter nodded negatively. "Had enough. Thanks."

Franco nodded. "I'll drain it for you. So, where'd ya say you're from?"

"I didn't."

"Yeah. Right." Franco tried to hide his suspicion. He chuckled. "We're all from somewhere. And God willing we're going back there. You sound like Tex. Where were you born?"

"Oh, you got a Tex?"

"Yeah. I guess we all got one. So where in Texas?"

"A little town ya never heard of."

"Try me."

"Shumannsville. A little farming town. Nothing much."

Franco laughed. "You gotta be kiddin'. Tex's from Shumanns-ville. What's the odds of that."

Peter's brow fell and his cheeks raised to meet them in a forced smile. His cover was over. His men were relaxed, their weapons not at the ready. He could take Franco, but his men would be vulnerable. And then it came to him. "Ya asked where I was born, not raised. My momma got stuck in that crappy town on her way to Houston. Truck broke down. Had me there. A month later I was in Houston. Glad to meet your Tex though. Still a brother from the greatest state in America," he said with a grin that covered his tension.

"Yeah. Let me take you to him. He's a special guy. "

"Special?"

"Yeah. Don't know how the hell the army let him in. It's been my mission to take care of 'em.

Ya know? Just somethin' I gotta do."

Peter shot him a nod and forced an appreciative smile.

* * *

They entered Noah's tent and saw him asleep on his side, his face turned away from them. "Noah. Wake your lazy butt up. Got a Texan here who wants to meet you."

Noah rubbed his hand down his face wiping his drowsiness away. He sat up and slowly turned to meet them.

Peter's eyes widened in shock, and he quickly dropped his hand to his side iron. He stepped back behind Franco gripping his gun tightly with his deft fingers. *How could this be? It can't be.* He waited for Noah's response. He would kill Franco, but then what? *I have to kill him too? My cover's gone. Julia, I'm sorry.*

Peter waited for Noah's surprise, but nothing came. Just a stupid smile, and lazy eyes that told him something was wrong with him.

"Poor guy. Got some disorder. He's damn blind," said Franco compassionately.

Peter's mouth fell agape. He pulled his hand away from his gun. "He's blind?"

"Can't see a damn thing. Poor guy."

"Hey, stop callin' me a poor guy, Franco. I'll be back."

"He's getting shipped out tomorrow. Poor guy," he said teasingly.

Noah shook his head frustratedly. "Yup...Franco here just wonderin' how he's gonna get along without me."

"Yeah, yeah, yeah. Anyway, this is Sergeant Jenkins. He's got a problem like you."

"Your vision gone too, Sarge?"

Franco chuckled. "No. He's a damn Texan too. And get this. He was born in Shumannsville."

"What? You're kiddin'."

"Like I told Franco. Just born there. Raised in Houston."

"Ain't been back?"

"No. No reason to."

"Houston, huh? City boy?"

"I guess so. Compared to Shumannsville."

"You know the Guadalupe River?"

Peter paused under the pressure of his memories. He saw the river. He saw Julia again. And then he saw her lips, his first kiss, and all the times they shared nestled close together on the riverbank dreaming about their tomorrows. His voice cracked with an unexpected emotion. "Yeah. Yeah, I heard about it."

"I live right up next to it. Ain't nothing more beautiful…" Noah's eyes moved back and forth in a fond memory and a smile pulled across his face.

Franco snapped his fingers near his face.

Noah shook the memory away. "So how long were you there?"

"Just a bit. Just born there."

Noah rose to his feet and tilted his head slightly as if trying to see through his blindness. "Ya know. Ya sure do sound familiar."

Franco absorbed Noah's curiosity and studied Peter's response.

"Well, who knows? But I think you're just missing home. Like me, I heard a dog barking yesterday. Swore it was mine."

Noah laughed. "Yeah. You're right. Anyway," he reached out his hand. "Glad to meet you."

They shook.

Franco slapped Peter on the back. "I got watch. You take my cot."

"Ya sure?"

"Yup. Just don't let this fool talk your ear off. You hear that, Tex? Let 'em sleep."

"Roger that."

Franco left. Peter tossed his gear to the floor and sat on his cot.

"Hey, I'll let you sleep, Sarge." Noah backed up until his leg pressed against his cot. He lay back in and whispered to himself. "Born in Shumannsville. What's the odds of that?" He shut his eyes and fell fast asleep.

Peter was split in two—one side wanting to run away, the other fixed by the thick, iron spikes of duty. His hand shook uncontrollably. He grabbed it and tried to squeeze away its advance. He lay in his cot, his lips uttering silent pleas. "Julia, forgive me, forgive me…"

* * *

It was 15:45 exactly. Peter's men stood in formation in the darkness, their mission complete. They were quiet, still, their faces stoic and their chests still expanding and contracting like they'd just sprinted, warm blood still dripping from their knives. They entered like ghosts in the night, just as Lieutenant Colonel Shmitt said, translucent, floating, silent executioners with quick, sharp thrusts that killed their targets in their sleep.

Peter addressed his men. "You're Germany's finest men. Return as instructed. I'll follow shortly."

One of his men spoke respectfully. "Sir, you're not returning with us?"

Peter looked toward Noah's tent. "No, my mission's not done."

"Yes, sir."

They saluted their leader and headed north for Berlin.

* * *

Peter stood outside Noah's tent. He entered and poured a solution into a handkerchief and then covered Noah's mouth and nose with it. Noah struggled, every muscle in his body tightening, his hands squeezing and pulling against Peter's hands, but they were steel vice grips impossible to break.

His legs kicked violently beneath his blanket. He punched and clawed, but nothing could break Peter's hold. Noah heaved in a chemically tainted air and then felt a coldness cover his body. He heard his own muffled cries for help slowing. Then he heard Peter's voice speaking in German. "It's okay, it's okay. Sleep, my friend. Sleep," he said compassionately.

Peter removed his grip and lay Noah's still body gently back onto his cot.

* * *

The next morning Noah struggled to lift his head, still feeling the power of the chemical he was forced to breathe.

Peter stepped close, tilted his head, examining Noah's eyes.

"What happened? Where am I?" he asked.

Peter grabbed his shoulders and sat him up against a tree. "Can you see?"

"No. Where am I? Am I in the hospital?" Noah tried to lift his hands and discovered they were tied behind his back. "What's happening? Why are my hands tied?"

Peter wiped the sweat from his brow and lowered a shovel that rested on his shoulder, shoving it into the dirt. "You'll be fine. It'll wear off soon."

Noah tugged at the ropes that bound him. He felt the red tide of his temper rise through his body. "What the hell's goin' on?"

Peter fetched a canteen. "Here. Drink. You'll feel better."

"Who are you?"

"You know me as Sergeant Jenkins, U.S. 101st. But I am a Lieutenant of the Wehrmacht. We eliminated your Colonel." He let his words sit. "The rest are dead too. I just finished burying them."

Noah struggled to stand but fell back against the tree. "You killed them? Franco. Where's Franco?" He yelled in a panic. "Where's my brother?' He screamed.

"He felt no pain. None of them. They died in their sleep."

"You killed them?" Come on now, Sarge, quit the kiddin'," he said with a nervous smile. "Where's Franco? Franco, Franco!" he yelled. He nodded to himself. "Oh, I see. This is some sort of training. Come on Sarge. Cut me loose. Game's over."

Peter came closer and spoke softly. "Franco was a good man. He cared for you. I'm sorry for your loss, Private."

Noah felt sick to his stomach and then vomited violently. When he was done, he wiped his mouth with his shoulder. His lips tightened with determination. He shot to his feet, "You son of a …" He took two steps and fell on his face. His tears spilled onto the fresh dirt that fell from Peter's shovel. He tried to lift his face from the ground, but his agony overwhelmed him. "No. Please, God, no."

He wept until he passed out.

★ ★ ★

Noah awoke to a crackling fire. It was dark now. He tried to sit up but was still too weak.

Peter lifted him and sat him against the tree again.

Noah's eyes were swollen and red, and dirt covered half his face. He cried throughout an entire six hours of sleep. His throat hurt and his mouth was dry. "Who are ya?" he asked with a weak, raspy voice.

Peter stood across from him stoking the fire. He tossed a casual glance and returned to the fire.

Noah's lips stiffened as he choked back a sob, and his vision swam in hot tears he felt shouldn't be released until he knew more. "Who are you?"

Peter sat down and lifted his hands toward the fire, rubbing them together. He looked up at Noah and tried to speak but no words came.

Noah looked away in disgust. He took in a deep breath and leaned back against the tree. "They were good men."

Peter nodded slowly and spoke as if to himself. "Good men?"

Noah struggled to get up, but his legs shook and gave way. "They were good men, you bastard."

Peter sighed. "Good, evil, it's all lost now." He stood and blinked his eyes against the smoke. He paused for a long time and waved his hand over his brow gently rubbing his forehead of a sadness he could not afford. "Simple soldiers like us...we don't get to decide that."

Noah looked back toward the smell of the graves and felt an overwhelming anguish entangled with all the curse words he knew. He shut his eyes tightly and his body shook uncontrollably, his thoughts raced without mooring. He was back home, then back at the mass grave, in his bedroom, then laughing with Franco. And then he saw Franco dead in a hole, dirt being thrown upon him. He was losing his mind. He prayed desperately trying to hold his sanity. He lifted his head when he heard Peter filling his pack.

Peter swung his machinegun over his shoulder. He looked back at the graves again. "You have a few minutes. Then we move. I can direct you to his grave if you want." He pulled out his knife and cut Noah loose, lifting him to his wobbly feet.

★ ★ ★

Noah stood over Franco's shallow grave, his eyes arid and useless. "Why, buddy?" He looked at the other graves. "I was supposed to be your good luck." He looked over his shoulder at Peter who stood nearby. "I'm sorry, brother. Wish I had gone with ya." He began to step away then stopped and returned to his grave.

"Let's go," commanded Peter.

Noah bent over and scooped up a handful of the fresh soil that covered his friend. He squeezed it in his fist and prayed silently. He threw the dirt back on the mound and turned toward Peter.

Peter grabbed his arm. "Wait. Why didn't I die too? It would be so much better for me to be dead." He pulled away from Peter's grip and shouted. "Why didn't you kill me?"

Peter tugged on his machinegun strap bringing it closer to his chest, as if to conceal the truth that wanted to leak from his heart. "Death is the master, above mere mortals, stupid soldiers like us…we bow to him, thousands at a time, one at a time… his time…" He tugged his arm. "Not your time."

Noah pulled away again. "No. This is my time. Kill me now," he demanded.

Peter tugged him hard. "Let's go."

Noah fixed his boots firmly into the ground and forced his face in Peter's direction. His words, burning arrows pointed at his heart. "I swear to you. I'm gonna kill you. Someday I'm gonna kill you. I swear to God."

Peter sneered and grabbed him again with a grip that gave no room for Noah's defiance. "Death is a mocker, Noah….and he doesn't listen to prayers. He's a prodder, slicing, scaring, making life ebb away a thousand moments in his time."

Noah stumbled along, peering over his shoulder at Franco's grave, into an utter darkness that covered his eyes, and now his heart. *I'll get 'em, Franco. I promise ya. I never break a promise. I'll get 'em.*

GREENBERG'S NOT A RABBI

Tegel Penitentiary

Two months passed since their first meeting. Greenberg was moved often and only brought to Max's cell a few times, sometimes only for a few hours. Today Greenberg sat on the floor, his twisted back pushing his chest against his knees where he rested the left side of his head so he could see Max who sat to his immediate right.

"Here, take my water," said Max. He lay the cold edge of his water cup against the old man's lips. "There you go. You must keep drinking." It was now summer, and the cell filled with stifling heat, humidity and the foul stench of their body odor and waste bucket.

Greenberg tapped Max's hand, signaling he'd had enough.

Max pulled the cup back exposing Greenberg's smile. "Thank you, Max."

"How do you do that?"

"Do what?"

"Smile like that?"

"The how is a physical phenomenon involving the facial muscles," he said chuckling. He lifted his head off his knees and straightened his neck. "You mean the 'why' of course."

Max nodded.

"Well, that is a very complex question, with an equally complex answer. Are you sure you want me to respond? It may take a while, my friend."

Max nodded and broke a smile. "Well, I may have a moment between my lectures and tennis."

Greenberg's lips spread across his face in a smile that belied his declining health and terrible pain.

"Wait. Before you answer that, you have yet to tell me about yourself. How you got here, and what they so desperately want from you."

Greenberg sighed heavily. "How I got here…I haven't spoken of it in quite a while."

"I'm sorry. I don't need to know."

"No, I think it helps. It reminds me of what is important." He took a deep breath and set aside his hesitation. "First, they took everything from me…my way of life, my reputation. It mattered little to me. I had my family." He shook his head. "That, they understood." He wiped his lips with his trembling hand and his eyes set above Max at nothing. "One morning, they pulled us out of our home, twelve Gestapo, in front of our neighbors, still in our sleeping garments." His eyes plunged to the cold concrete ground. "Without a word, they pulled my daughter-in-law from my son's hands and filled her with bullets." His eyes lifted at him. "'Relent,' they said. I would not. Then they made my son kneel next to her body. My only son." He shook his head against the memory. "They put a bullet in his head. One terrible bullet."

Max watched the man, his eyes telling the story, pain finding a reservoir to lay in, and he felt terrible for asking.

"We all knew this was coming. We all understood what was at stake and fully accepted…" He wiped the corner of his eye of a lone tear with his twisted, bony finger. "It is hard not to remember my wife's eyes at the end. They were so kind…no regret," he said, as a tender smile remembered her. "Her eyes still give me strength to this day…to never stop fighting this evil." He chuckled and cried simultaneously. "What a gift she gave me." He rubbed his eyes vigorously with his bent fingers and his voice quivered. "They died honorably, Max, never once doubting my decision." He looked away as tears fell in thick, wide lines from his old, weary eyes. "Never doubting, Max. That is the 'how' for me."

Max wanted to say he was sorry, but the old man's words were now stuck in his throat, slowly slipping into his gut, festering, bubbling, forming something there he was too sick to comprehend.

"They say my two grandsons are alive in a camp. But in my heart…I know they are already dead."

"Perhaps you're wrong. Maybe you will see them again when the war is over."

"If only that were true, Max. There is something that happens to the human heart when a loved one is taken forever. It is undeniable." He pressed his finger against his chest. "It is felt here. One knows."

Max's gaze shot to the darkest corner of the cell. "Yes," he nodded, agreeing. "Yes…one knows."

"I have been tortured for years, every time closer to death. But I'm still alive, an old man like me." His face brightened with his characteristic grin. "And then you came. So now I know my end is near."

"What do you mean?"

He nodded to himself as if already hearing his words and agreeing gleefully. "You are an answer to my many prayers, Max," he said as a new flow of tears streamed from his bright, hopeful eyes.

Max covered his mouth with his hand not wanting to speak the words that would betray Greenberg's joy. He looked away into the shadowy corners of their cell again. "Are you a rabbi? I knew many rabbis."

Greenberg chuckled. "No, no. Me, a rabbi? I am a devout Jew, but what reason would they have to keep a rabbi alive? Perhaps Hitler has seen the light and wants a bar mitzvah. Or better yet a circumcision. Now *that* I would be glad to provide," he said as he raised his shaky hand.

They both laughed and he ended with a nod of his head and his singular smile again. "No, my friend, not a rabbi."

"Then who are you? What do you have?"

"Oh, my friend, you are not ready for my answer," he said as he wagged his finger at him.

"Ready for what?"

He waited too long seeing an anxiousness in Max's eyes. "To everything there is a season. I have little time, I know. But I must wait for you."

"For me?" Max looked out toward the guards that sat nearby. "You want us to break out? You want me to kill these guards?" He looked down at his bony legs. "I'm sorry, friend. It isn't in me. I haven't the strength, nor the care."

Greenberg rubbed his forehead with the palm of his hand. "No, no, Max." He dropped his hand and smiled. "Something greater must happen. Something that cannot be constrained by these bars, or by any man, not even you, Pastor Engle."

Max pushed his head back against the wall, his neck stiff with resistance. "Please don't call me that."

Greenberg nodded in acceptance. "Yes, yes, I understand… you are not ready."

Max struggled to his feet and shook his head angrily. "I'm sorry, my friend. You're mistaken. I'm not …maybe there will be another one."

Greenberg's eyes fell, discouraged, his hope deflated. "I'm sorry…this is not the time."

Max stepped closer and dropped to one knee looking directly into his eyes, searching for the mystery of his strength, speaking as calmly as he could. "I…I can't be who you need, whatever you think you need. Sorry, my friend." He put his hand on his shoulder. "You have something, something that keeps you alive. I don't understand it, how you still fight to live." He lifted his hand from his shoulder and let it fall limp at his side. "All I want is my death." He nodded at him like one looking for agreement. "Is that asking for too much?"

He forced himself up and backed against the bars, his body heaving in a silent cry. Greenberg nodded compassionately. "I understand. Like me, torture is our brother, death a distant cousin." He leaned forward catching Max's darting eyes. "Like me…you hold something more precious than gold, more precious than life itself."

The weight of his words forced Max's nose against the cell bars. He pulled his dirty blanket over his head to hide his burning opposition.

Greenberg looked away, too tired to hope. *Oh Adonai, my heart beats weaker by the day. Am I wrong? Is he not the one?*

Max stumbled to the door, gripping the iron bars. "Guard, guard. Move me to another cell. Move me," he demanded.

Greenberg felt a heaviness in his heart that began to crush the hope that kept him alive. He put his hand over his eyes and wept.

JUST A SOLDIER

Noah rested near a brook that would ultimately feed into the English Channel, a few miles from the Port of Cherbourg, France. Peter filled his canteen with the brook's cold water and drank it without a pause. He refilled it and walked over to Noah, handing it to him. He heard the soft babble of the brook and it reminded him of hunting with his father in the forest.

Max pointed to a pile of elk droppings and then motioned eastward with his head. Peter followed his father as they navigated the slippery side of a hill. Two steps forward and they both slipped, tumbling down the hill and falling face first into the muddy base. Max quickly sat up and pulled Peter to a sitting position. Peter, clearing the mud from his eyes, looked up to see his father's face smeared with the same muck. A quiet chuckle began with Max, soon joined by Peter's muffled laughter. Before long, they were both laughing uncontrollably. They walked back to the farm, his father's arm around his shoulder, both still covered in mud.

Peter rubbed the memory from his eyes and sat down, giving his back to his prisoner as if tempting him to make his move.

Noah felt a large rock near his foot. In two seconds, he could take him out. He inched closer to it.

"So, you want to know why I spared you?"

Noah stopped and sat back down. "I don't…I don't care anymore."

Peter chuckled. "Maybe you don't. Maybe you're just like me; you care about nothing."

"The hell with you. I'm nothin' like you."

"You're right…nothing like me."

Noah kicked the rock near his boot, sending it into the brook. "You don't know a thing about me."

"Enough. I know enough." Peter turned to face him.

Noah turned toward his voice, his lips stiff with anger. "Like I said, I'm nothing like you. You're a cold-blooded killer."

Peter's hands swept through the tall grass that abutted the brook. He smiled softly. "I'm just a soldier. I kill, like you, like your friends. That's what we do."

Noah's fingers felt the ground searching for a rock, anything to vent his hate, to kill Peter, but found nothing but loose soil. He picked up a handful, squeezed it before tossing it to the ground. "I wish I had a knife. I'd cut ya into a million pieces."

Peter nodded and his lips curved in thought. "You haven't killed yet, have you?"

Noah's stare narrowed in a hate that loosened in a cold calculation. "I'll tell ya one thing. Nothing would give me more pleasure than killing you right now."

Peter pulled his machinegun strap over his shoulder. "Well then, maybe we're different after all…very different." He stood and stared off at the brook as it turned west and out of sight.

"Damn right," yelled Noah.

Peter returned his gaze with a softness in his eyes that held no judgment. "I've never taken any pleasure in killing anyone. Never will."

Noah felt the heftiness of Peter's words. He tried to extricate his passion to hate him again—it was eviscerated by Peter's truth, and all that held him now was the thought that Franco was gone forever. He heard the sweet rouse of the brook for the first time and began to cry.

"I'll leave you here. This is where the Brits will find you. Just sit and wait."

Noah stood slowly still wiping mucus from his nose. "Why ya doin' this?"

Peter considered his words for a while. He looked down into the brook, catching his reflection, seeing someone he barely recognized. He squeezed his machinegun handle tightly. Then he looked down at his dirty boots fighting a growing compassion that had long been chilled.

"I need a reason. Please," begged Noah. "I'm alive and all my buddies are dead. I need a damn reason why ya didn't kill me!" he yelled.

Peter turned away from the brook and faced him. His eyes narrowed with a kind inspection. Then he looked past him toward the rumbling of a distant British transport truck. "Make it to Shumannsville, Noah. That's where the answer is." He marched away never looking back.

Noah fell to the ground, covered his face with his hands, and sobbed.

* * *

**Texas Correctional Institutions Division,
Mountain View Unit
Gatesville, Texas – Summer of 1977**

Peter wiped his tears with the back of his hand. The guard on his side stood a little closer, his face scornful. "Maybe you should be done with your story now, Mister. And how the hell our government let you live here is a mystery to me." He shook his head. "Ya killed them boys…don't really wanna hear anymore."

"Hey, wait a minute…I got a right to hear this crazy fool's story…all of it," said Lisa.

The guard at her left pulled the phone from her hand and spoke heatedly to Peter. "You got half an hour, Mister. That's it. And if ya got more Americans killed, we don't wanna hear about it."

"I wanna hear 'bout every killin'. Don't care who, don't care why. You fools act like ya care. You don't care." She stuck her hand out for the phone. "Killin' just gotta be done…y'all never done it. It ain't nothin'. Now give me my phone. I wanna hear how this thing ends."

The guard shoved the phone back into her hand. "Shut the hell up. And I swear, if I could, I'd kill ya right now."

She spoke into the phone, her head tilted at Peter, inspecting his eyes. "He won't kill me because he ain't like us. Right, Mister? Ain't got what it takes. Ain't that right, Mister? Ain't it right?"

Peter said nothing. He just dove into her eyes and watched her heart beat, just like his had years before. Slow and cold…icy cold.

"Why ya tellin' me this story anyway, Mister? Whatcha after?" She grinned. "Ya after somethin'." She shook her head slowly. "Ya after somethin', for sure."

Peter faced the guard who flanked him. "May I continue?"

The guard looked at his watch. "Ya got thirty minutes left."

NOT DONE YET

Camp Bravo
One Week Later

Noah looked into a small, square mirror that hung from a tree limb. His vision had fully returned. The British transported him to base camp Bravo after what felt like two days of interrogation. He had a shower and shaved the little chin hair that grew since his encounter with Peter. He tossed his razor into a can of cloudy water and wiped his face with his shirt. He spoke to no one in his new platoon, and no one seemed eager to know the lone survivor. He was bad luck. He awoke before everyone because he needed time to wrestle away the claws of guilt that pinned him against his bed in another restless night. He thought of Franco all the time. There was no one to replace him—no one like the brother he was. And he couldn't stop thinking about why he was spared.

He gathered his pack and walked eagerly toward a small cornfield that lined the base camp. It reminded him of home, of a place where God spoke the clearest. He walked into the first row and waited to hear the rustling of the stalks. The breeze animated the tall, tight stalks to-and-fro. He waited for an hour hoping for an answer. But nothing came and the stalks seemed like teasing children who had a secret they wouldn't tell.

Then he heard the tired whimpers of a trapped animal. There in the last row, he found an adolescent, emaciated fox caught in a rudimentary trap. It looked at him with hollow eyes, its head low in defeat and acceptance of its demise.

Noah forced the trap open, but she lay frozen, near death, too weak to escape. He reached toward her head to stir her to life. The fox snapped at his hand, narrowly missing her mark.

Noah jumped back. "Damnit. I'm trying to help ya."

She leapt to her paws, pupils constricted, instincts awakened, motionless, peering into his eyes as if trying to understand. She lifted her head picking up a scent, remembering her intense hunger. Then she took off in a confident trot.

He watched her until she entered a nearby woods. " Ain't your time," his words returning in a cold wintry breeze.

★ ★ ★

Captain Peterson sat in the passenger seat of a Jeep transport painfully absorbing every bump and hole against his fragile lower back. His driver pulled into Camp Bravo skidding to a careless stop. He jumped out of the Jeep and pulled the captain's bag from the back. He saluted stiffly. "Camp Bravo, sir. Made it with time to spare."

He fought his way out of the Jeep, every move shooting pain throughout his back and leg. He held his breath until his feet hit the ground and he could straighten up. He saluted weakly. "Pleasant ride." He looked down and saw that he was a foot deep in mud. He shook his head and let out an exhausted sigh.

"Thank you, sir," replied the private.

"Your quarters are over here, sir."

He escorted him to a large canvas tent in the interior of the camp.

★ ★ ★

Noah sat inside the quarters flanked by two burly soldiers as if he were a prisoner. Captain Peterson entered, and the two soldiers snapped to attention. Noah began to rise.

"Sit, Fischer," he said. "Leave us." He tossed his attaché case onto a sloppy desk and dropped his hand in an aloof salute excusing the guards. He lowered himself gingerly onto his chair, his face tightening in pain. He pulled a file from his case and reviewed it quickly. "I've come a long way to ask you one simple question."

"Yes, sir," answered Noah eagerly.

"Why the hell did he spare you?"

"Sir, he didn't say."

"Oh. Well, he didn't say. Didn't write out a nice little note proclaiming his love for you?"

"Sir, I don't rightly know why he spared me. Didn't make any sense. Don't think he knew why."

Peterson shifted his weight and his eyes closed tightly against the knife that bayoneted his back. His words escaped through clenched teeth. "Where you from, Private?"

"Shumannsville, Texas, sir," he answered proudly.

"They have schools there, right?"

"Yes, sir."

"And you went to these schools?"

"All the way to grade twelve, sir. I graduated."

The captain's eyebrows lifted and his face brightened. "Oh, that's great, Private. I'm really happy to hear that." His brows lowered as he inched closer, grimacing against a yelp he was too proud to release. "Look, I've come a long way to get some intelligence from you, and I'm not getting anything that's gonna make this trip worth the hell I've been through." He grit his teeth and spoke slowly. "Why did he spare you?"

Noah shook his head. "Ain't nothin' I can add, sir." He took a deep breath then spoke through a nervous grin. "Just not my time, sir. I guess."

The captain sat back in his chair and exhaled strongly.

"I begged 'em, sir."

"Begged him?" he questioned as he pressed his fist down onto the desk, his pain surging.

Noah's eyes widened in concern.

"Okay. Let me try this. This German operative, incognito, we know all about him. He's a very dangerous man; he leads a dangerous group. They've caused us setbacks we can't afford. We gotta find out when he'll strike again. Maybe knowing why he spared you will help. You understand?" He struggled to get up and then sat on his desk bearing most of his weight on his right side. He reached into his pocket, snapped open a bottle and swallowed a pill.

"Yes, sir. I understand."

"Now tell me. Think hard, Private. What else did he say?"

Noah shrugged his skinny shoulders. "Ain't nothin' else, sir. Wasn't much on talkin' terms." He looked away, shielding the tears grouping in his eyes. "Ain't nothin' I wanna know more. My buddies are dead. I'm still here. Hurts, sir. Hurts real bad."

Peterson felt a wave of compassion subdue his pain. He squeezed the tension in the back of his neck. "You've lost a lot, son. I'm sorry about that."

Tears broke and he quickly wiped them from his cheeks. "Yes, sir."

"Sorry about my anger." He touched his lower back. "This pain's got the best of me." He stood and felt a debilitating pain break his stiff posture.

Noah stood and grabbed Captain Peterson's elbow. He steadied him back to his desk. "Sir, before ya sit, may I help?"

"Help? What the hell are you talking about?"

"Your back. I can fix it. My father has the same condition. It's your hips. Also worked with our cows; sometimes happened during birth."

"Are you out of your mind, Private. Cows? Are you nuts, boy?"

"Sir, done it many times for my father. Ya got nothing to lose."

He looked around and then spoke quietly. "What kind of remedy are you talking about?'

Noah was already behind him, his hands wrapped around his upper chest.

"What the hell?"

"Sir, cross your arms over your chest."

"What the hell is this?"

Before he could free himself, Noah had already made his adjustment.

The crack was almost as loud as the captain's scream. He stood motionless, uncertain if he was paralyzed or healed. He rolled his lips inward, took a deep breath through his nose and then released it slowly. He cautiously wiggled his shoulders, his arms, then his hips and legs. His eyes examined Noah with wonderment. "By God, boy. What the hell!" He paced back and forth with jubilance. "I haven't felt this good in over a year."

"Good, sir. I'm glad."

He shook his hand. "Thank you, son. We're done here. If you think of anything else."

"Yes, sir. Oh, sir there's one thing."

"Yes, Private."

"If you find him, I sure would like a chance to take a crack at 'em…well, before he gets what's comin' to 'em."

"Son, he's not the kind of man that will be captured alive." He shook his head. "You won't get that chance."

"Yes, sir. One more thing. He knew my first name. He called me Noah. No one calls me Noah, sir. I'm Tex, to everyone."

"Well, maybe someone mentioned your first name, Private. Not a big deal."

Noah shook his head. "No one even knows my first name, sir."

The captain blinked in surprise, then etched into Noah's innocent eyes. "Thank you, Private. I'll think about that."

Noah saluted and walked out.

ONLY DEATH WILL SEPARATE US

Berlin, Reichstag Building
Four Months Later

Peter earned his rest in Berlin. Operation Greif ran its course. His American uniform was burned and buried. Lieutenant Colonel Shmitt had taken care of Peter's diversion sparing no expense. Peter stayed at the finest hotel in Berlin and all the pleasures of the day were at his disposal. He chose instead to rest, sleeping two days straight. It was Tuesday morning when he finally woke up. That afternoon, he sat in a plush, leather chair dressed in a formal, custom-tailored German army uniform, blindfolded, waiting for Shmitt…for what was next.

★ ★ ★

As instructed, he removed his blindfold and sat quietly in what he surmised was Shmitt's new office. It was neat and meticulously organized. Every book in its place, spines rightly displaying titles in alphabetical order. His eyes fell on *Simplicius Simplicissimus*, then *The Sorrows of Young Werther*, then over to *Hyperion*. On the desk sat *The Devil's Elixirs*. He had heard of these great German works but had never read them. He fixed on a globe that sat at the right corner of the desk. It was large, too large it seemed for the chair that sat behind it. The globe's colors were weathered and its brass base worn. It was from a bygone time when such artifacts spoke of wealth and excess. He noted fresh, red lines encircling parts of Northern Africa and he wondered if they were clues to his next assignment. Perhaps it was time to leave Europe and see the world. He released a compressed sigh and with it any remnant of concern about his future.

He heard footsteps from the adjoining hallway—soft, precise, feminine.

"Lieutenant Engle. I'm sorry for your wait."

He turned to the voice behind him and immediately stood. Her beauty overwhelmed him, and he felt his lips separate slightly with an immediate longing. He grunted instinctively then tried to recover with a soft, guarded smile that said he was still the impervious war hero.

She expected his restraint and the attraction; the latter had always been part of her life. She did not however carry any unkind confidence that commonly deflates the male ego. She smiled in return, but without Peter's constraint. And she was genuinely impacted by his masculine looks. She had read his dossier and was glad to know that Peter's appearance exceeded her imagination. She shook his hand and felt a sensual lucency release into her body. She tried to stifle a slight gasp with the tip of her fingers over her ready lips. "May I get you some coffee or tea, Lieutenant Engle?"

"No, thank you."

"Are you sure? It's no trouble at all."

He released a carefree smile. "I am fine, thank you…ah… Fraulein…"

"Oh, forgive me. I am not permitted to give my name."

"Oh, I wasn't aware. The blindfold. This is more secretive than last time."

"Yes. It has become necessary. Please sit." She gestured elegantly with her slim hand. "Lieutenant Colonel Shmitt will not be meeting with you. He has been transferred. You will meet with an SS representative. He will be here shortly." She handed him an envelope. "I am to give you this."

He received it and slid it into his coat pocket. "All will be explained shortly. Please, is there anything I can get for you?" she asked with eyes that floated the word 'anything.'

Peter smiled at her advances, kindly nodding away what could not be—at least not now, not here.

"I wish to tell you something else, Lieutenant." She looked over her shoulder. "What you have done for our homeland… your great accomplishments. Your name will never be forgotten."

He bowed his head respectfully, holding back the words he really wanted to say and instead giving her what she wanted. "I'm just a soldier doing my duty for my homeland."

She shot him a smile mixed of arousal and pride, fighting her urge to wrap her arms around his broad shoulders. She bowed her head and walked out.

Peter leaned on his chair back watching her walk out, admiring her form, expecting she could feel his stare. He sat back in his chair and pulled out his orders. He looked at the envelope, his eyes lazily inspecting what was always written on the outside. 'Destroy after reading.' He stuffed the envelope away and looked at his watch. He stood and stepped toward the many books arranged neatly on the bookshelf. He picked one that lay opened on the desk. He turned the pages and his eyes fell on this: 'Crows exhibit human characteristics: They are intelligent, they play, communicate and have the capacity to deceive.'

"Don't turn around. Do nothing. Just breathe," said a familiar voice.

Peter calmly shut the book on the table trying to steady himself. He considered what this reunion would mean. *Death…this is your time?* His hands collapsing into hard fists as he remembered what he had done in Belgium, where Death had laid its mark. Or was it the pond in Ostbrandenburg, when they were carefree boys, bound by an enduring bond stronger than the whims of hatred that drive men, even brothers to murderous intent?

"It can't be. It can't be. If I disobey, will I be shot?"

"Kill Germany's greatest hero?" the voice answered blithely.

Peter spun around. "Martin!" he said. He wanted to embrace him as he did when they were boys, but the events of their last meeting, the killing of Elise, flooded his mind. His eyes bloated with tears. He dropped his stare to his feet and shook his head in disbelief. "I never thought, never thought…"

Martin's shoulders fell, his professional countenance drained as his teeth chattered against the uncontrollable pang of disquiet that twisted in the sadness that separated them. He could not look at his friend; not because he hated him, but because he suddenly understood that Peter had always carried the weight of the execution with him. Martin, now a man of influence, a man that made many such decisions since then, also knew the sadness of leadership. He wiped his cheek of his tears and lifted his head slowly, forgetting his rehearsed lines. "My brother."

Peter looked up and their eyes connected. Peter embraced Martin, lifting him off the ground so tightly that Martin gasped for breath. Setting him down, they stood motionless, inches apart, cocooned in a shared silence that broke apart freeing what would be a new flight neither one could imagine.

Peter started to speak before Martin cut him off.

"No, my brother. I know what you want to say. Don't say it. I've made many heartbreaking decisions since I last saw you. I understand now." He swallowed deeply and looked at him with his dark, wistful eyes. "I know now…this is war… just one necessary, horrible choice after another."

And though Martin's resolute eyes said he had forgiven all, Peter caught an infinitesimal tremble in Martin's lips as he spoke. "I was weak. I've moved on. I'm so much stronger now." He nodded, agreeing with his own words. "You taught me well."

Peter grabbed his shoulder and shook it lovingly. "I can't believe this. Together again."

Martin's broad smile wiped away the tension in the corner of his lips. He gestured to his desk.

"Please, Peter, sit. Can we get you something?"

"No, thank you. Your mystery host has done a perfect job."

Martin sat at his desk and poured from a flask of whiskey. He set a full glass before Peter. He was dressed in a regal black SS uniform adorned with countless medals. He forced a long exhale until he could bring himself back to decorum. "We'll have time to catch up, but I've got to tell you about what's changed, and why you're here." Martin took a short sip letting the amber liquid warm his throat. "Did you read the orders?" He smiled and answered himself. "Of course not."

Peter sipped his whiskey feigning appreciation with lifted eyebrows. "My orders?"

"Yes. I won't be part of it. I begged to be part of it. But it's been decided. The Fuhrer himself has chosen you. Only you." He leaned forward and gazed at him. "You have no idea what he thinks of you."

Peter forced a faint, contemptuous smile.

"You're a savior in his mind."

Peter chuckled and frowned cynically.

Martin took another sip and nodded. "I know… Peter Engle, the great German Savior, the Chosen One," he said with like cynicism, only it had a sharp tip to it that Peter could feel.

Peter's smile faded and his eyes tightened in inspection as he touched the globe in front of him. "Maybe you should have a talk with him. I'm no savior. I don't care to save anything, Martin." He leaned back in his chair, his shoulders pushed down by what he knew he had to say. "I'm done, Martin." His head shaking in advance of his words to make them more convincing. "It's over."

Martin felt his lips tighten like a locked door. He glanced at the many medals on his chest, then pinned his eyes piercingly on his friend. "Yes," he said with an agreeing nod. "You're tired. You've been through so much, my friend." He inhaled the discontent that filled the gap between them. "My dear friend, my brother. There is so much you do not know. But, I understand, you are consumed by what you do know. All I will say now is that… all that we have fought for…our very victory is in jeopardy," he closed with a heavy, broken brow.

Peter stood and gave the globe a twirl. "Victory?" He shot him a vacant smile. "I'm afraid no one knows what that is. I know I don't." He chuckled. "I feel like a man who clawed his way up a mountaintop…where victory should be, but there's just a thousand more mountains." He stopped the globe's spin with his finger. "When does it end, Martin? That's all I want. And I don't care how it comes."

Martin drained his whiskey and laid his glass down gingerly onto his desk. He looked into its emptiness. "There will be an end, Peter." He paused, considering the dangerousness of his words. "You can choose our end, my brother. Our victory."

Peter walked to a window and lit a cigarette to calm his nerves. He nodded slowly. "Choose? The choices have all been made." He blew a line of smoke out the window.

Martin walked over to the window and took an offered ciga-rette. "The die is cast. Maybe you're right. Maybe." He put his hand on his shoulder. "If it is, we were destined for brotherhood." He dropped his hand from his shoulder and looked out the win-dow. "Nothing can separate us."

Peter exhaled the last of his cigarette, nodding agreeingly. "Yes, my brother. All we have is each other."

Martin cleared his throat of the tension that suddenly gripped it. "There's something else." He took a long draw from his ciga-rette, expelling it just as long. "Our village…I was there."

Peter's eyes widened with expectancy.

"There's nothing left. The Russians bombed it. It's terrible. Your farm…everything's gone." Martin threw his cigarette on the ground and crushed it. "Damn Russians, they destroy every-thing in sight." He looked at Peter hoping for a response, seeing nothing.

Peter nodded with callous acceptance.

Martin forced a smile. "And yet my father's home still stands," he said with a sarcastic chuckle.

"Your father?" asked Peter.

"He got out before. I made sure of it."

"You're a noble man." Peter turned to look at him. "He doesn't deserve your kindness."

Martin walked back to his desk and stood behind it, his broad, strong shoulders pulled back. He shook his head and his shoulders fell soft. "Well, what's done is done."

Peter forced an approving smile. But he knew his friend all too well. Martin's wounds were deep like his. They were both men in search of something. For Martin, it had always been his father's approval. Now, it was the Fuhrer, it was Peter, it was anyone in a uniform, and it was Germany. Peter saw it in his destitute eyes…the same eyes of his childhood.

Martin sat down and cleared his throat of all emotion. "So, my friend, your new assignment is more important than anything you've done."

Peter's eyebrows climbed up. "Really?" he said sarcastically.

Martin shook his head and cracked an understanding smile. His smile fell as he leaned back in his chair. "I've fought beside you in battle, I know, I know…I won't waste your time trying to appeal to virtue." He tapped his desk with his finger, pausing for effect. "Our enemy is our brother, and he wants our father's head."

Peter looked up at the ceiling avoidably. "Like I said, Martin, I'm done."

Martin held the additional orders firmly in his hands wondering if he'd made a mistake. *What have I done? You don't care…you care about nothing…Germany needs you to care.* Stress lines formed across his forehead as he slid the orders across the desk. "Please, just hear me out. Then, whatever you wish, a nice trip away from it all. I'm sure I can arrange it. You've earned it."

Martin leaned forward forming his words in his head. "We've stopped several assassinations against the Fuhrer, but we need your help. It's very complicated. We have a list of leaders that ignore his orders. Some have openly vowed to assassinate him. We can't get to them. Many are protected by brainwashed underlings, and some are too isolated. And we can't be open about our efforts…they know it."

"So you want me to assassinate them, one-by-one, quietly."

"Exactly. An assassin of assassins. We've executed those we know. But yes, they must be eliminated quietly, covertly. Every death must look like an accident, a suicide, at the hands of our enemies. You'll start in Vienna, with a Field Marshal Conrad Becker." Peter nodded slowly, his eyes tight and curious.

"We've followed these men. We've corroborated the Fuhrer's suspicions. Each order is very specific—the how, where, and when—all has been considered."

Peter carefully placed the orders into his jacket. He scanned the books on the shelves and then set his eyes back on his friend. "Are these your books, Martin?"

Martin snickered suspiciously. "I've inherited them."

Peter nodded. "Do you think the answers are there?"

Martin grabbed the book on his desk, his right hand weighing it in the air. "Answers? There are no answers." He tossed it onto his desk, like it was a waste basket. "Duty. Just duty…that's all there is," he answered with a pride that belied his vapid eyes. He stepped around his desk and pointed a finger into Peter's chest. "You taught me that. Have you forgotten?" He raised his hand to his friend's shoulder giving it a loving squeeze.

Peter slowly re-scanned the books and then his eyes floated boundlessly, hopelessly. He shot him a faint nod hating that his primal words had returned with stronger ropes and chains. "It was good seeing you, my brother."

Martin embraced him, one hand around Peter's neck, and he whispered in his ear, "Only death will separate us, my friend, my brother."

Peter pulled away and saluted formally.

Martin watched him walk away, and he recognized his long confident strides, like those of a loyal workhorse never bucking, fully obedient until its last breath.

NOT THE WAR

When we kill our own, the war is lost.

Vienna, Austria
Three Weeks Later

General Field Marshal Conrad Becker sat outside with his wife at the Café Mozart under a faded tan awning. He donned his formal uniform—a red high-collar, blazed with thick, gold-leaf fit snug against his sturdy neck, and an iron cross on his chest reflecting the morning sunlight that escaped the awnings protection—befit for the highest-level military meetings. He was in his mid-fifties, graying at the temples, with no other sign of aging. His fingers shook nervously around the butt of a nearly spent cigarette. He brought it to his mouth and inhaled. He turned his head from his wife, looked nervously over his shoulder, and freed the smoke. As he put out the cigarette, he heard muffled words in front of him.

"Conrad. You haven't listened to a word I've said." With a dignified agitation, his wife sipped her tea and looked away toward a small child who scurried from his mother's grasp. "You don't seem to care. Must we stop living?"

"My dear, I won't be attending Michael's birthday," he said sadly. "I won't make anyone's birthday."

She lowered her teacup with a slight tremble in her hand. "Conrad, what are you talking about?"

His fingers interlaced before his chin, and he rested it there surveying his words. "My love, haven't I always done what was right before my people, before God himself?" he asked as he softly touched the tip of her chin.

Her eyes widened in alarm. She had never seen such sadness in him. "Conrad, what's happened?"

"My dear, I can't explain. It's better for you, and for our family, that you know nothing."

He was a man of few words, a loyal, good man that she never questioned. She held his hand tightly. "You're on the list?"

His eye winked a tear free. "I'm not sad about what I have done. I'm only sad that I'll never see your beautiful face again."

"No, my dear. We'll run. We'll hide."

"I can no more hide or run than I can resist loving you."

Two men approached and stood at her side. "I've made all the arrangements for you and the children. It's all in motion. But you must leave immediately with these men. They're trustworthy men."

"I'm not going with anyone. I will stay with you until the end," she said through trembling lips.

He nodded at the men, his eyes now in flight.

They held her arms and lifted her. She resisted, though without any success. "My dear, I don't want to remember you like this. Please look at me," she said, her hysteria confined by the eyes around them, now suddenly suspicious, one or another possible executioners of the list.

He kept his eyes distant, unable to see her, unwilling for her to see his agony. His words narrowly escaped his throat. "Please go. I am with you always." He turned to see her forced into a waiting car. He stood, laid his hand across his heart watching her leave forever.

* * *

Peter sat on his *Zundapp* motorcycle, dressed in a full-length black leather coat, dark sunglasses, and a leather cap that he pulled off and placed into his pocket. His purple scarf now tattered and discolored lay in deep contrast across his neck. He looked across the square at the Field Marshal, his hand still on his chest, his head pressed down by the weight of his loss and what he knew was inevitable.

Peter felt a seed of sadness germinating in his heart. He whispered against it, "duty." Martin's words, his words surrounded him. "There are no answers. Duty, all that matters is duty." He pulled off his gloves and let his hand rest on the butt of his gun. His hesitation made him think too much. And that was dangerous. "No answers," he said to himself.

He looked around the square one last time making sure there were plenty of witnesses, as ordered. He knew he was being used to make a statement, and perhaps to simply pacify the anxieties of a mad man. But what did that matter? His greatest strength came from a mind devoid of such concerns, a mind deep with icy water where incredulity drowned and sank, unretrievable forever. Duty…that was all that mattered.

Then suddenly, words broke from his lips he had no control over: "Get thee behind me." His neck tightened and pulled his head back away from his words. They were not his words, nor his thoughts. They were his father's words, commands against the devil himself. They were foolish words that placed confidence in ghosts, goblins, and spirits that could not bleed. His mind told him only that which bled, felt pain, and that which could deliver pain was real. This was truth, not the empty incantations that represented the last, desperate gasps of a past deceived by a false sacredness. Nothing was sacred now. He had only his duty: only to do…never to question. He slipped his hand slowly down his face wiping any trace of consternation, stepped off his motorcycle, firmly tightened the waist strap of his leather coat as if to harness all his hesitation, and walked slowly toward the Field Marshal.

He cut through the square passing a young mother holding her crying toddler. She looked at him sadly as he passed by, as if she knew what he was about to do. He was fifty meters from his target, subconsciously searching for the cues of battle—the call of bullets and bombs, the screams of wounded men, the smell of spilled blood, the kill or be killed modus vivendi—the very fuel that had always inspired him to kill with passion and unmetered force. But there was nothing. This was not war. There was only the Field Marshal sitting, desperately trying to light his last cigarette.

Peter quickened his pace, tugged his scarf over the lower half of his face, and poured his hand into his jacket pocket where his pistol waited.

Field Marshal Becker saw his approach and dropped his cigarette. He reached for his gun, doing what he had decided to do from the day he learned he was on the list. He broke from his chair, his shoulders tucked back, formal and declared, "Only God can judge me. I have done what is right." He set the barrel firmly against his temple in a final act of defiance against the evil that dispatched his assassin.

One shot.

His face fell into the ashtray before him, and his body went limp in his chair. His right hand fell slowly to the floor dropping his gun.

Peter's arm extended stiffly, his hand gripping his gun tightly, still directed at his target. He returned his gun to his pocket, no bullets expended, the job done with the greatest of efficiency. He turned and walked by the woman with the crying baby as she sat crouched low on the ground, her baby tucked into her bosom in safety.

His eyes met hers—wide and fearful as if she'd seen the devil. He stopped for a moment wanting to lift her to her feet, but his gesture only caused her to scream in horror. He moved toward his motorcycle and suddenly remembered his orders. He stopped and shouted in Russian to all that could hear him, "Death to Germany. Death to the Fuhrer."

Two police officers on the other side of the square ran in his direction. He put his hand on his gun and noticed it shaking uncontrollably again. He balled his fist tightly, put his motorcycle in gear, and sped away.

★ ★ ★

Two hours later Peter was aboard a train headed to Berlin. He was tired and his eyes were heavy from looking into the darkness that covered the escaping countryside. A stranger passed by him headed to the next car. He caught a quick glimpse of his back—tall, strong, well dressed. There was something familiar about the way he moved. He watched as the man opened the door to the next car. Then he shot a quick look over his shoulder at Peter.

Peter gasped and strained his eyes. He jumped to his feet and followed. He opened the door to the next car seeing no one in the aisle. He walked gingerly looking for the man wearing the black eye patch. If he found him, he wasn't sure what he would do. He stopped for a moment and considered turning around, but his resistance turned quickly anemic. *What will I do? Why are you here?* He looked carefully into each row down to the last seat, and there he was. A black band encircled the back of his head.

He stood behind him unable to move forward. How could he still be alive? Should he embrace him, or would he strangle him? There was no in-between for Peter. He shook his head trying to air out his confusion.

The man rose to his feet and slowly turned.

Peter mouthed the word "Father," but it stuck in his throat.

The man walked toward him, bumping Peter gently. "Sorry," he said insincerely.

Peter breathed again. As he watched the stranger walk past him, he was glad the word had failed. He never wanted to say 'father' again, the way he did when he was a child, its meaning more precisely 'abba.' And it was much more than just a word to Peter, but an idea that could no longer exist in his world, in his being. He looked over his shoulder watching the stranger disappear.

'Father.' Its mere utterance had a power and a potential to change the entire course of his life. So he vowed to himself to never say it again, to never free it from the primordial, unremitting mire that lay at the bottom of his consciousness. He felt weak on his feet as he steadied himself against a passing porter.

"Are you okay, sir?" asked the porter.

Peter looked at him and stumbled back to his seat.

GOODBYE GREENBERG

Tegel Penitentiary

Months passed since Max's last encounter with Greenberg, but now the old man lay near him, death close, captured in another nightmare. Greenberg's lips trembled in another round of weak, painful murmurings.

The old man had been hung by his arms for days with no food or water. He was transported back into Max's cell in the middle of the night. And now Max was sure he would not live through the night.

Greenberg's words ebbed and flowed weakly. Max recognized the Yiddish, a few familiar words. "There, there, my friend. Rest. Rest," he said as he gently stroked his head. But Greenberg would not relent. He had just enough strength to release his words. "For…given," he moaned.

"My friend, sleep. Please save your strength."

"For…given," he repeated over and over.

"Yes, my friend, rest. There's nothing to forgive."

Greenberg looked at Max with alarm in his wide, red-laced eyes shaking his head in disagreement. His eyes spun in their sockets, then rolled back into a coma.

* * *

Two days later Greenberg awoke before sunrise. He sat up with no assistance, startling Max from his sleep. "I thirst."

Max jumped to his feet and fetched water for his friend.

He drained the cup with his shaky hands. "I've been asleep?"

"Yes, quite asleep."

"I have seen things."

"Yes?"

"In my sleep, I have seen things."

"Food, you need food." Max pulled a crust of bread he saved from under his blanket. "Here. Eat this." He handed it to him, but he would not eat.

"I must tell you what I saw."

"After you eat."

"No. I must tell you now."

Max nodded.

The old man spoke quickly and energetically looking past Max as if still in a dream state.

"There was a field, a long field, hills on either side. In the middle of the field were buried hundreds of soldiers in unmarked graves. And then I saw you; you were frantic, like a mad man, driven by some demonic force shoving your hands into the fresh soil, pulling the decaying bodies out one by one."

Then he fixed on Max with eyes so large they threatened to push out of their sockets. His voice shook with an intensity he could barely contain. "And on one of the hills stood a man, a majestic man, a glow about him, looking down at you, crying for you, beckoning you toward him, begging you to stop." He slowed to catch his breath, returning to his exuberance. "He called you by your name. And he said…" He paused, his throat weary and dry. "He said, 'Your shame…" He closed his eyes as if to gain the strength that weakened with his words. "Your shame is gone forever. Do not unearth what I have buried.'"

Max's eyes widened and froze. He fell to his knees and looked up.

Greenberg repeated, "Do not unearth what I have buried."

Max slowly lifted his hands from his side and let his face fall into their cradling. And he sobbed, unlike any cry he had ever experienced, even greater than the day of his family's death. Tears guarded for many years in an old, decaying cistern broke free in great torrents. "My God…my God…" He raised his hands high above his shoulders in contrition and praise.

Greenberg extended his crooked arm and gently placed his hand around Max's neck. He pulled him close and spoke compassionately. "This I say with my own heart…you are free now, my brother. And now you can receive what you could not receive before."

"Receive?" asked Max with his sobs.

"Yes, receive. That is why you were brought here. Don't you see?"

They heard the sound of the guards coming.

"Hurry," said Greenberg. "Put on my pants. Give me yours."

"What? Why?"

"Sewn in the hem through the waist of my pants is a paper. On the paper is a long formula, a complex mathematical formula."

Greenberg removed his pants while Max still struggled to understand. "I am Professor Greenberg, the leading physicist of Germany. You must memorize the formula, destroy the document, and relay it to the Allies. If the Germans get it, millions will be destroyed."

Max handed him his pants and put on Greenberg's. "But I know nothing of mathematical formulas."

"God is with you. You are chosen, Max," he said as he pulled Max's pants to his waist. "This is the day I have longed for. You will save millions, Max, and today I will no longer resist death. My call is over." He smiled lovingly and then his face stiffened. He clasped his hands tightly around Max's hand. "Do you understand Max…the formula?"

Max nodded slowly.

The guards threw the iron door open and peeled Greenberg away. They grabbed him by his frail arms and dragged him out of his cell.

"Goodbye, my friend. Goodbye, Pastor Engle!" shouted Greenberg, his words trailing off as he was whisked away for the last time.

Max shot to his feet, his hands squeezing his cell bars tightly, fighting for words to break from his sobs. "Goodbye, my friend," he whispered to himself. "Goodbye." He forced a heavy breath into his lungs and freed a shout that echoed down the cold, long hallway. "Goodbye, my friend. Goodbye, my brother," he repeated until he heard the dead, faithful thud of the last iron door.

★ ★ ★

The next day Max gingerly pulled the end of a tightly rolled paper from a small hole at the front of the waistband. Under a block of light, he unrolled the document, and to his shock, he found the writing to be much more complex and longer than he had envisioned. It seemed impossible to memorize every sign, symbol, and number. And then there was the other consideration. It was clear this was a formula to a weapon that would produce terrible destruction. What would the Allies do with it? Would they use it for evil purposes? He had no answers to his questions, but it was undoubtedly clear that Germany had shown her hand. She would do exactly what Professor Greenberg said. *I cannot let this happen. I must intercede.* But for a moment his thoughts convicted him. *And yet I did not intercede for my precious wife? I did not intercede for my son?* And then he remembered Greenberg's dream, and he felt a rush of warmth throughout his body. He was free. All was forgiven. He would not unearth what was buried forever.

Free from the burdens that once enslaved his mind, he let go of his concerns about the Allies and began to imprint every line, dot, and symbol, a quarter inch at a time.

A WORTHY FATHER

Peter sat in the back of a long, black BA-10 armored car. He opened his orders for his next assassination. He read the document once and returned it to the envelope. On the backseat lay another package with a set of clothes for the German envoy he would portray. He was to make contact with Field Marshal Stein, a war hero from the first Great War who commanded a platoon of loyal and courageous soldiers. Stein had defied orders again, breaking from the coordinated movements Hitler had orchestrated. And yet he was successful in pushing back the Allied entry into Germany. But that didn't matter. He was on the list. Conventional means to stifle him and to redirect him had failed. He was too insulated and his men were willing to die for him. Peter would assume his new identity and catch a train in the morning.

★ ★ ★

Grunewald Forest, Germany, West of Berlin

A solitary duck rested its outstretched wings on the wave of a strong updraft that carried it precariously away from its flock. A shot exploded a few hundred feet away, instantly ending the errant duck's life and breaking the flock's solid formation into a panic of many arrows diving for the foliage below.

Field Marshal Stein whistled a command and his dog jumped into a cold lake. The dog returned in seconds with a limp prize in her mouth. He patted her and tucked the duck into a leather pouch with the others. He whistled again and the dog followed him closely as he walked back to his quarters. Like the dog, two German soldiers followed him in lockstep.

"There is security in unity," he said with a sad smile. "Though there are times when it is right to venture from the collective. But there is always a cost." He stopped and turned to face his young loyal soldiers. He spoke with a compassionate, fatherly tone. "Those with such courage will always be judged unfairly. They will suffer for doing what is right. Do you understand?"

They saluted sharply. "Yes, sir." They understood the importance of his words and had counted the costs. If Germany was to succeed, it had to be governed by local, tried and true wisdom, not by men in far off towers. His men did not know the full extent of their leader's rebellion, but they trusted his judgment and because of it, they were alive and had tasted one triumph after another. They were a special band of men—his men, his family.

★ ★ ★

Peter read his orders again. He revisited the reports about Field Marshal Stein's rebellious decisions. But Peter also completed his own investigation and became aware of the man's many successes. He was a brilliant military strategist. His rebellion began when he turned down Hitler's first assignment to oversee all military strategy and logistics. His response was simple: "I will not stand in an office, with shiny boots." The Fuhrer hated the comment, as did all his generals insulated from harm. That was two years ago. It would have been easy to eliminate him then, but he was needed.

And now, he was a disruption, a thorn in Hitler's side that would not go away.

Peter's orders were clear. He was to offer a resolution that gave Stein total independence as long as he did not disrupt the Fuhrer's general plan, and he would be supplied all he needed. And when the war was over, he would have a hero's welcome. But everyone knew he would turn down the offer. So, he was on the list.

Stein was guarded at all times, and Peter would be thoroughly searched. If he was going to eliminate him, he would have to do so with his bare hands.

He was an hour from his destination and growing tired. The train rocked his body soothingly and the hum of the wind that cut against his window made him yearn for sleep. His eyes felt heavy, and his thoughts went to another place.

He saw himself lined up with other soldiers in formation, their eyes fixed on the Field Marshal, a gallant man, tall and strong, with intense eyes, no pretense or pomp, dressed like them in a simple, battle uniform, pacing back-and-forth preparing them for battle.

"My sons, this is our hour. We have been called to fulfill a simple calling, to fulfill a sacred oath as brothers-in-arms, to do what is right and noble." He stopped and raised his gun high in the air. "You are my sons," he said with a breaking voice overcome by his love. "And I fight with you, ready to die at your side. Are you with me?" he shouted.

Peter's hands squeezed his rifle as he shouted with the others. "We are with you. We are with you."

An hour later the train came to a stop and Peter's eyes opened bright and ready. He tucked his orders back into his jacket pocket and headed for Grunewald Forest.

★ ★ ★

Field Marshal Stein sat at a table alone cutting into the freshly cooked duck. Five days earlier, the chateau had been commandeered and its owner, a wealthy Frenchman, was allowed to flee with his family. The Field Marshal never hesitated to kill the enemy. The Frenchman was a simple opportunist who cared little of French resistance. He gladly gave over his chateau to save his life. He made sure the Field Marshal's men had all the food and drink they wanted and found them bedding. His wife, a beautiful woman, much younger, eyed the Field Marshal with a deep disdain only exceeded by that which she had for her cowardly husband. Other men would have taken advantage of her, but not the Field Marshal. He showed respect and expected it from his men.

His sergeant knocked at his door. He put his fork down and slowly wiped his mouth with his napkin. "Come in."

The sergeant stepped in and saluted. "Sir, they've sent another envoy."

He folded his napkin and sat it on the table before him. "Alone?"

"Yes, sir."

The Field Marshal smiled kindly and spoke softly. "Send him in."

Peter was searched a third time by two soldiers who roughly poked and prodded. He put his coat back on and straightened his tie. They returned his attaché case with a strong shove and glared at him with suspicion.

"Still not satisfied?" asked Peter.

"Maybe you have a knife up your…," responded one of the searchers with a hostility that would have led to a beating but for the Sergeant.

"That's enough," interceded the Sergeant. "Is he clear?"

The soldier nodded while his eyes cut into Peter's stare. "Three searches, sir."

"This way," said the sergeant as he motioned toward the Field Marshal's room.

The Field Marshal stood and approached Peter with a warm smile and a hearty handshake.

Peter looked upon him with amazement. He was not at all what he had imagined. He looked so much like Mr. Wenzle, a simple cobbler from his hometown. Like the cobbler, he was a very average man. He was of average height and weight, his hair gray and receding, his eyes kind and conspicuous. He spoke with a meekness that commanded nothing. And there was an empty left sleeve tucked into his waistband. Peter assumed he had lost his arm in the Great War. He was so taken aback by this man's plainness that he forgot to introduce himself.

The Field Marshal gestured toward two well-cushioned leather chairs that sat near a large open-faced fireplace. "Please, sit."

Peter approached the seat.

"I'm sorry I didn't get your name."

Peter gave his feigned name. "Yes, of course. I am sorry. Bauer. Hans Bauer."

They sat in their chairs facing each other while the sergeant stood nearby.

"Bauer? Any relation to Gustav Bauer?"

"No, sir. Don't believe so."

"Oh, if you were related you would know. He's a great concert violinist. Overlooked I'm afraid. Far too overlooked." He smiled at Peter now with a broad, toothy smile that made Peter smile instinctively.

It had already begun. The Field Marshal had so quickly disarmed him. Peter knew the devices of men in power, their hypnotic charm, their thin disguises. He had never been under their sway. He could smell their true stench from afar. But not this man. He was like the men of his town—kind, fair, helpful, humble—honorable men. He was like his father. He immediately understood why his men would die for him without hesitation.

"Herr Bauer, have you had dinner? You must be hungry. Sergeant, prepare a meal for our friend."

"That won't be necessary, sir. I'm not hungry."

"Are you sure? We have some duck. It's delicious."

"Very kind, but no, thank you."

"Where are you from?"

Peter recalled his bio without hesitation. "Berlin. Born in Berlin. My father and mother come from Brandenburg."

"Of course," he said enthusiastically. "It's a beautiful place, spruce trees in spring…a beautiful scent, life giving."

"Well, I've never been."

"Never been to your parents' home?"

"My parents died when I was very young."

"Oh, I'm sorry," he said compassionately. "You have had a difficult life."

"I've managed, sir."

"Here you are an important envoy for the Fuhrer." He chuckled. "You have managed well. I am proud of you."

"Thank you, sir. And you, sir, any family?"

Stein eyed him with a penetrating stare. "You, an envoy of the highest rank, I am sure you have your answer."

"Sir, you make too much of me. I am simply a courier. I honestly know very little about you, or your personal life."

He nodded. "That may be. The others seemed to have known everything, even down to where I kissed my first love in the woods of Mittenwald." He chuckled again.

Peter joined in the chuckle and rested into a smile that felt unfamiliar to him.

"A wife, a child, Herr Bauer?"

"No, sir. No one."

"I am surprised. Despite not having parents, I can tell you were made for family."

Peter felt uneasy as if being probed, but curious. "May I ask how? How can you tell that, sir?"

"I am the father of many men. I know them all. I know their names, their pain, their dreams. I study them. I think of them always. I have learned to sense things about each one. I am a shepherd that loves his flock."

"Yes. A shepherd," he agreed, fighting the childhood memories the word inspired.

Stein's tone turned serious, his eyes sharpening as if attempting to pierce the protection about Peter's mind. "We think we can hide our innermost being. We all try to hide who we really are… with our uniforms, our guns. But we are just men…just simple men who wish to live, to love."

Peter felt his heart pounding in his chest. Was this the time? Should he take him now? Could this man discern his lie?

"Now why don't you tell me why you are here?"

Peter fought his instinct to attack and fixed his mind to the plan. He reached for his attaché case and then stopped, looking over his shoulder at the sergeant who nodded. He pulled out the communication and handed it to Stein.

Stein read it carefully and handed it back to Peter. He inched his chair closer and rested his chin in his hand. "Hans, we will not win this war. I have tried to convince the Fuhrer, our generals, that my tactics, which are simply defensive in nature, should be our aim. We need to protect our homeland and negotiate a peaceful end before it is too late, and my sons go home to nothing. Does that seem reasonable to you?"

Peter sat back in his chair as if pressed against it by the force of the unexpected. "It's not my place to say, sir."

"My son, what really is your place?" Stein looked away at the empty fireplace and sighed heavily. "You are not this Hans Bauer, no simple envoy." He sat back in his chair and rested his hands calmly on his lap. "Your suit, your manner, your story cannot hide what your eyes tell me. The moment you walked into this room I knew. You are a man who has seen battle, a man who has killed and led men. You are a soldier's soldier."

Peter looked away toward a window that he had considered as an escape when the job was done. He knew he could take them both without a commotion, without a sound, but he chose not to.

He looked over his shoulder and saw the sergeant pointing a handgun at the back of his head. He looked back at the Field Marshal. "You asked me a question earlier. Is it reasonable to negotiate peace? And this is my response. You should do what you have always done. Simply be the man you are. Nothing more, nothing less."

"We can't let him return, sir," added the sergeant.

Stein rubbed his bare chin again as he continued to examine Peter. "You don't want me dead?"

"I've never wanted death for anyone. I've simply conspired with it, hundreds of times, never questioned, never reconsidered my orders, until…." He paused feeling his hand begin to shake. "I've simply done my duty. That's all."

Stein nodded compassionately. "And you're tired? That is the look I see in your eyes. You tired of death, of the blood on your hands, of just following and never questioning." A smile stretched across his face, the corners trembling in an emotion that wanted to push his words into Peter's heart. "No matter how hard we try, we can't run from it. We think we can drink it into oblivion or build walls of our own strength to keep it out." He put his hand on Peter's wrist. "Truth, son…it will never leave you. It always finds a way, now or at the hour of our death." He stood and walked to the window that was Peter's only escape. "Perhaps it finds its way today," he said with his back to Peter.

He glanced over his shoulder at his faithful sergeant. "Give him your gun."

The sergeant's eyes widened in disbelief. "Sir, I will not. He's an assassin, an enemy sent to kill you, to end us."

"Give him your gun," he ordered.

The sergeant fought the force of the Field Marshal's words. "I can't sir. I can't do that."

The Field Marshal turned on his heels. "Sergeant, if it is my end, if this is meant to be, I wish to remember you as my loyal son."

"Please, sir. Please don't make me do this."

The Field Marshal stepped forward and pulled the gun from his sergeant's grip, patting him compassionately on his back. He handed the gun to Peter and returned his gaze out the window.

"Hans, whatever your name is…I bow to what is true, nothing else. You choose now who you shall be."

Peter held the gun loosely in his hand and forced his steps toward his target. He passed by the sergeant whose eyes filled with terror. He pulled his purple scarf from his coat pocket and held it in his hand, examining it with repulsed eyes, like it was torn from the devil's favorite coat. He lifted the scarf to his face in a pointless attempt to conceal his shame again, smelling a putrid stench of sulfur from it.

He lifted his hand slowly and took aim.

BE TRUE

A large piece of timber lay heavy across Peter's chest suffocating him. His ears rang loudly as he choked on the cement dust that filled the air. An American M2 mortar hit the Field Marshal's room ripping the northern and western walls to their foundations. A gaping hole peeled back the roof exposing the bright blue sky. Peter pushed against the beam that ensnared him, giving him a few centimeters to breathe. He looked to his left and saw the sergeant crushed beneath a concrete slab.

As the dust settled, his eyes were drawn to the Field Marshal covered in blood and dust sitting against what was left of the north wall. With each breath, blood shot from his upper torso.

Peter felt a burst of strength run through his muscles. He lifted the beam and ran to the Field Marshal's aid. He did all he could to stem the bleeding, but it was futile. His face was already ashen, his pulse undetectable.

"My son," whispered the Field Marshal.

Peter came close and held his hand. Peter recognized death's intrusion. He sat next to this stranger who had so quickly broken through all his defenses. "Sir, I am here."

"My son, be..." He coughed from the blood that filled his lungs. "...be true." He coughed again, choking out, "...be true," and then quietly gave into death's command.

A second mortar hit the lower level of the chateau and then machinegun fire peppered the remaining walls. Peter heard the chaotic yelling and screams of men without a leader. He jumped to his feet and joined the fight.

★ ★ ★

Thirty minutes later he wore a purloined American soldier's uniform. He ran out the chateau with the soldier's gear and rifle covered in dust from head-to-toe nearly unrecognizable. He trotted past three American GIs headed for a second assault against the few Germans held out in the chateau.

"You okay?" they shouted as he ran past.

He avoided eye contact. "Okay, okay, keep going. Out of ammo."

One of the three, turned at the sound of his voice and his eyes widened in recognition.

Peter looked up as he passed him, unintentionally catching his eyes. He stopped in his tracks squinting his eyes past the dust that betrayed him. "Noah?"

Noah cut the space between them pushing the other soldiers aside. But they grabbed him and turned him around. "Tex, Tex, come on. Where the hell you going? The battle's this way."

Peter wiped the cement dust from his face, shot Noah a final nod and ran off.

Noah pulled his rifle back and turned toward the chateau saying nothing more.

A FOOLISH THING

Tegel Penitentiary
The Last Days

It had been weeks since Greenberg's death. Max used every moment of sunlight for his task but was no more than an inch-and-a-half from the beginning. He fought the frustration that chewed on his resolve. He could remember one segment, but then immediately forget the segment before. He began to pray again but in a manner he had never known. His prayers were clear now, focused, unencumbered by a powerful shame that previously killed his petitions at his lips. He knew this new task was Divine, and that it flowed from an unearthly forgiveness and love that could not change with his success or failure. His eyes had seen God so dimly before—a God that required too much to attain his favor, a God that pointed an angry finger at one's past, a God who shakes his head against fears and doubts. But now he saw Him, His arms open, beckoning his child to his warm embrace, always beckoning forward, never back where all is buried for good. Max had never felt such hope.

★ ★ ★

He heard the clanging of keys from an approaching guard. He rolled the document up and inched it back into his waistband. To his surprise it was the portly guard he had not seen for several months.

The guard motioned Max over. "I have arranged something for you. The warden is out for a few days." He unlocked the barred door and waved him to follow. They walked down a long, dimly lit hall to another series of metal doors. Just before he opened the last, he whispered. "Remove those filthy rags. You get a shower. It's been months, and to be honest, Pastor, I can't take the stench."

Max smiled. "My clothes?"

"Yes, you can't shower with them on."

He considered what might happen to the formula. *I've had a few showers. I always put the same dirty clothes back on. Why would this be any different? If I ask, I'll raise suspicion.*

He smiled again and nodded with a strained acceptance. He removed his clothes and stepped into the shower area. The warm water and filth falling from his body felt good. He wanted to stay there forever. When the water turned cold, he turned off the faucet, quickly dried and opened the door to retrieve his clothes.

They were gone.

His heart lurched in his chest, and he felt a panic overtake him. He looked around to find no one. He considered yelling for the guard, but instead began to pray. *Abba Father, please. I don't know what to do.*

He heard the hurried footsteps of the approaching guard. He tried to calm himself. The guard carried a paper bag and a big smile. He handed the bag to Max. "Here you go. Should fit. They are donated," he said happily.

Max looked inside the bag. "My clothes, where are my clothes?" he pleaded desperately.

"Oh, Pastor, I got rid of them. You can't put on those filthy clothes. We burned them."

He dropped the bag and grabbed the guard. "No, no you can't."

The guard pulled himself away. "What's wrong? I brought fresh, clean clothes for you."

God, it can't be. Please help. He tried to calm his spirit, but his words broke through nervously.

"I need them," he said, watching the guard's confusion. "Yes, thank you for the fresh clothes. It was very kind of you. But those old rags mean something to me. They're a reminder of who I was. I need them."

The guard smiled. "I understand." He touched his wooden cross. "This is a reminder of something. I was five years old…"

Max interrupted. "I'm sorry, but you said the clothes were burned?"

He nodded. "I threw them with the things that are to be burned."

"Please, please, could you get them for me before they're burned?"

"Oh, I'm sure they're already destroyed. I'm sorry."

"It would mean a lot to me if you would try."

"We can't keep them. The smell, the bugs. They were to be burned immediately. That is protocol." He wondered at the desperation in the pastor's eyes and conceded. "I will check."

Minutes later a second guard approached and escorted Max to his cell without a word. The door slammed behind him. "Excuse me. The other guard, is he returning soon?"

"Do I look like a fortune teller? Sit down and shut up."

He sat on the floor in the darkness of his cell, all hope slipping away, confusion swirling in his head.

★ ★ ★

The next morning Max was awakened by the rattling of keys. The portly guard stepped in, looked over his shoulder, and then returned with a friendly smile. "Good morning, Pastor. I wanted to say goodbye. We are being transferred; the jail will shut down. All the guards will be sent to the front. We are too old and broken for war, but things are terrible. I feel it." He looked over his shoulder again. "I was hoping you could pray for me. I don't think I'll make it."

Max knew the formula was gone. He felt a despair, a confusion with God that he thought had left forever. *Oh Lord, none of this makes sense. My friend suffered for so long for nothing. The formula is gone. What is left for me to do? I feel lost again.* Then, he looked into the guard's eyes and felt his sadness. He gently placed his hand on his shoulder and closed his eyes, praying, pleading for his safety, fully present with him, with his God, with no regard for his own concerns.

"I wish I could do something for you, Pastor," he said with a quivering lip.

"You've been kind to me. That's more than enough." Max hugged him and watched him walk away.

The guard stopped suddenly and turned around. He reached into his pocket and pulled out a folded handkerchief. "I almost didn't bring this. It made no sense to me." He reached between the bars and handed it to Max. "It's a foolish thing."

Max unwrapped the handkerchief and lifted its contents above his head into the morning sunlight.

The guard chuckled kindly. "I'm sorry. It was all that was left. A waistband, button, belt loops. It would have been better to leave it behind. But maybe it will have some meaning, like you said." He wiped the tears from his round cheeks and glanced over his shoulder to make sure no one could hear. His countenance dropped as he shook his head. "There's one last thing. I hoped the war would be over before…" He took a deep breath. "They plan to execute all the remaining prisoners. I'm sorry." He touched his cross and spoke with a heavy rasp. "We will see each other again. I'm sure of it." He turned and walked away.

Max felt his lungs collapse. He stumbled to his window and tried to breathe in the morning air. He frantically searched the waistband, finding the formula intact. He turned away from the window and collapsed onto the concrete floor.

AN ASSASSIN'S RELIGION

Martin cleared his anxious throat as he read the updated list of rebels. He was concerned about Peter. He could sense his growing resistance. He shifted his mind to a few days earlier when meeting with the Fuhrer. His words were seared in his mind. "Well done, my son. I am proud of you. I have added to the list."

'My son. My son.' How many soldiers had heard these words from their great leader? And yet they were not enough. The Fuhrer's words seeped down into his soul and were immediately strangled by his father's words: *"You're worthless. You'll never be a good man. Why didn't I drop you off at the orphanage?"* He hated himself for letting his past live so strongly in his present. There was nothing else he could do to change how his father felt about him. So he forced himself to live in the present, to accomplish the mission, to win the war, no matter the cost. If he couldn't have his father's love and acceptance, at least he had the salve of Hitler's words; whether they were sincere or not didn't matter. But that too would be lost with Peter's growing apprehension.

He watched Peter's hand resting on his desk, strong, immovable, disinterested in the orders that lay before him. "My brother,

I know something's happening to you." He pushed his chair back from his desk about to stand and then decided to remain seated. Peter never cared for theatrics. "I know you too well. Something's happening in that head of yours. Tell me."

Peter looked out a window toward the sunlight that warmed his face. "I've been dreaming of my father. He was dead to me, never a thought, like he never lived." He looked back at his friend. "That was best for what he did to us."

Martin inched forward. "Yes. What he did was inexcusable."

"But now he haunts me in my dreams."

"He's dead, Peter. And thank God, his foolish ideas are dead too."

Peter chuckled bitterly. "Ideas can't be killed, Martin. Good or bad, no matter how deep we bury them, they're seeds just waiting for their time." He ran his fingers restlessly through his hair. He stood and walked to the window watching the anxious, hurried pace of those below. He shook his head slowly, sadly. "The Field Marshal was a good man."

Martin nodded reluctantly. "Yes, he was. But he wanted to surrender, Peter. We will never surrender, especially when we're so close…"

Peter sighed, taking his time, examining the worth of his words. "He said something to me before he died."

Martin felt the mission slipping through his fingers. He tried to hide his desperation with a feigned, interested smile. "What did he say?"

"He said…," Peter paused again, still afraid of his words. "He said…be true."

Martin joined him at the window. He put his hand on his shoulder. "You are the truest man I know."

Peter turned his head to face him.

Martin grabbed his shoulder. "I can't think of anything truer than a man willing to lay down his life for his country."

"Is that what my father would say?"

"I don't care what your father would say. He's proven to us, to all of Germany, how foolish his ideas were. He didn't lift a finger to stop those soldiers. That can't be right." He shook his head angrily releasing a thin snicker. "What are we to do, just pray over evil the way he did and hope it goes away?" Martin perceived the pain and anger in Peter's narrowed eyes. "I'm sorry. What do you want me to think? He was good to me, to everyone, but he didn't lift a finger when he should have. I can't forgive that. I know you can't either."

Martin felt Peter's resistance weaken. His words gushed out rapidly. "We're so close to victory, closer than we've ever been. There's no time to second guess. No time to look back. You must finish strong." He searched his mind for the words that would put an end to Peter's questioning. "And Germany will forever sing your praise. Whether you care or not, no one will ever forget the great Peter Engle."

Peter's lips tightened against the urge to laugh bitterly. "And all I want is to be forgotten. To be like my father…buried, forgotten." He placed his orders in his pocket and marched out without a salute or goodbye.

Martin watched him leave. He knew Peter was unstable, compromised. And the next assignment would be too much for him… too much for anyone.

★ ★ ★

Peter opened the envelope and read Martin's handwritten message:

You've done enough for Germany. I suggested others for this mission, to save you the agony, but the Fuhrer insisted on you. I'm sorry.

He studied the young General's picture. He was familiar with his victim's name and reputation. He came from great wealth but had given it all up for the cause. Hitler rewarded him and made him part of his inner circle. But he began to question. First with minor inquires, then letters written to other generals carefully intimating a concern over the Fuhrer's judgment. He was the latest on the list, and this assignment was meant to send a clear message that would finally stop the flow of treason that wreaked havoc in Berlin.

In the file was a picture of his beautiful young wife and three small children. He found that curious. He read the rest of Martin's note:

> *This insurrection must end. We must take drastic measures. You will execute the General and his entire family. You'll do it without any cover or disguise. Kill them as a German hero. The rest will learn that they cannot oppose the will of the Fuhrer, the German people, of God himself.*

The note fell from his trembling hands. Martin was right. He had done enough. He walked to the bathroom and splashed water on his face and looked in the mirror staring at a stranger. His hands trembled from the anxiety that overtook him. Stumbling back onto his seat, he hid his head between his knees. "Kill the entire family…help me, help me." His eyes wrenched shut and he fell back into his bed, into a vision.

Pastor Engle gripped the lectern tightly with his strong hands. He looked down at his notes, his open Bible, then at his wife and Peter seated in the front row. Behind them sat the Minister of Religion and his SS men. He shut his Bible and cleared his throat of the words caught therein. "I have seen the deepest dread of life, I have smelled the sulfur of hell hot in my nostrils, and my hands have conspired with the evil hearts of leaders, pawns in the hands of the devil himself." His hands loosened and he stepped away from his lectern. "And I have touched and been touched by a God who is above the worst that man can do." His eyes filled with tears and his voice quivered.

"Today he has given us a choice, as he gave those in Jerusalem, on the dark mount of Golgotha. We all have a choice…to do the will of God, not the will of men who will to be God."

Peter felt steely cold stares behind him. He turned and locked eyes with the Minister, seeing a soulless resolve that had already condemned his father, ready to condemn him too. "Mighty words, yes." He nodded with half his mouth turned up in a smile. "But how can you follow a man that did nothing to save his wife, to save his son?" He shook his head condemningly. "No son…do your duty."

He turned back to his father.

"What will you do, my brothers and sisters? What will you do?"

Peter gripped his wet sheets tightly around his neck straining to breathe. He sat up gasping like a man freed from drowning.

✳ ✳ ✳

Two days later he was dressed in a formal military uniform, his identity clear, his gun strapped at his side headed for the Hotel Adlon.

✳ ✳ ✳

The Hotel Adlon was Germany's finest hotel. It stood in the Pariser Platz, the grandest square in Berlin. Its rooms had a view of the many triumphant military marches entering the square from Brandenburg Gate. It was the Fuhrer's favorite place from which to deliver his most glorious speeches.

Peter sat at an elegant marble top table in the hotel lobby reading the Berlin Times. His face was concealed behind the paper with his sharp eyes darting from the print to the front entrance. An empty glass of whiskey lay near his hand.

A waitress approached again with a glass elegantly displayed on her serving tray. "Another glass, sir?" she asked with minimal interest.

190

He lowered his paper for the first time and exposed his face. His thick blond hair was neatly parted. He was freshly shaven and still tan from his last tour. He lifted his eyes and smiled at the woman, which took her breath for a moment.

Peter closed his paper and gave her his full attention. "I would appreciate that."

She stood there speechless, frozen in a passion she'd never known. He was the most beautiful man she had ever seen. She wanted to stay near him, to touch him, to feel his touch on her. She forced her words. "Can I get you anything else, sir?"

He reached over and took the fresh glass of whiskey and stood, all six feet four inches towering over her. She felt faint. Peter knew his effect was strong, though it had been a long time since he had interacted this way with a woman. He reached out and touched her hand wanting to steady her.

"Thank you." She looked at his strong hand, the source of the surge of heat that ran through her body.

She reached out for the glass of whiskey that had already been received and noticed her hand trembling in the air. She looked at him and they both smiled. Her face was flushed with embarrassment. "I'm sorry."

"I'm sorry if I caused you any discomfort," he said sincerely.

"No, no, of course not. I'll get that drink. Whiskey, was it?"

He gestured with the whiskey in his hand. "I already have it."

"Oh yes, of course. I'm sorry. Have a pleasant day."

"Yes, you too."

She backed away slowly, never wanting to forget the vision he was.

He nodded kindly and sat back in his seat. He picked up his paper and broke from the distraction. He heard a tiny giggle on the other side of his paper barrier. He lowered it and saw her.

"Are you my daddy's friend?" asked a little girl, five or six years old, in a lacy pink dress, hair set in two blonde pigtails. She stood inches from him. "You're my daddy's friend. I remember you."

He lowered the paper to his lap and instantly knew her face from the pictures he studied in his room. His hand began to shake. He balled his fist but had no control of it. He reached for the glass of whiskey and drained it. He looked around nervously.

"My name is Clara. What's your name?"

He fought the impulse to get up and run. He had never run from anything—not from battle, not from an enemy, even when the odds were completely against him. He had always overcome. But no force, no human power, or strategy had overwhelmed him like this.

She pressed against him and leaned comfortably there. "My mommy said we can have chocolate tonight. Since you're my daddy's friend, you must come. We're in room 407."

His eyes widened in despair. He could not retreat or regroup. He was enslaved, hamstrung, overwhelmed by a little child he was called upon to kill. He tried to respond but all he could do was nod in agreement.

"Clara, Clara, what are you doing, my child?" came a voice from behind him. He turned around and saw her mother.

"I'm sorry," she stepped in front of Peter and gently moved her daughter back. She made a quick inspection of his ribbons and added, "Lieutenant."

Peter knew his face could not hide his horror. He slid his hand to his face, his long fingers poorly covering his anxiety.

"Again, my apologies, Lieutenant. It's the uniform; she feels great comfort. She doesn't get to see her father often. Please forgive us."

He stood, saying nothing, forcing a nervous nod.

Her eyes narrowed in compassion and concern. She had been around the suffering of this war long enough to recognize its effects on the battle worn. "You have seen much, haven't you?" She pulled her daughter close against her hip. "I'm sorry. I shouldn't have said that." She smiled again and nodded politely. "Pleasant day to you, Lieutenant."

He watched them walk away toward a staircase and out of view. He called the waitress, "A bottle please."

★ ★ ★

Peter's strides were fast and deliberate as he walked the square for two hours trying to calm his anxiety. He wore his hat low shielding himself from any onlookers that might perceive his dread. He concealed a bottle of whiskey in his coat hoping to find its persuasion. Past the square, through the Brandenburg Gate, he saw a cross at the peak of a church about half a mile away. He cut through a narrow alley toward the church, passing an old woman walking gingerly with a bouquet of roses in her hand; a black crow perched on the index finger of the other, its head cocked in inspection.

"Flowers, flowers for your sweetheart. Flowers for love," she beckoned. She stopped just before him. "Just because I am blind doesn't mean that I cannot see you." She raised her hand offering the flowers so close he could smell them. "Flowers for your sweetheart?"

"No, thank you," he responded politely.

"You must have a sweetheart."

"No, thank you. I don't need them." He looked into the beady eyes of the crow and could see his own panicked reflection. He backed against the wall trying to make his retreat.

"Oh, sir. I sense my friend disturbs you. Not to worry. He's kind and smart. He tells me where to go and warns me if I am in danger." She laughed tenderly and put the crow close to her to give it a kiss on its head. "Am I in danger, sweetheart?"

The crow fixed its eyes suspiciously on Peter and cawed loudly. "Imagine that. He says I am in no trouble…but you are. Perhaps a flower will help," she said, offering one with her large, toothless smile.

Peter pressed his hands against the stone wall to steady himself, the whiskey pulling at his legs.

* * *

He drained the whiskey and stumbled into the church. The pews were gone, the lectern dismantled, and the pulpit was an empty space surrounded by boxes. Twenty swastikas draped the open rafters above. He found his way to the middle of this once sacred space and looked all around him, finding nothing that reminded him of the best years of his life—before the worst day of his life. He sat there in the emptiness of the church, wiping the nervous sweat from his forehead.

He was an assassin—a soldier, fearless and fully committed to do whatever was asked. But this chance encounter with an innocent little girl brought him so much anxiety that he could hardly breathe. She had penetrated a crack in his armor that led to the deepest part of his soul where his father's words lay under lock-and-key. Now she held a key in her hand that seemed to unlock the door to his heart. If he could not keep his heart closed, he would see again, and feel again, and that would be his utter destruction. He was still a soldier; he had his assignment. He could not let this child be his demise.

He sat quietly in the church searching for a power that could keep his soul locked down. There, in what was once familiar and comforting, he'd find an answer—a calm for the war in his gut, a divided courage from God, the devil, one in the same in his shattered mind—from whoever had his mind, for he knew he had lost it.

He laughed at the irony of what had brought him there. His gaze was captured by a discolored imprint of a cross on the east wall. "I've come to you to help me be the devil I am!" He surveyed the sanctuary one last time, taking it all in fighting the inner trembling, intermittent breaths, quickening his final words, strangled and bitter, "The devil I am..."

He heard a muffled chuckle coming from a dark corner swathed in old, discarded church banners. He leapt to his unsteady boots and stumbled over. He lifted the banners but found no one. From the opposite corner he heard the indiscernible words of a child. He stepped closer, cautiously, his gun drawn realizing the voice was a man's. "You are home now, Peter. Come, take my hand... my son. Peter, my son."

Peter turned the corner, his gun pointed in his shuddering hand at nothing. He grabbed a nearby chair, and heaved it against the wall, smashing it into pieces, smashing his resistance, a full embrace of the madness that possessed him.

★ ★ ★

Martin watched Peter plodding across the square toward the Hotel Adlon. He set down his binoculars and closed the curtains to his lavish third-floor hotel room. He sat on a chair, toasted a glass of whiskey in the air, "Alea Iacta Est, my friend."

★ ★ ★

Peter carried his hat in his right hand tucked tightly against his ribs. His eyes set on the front doors of the Hotel. Whether it was the whiskey or the realization that his mind was spiraling out of control, his moral hesitations had retreated back to the dark, lower levels of his consciousness, back under lock and key.

Now, he was captivated by a steady ticking in his head, like a watch, clear and distinct, ordering his steps in a warrior's march. He entered the hotel and headed directly to room 407. He ascended to the top of the red-carpeted staircase before pausing. The ticking in his head sounding more like a distant thud of cannon fire now. The cadence was steady, confidently driving him to battle as it always had. The whiskey stupor was quelled by a warrior's passion cued by the thuds in his head that commanded obedience, loyalty, and victory. His mind razor sharp, he picked the lock to room 407 and entered. He hid behind a thick, floor-to-ceiling curtain that outlined the east window.

He decided to kill the General and his wife immediately upon entry and then the children— though they were less children, merely targets now. He was in kill mode, a familiar state of mind that had served him well in countless battles. He was a surgeon with a scalpel cutting into human flesh to execute a purpose having nothing to do with feelings. This sterile detachment—his greatest strength—remained, even bolstered his strongest religion; the uncertainty about whose son he was, finally over. He was the devil's son now. He was Lieutenant Peter Engle, Germany's greatest war hero. Life had made him this...made him for this.

He tugged at his purple scarf until it ripped from his thick neck, tossing it to the floor. "I hide from no one now," he whispered to himself. He cocked his handgun, stunted his breathing, and released meaningless words, the final cue for battle: "Our Father in heaven... hallowed be thy name..."

★ ★ ★

The General walked down the hallway toward room 407. His son Otto, seven years old, held his hand tightly, occasionally looking up at his father with awe. His daughters Clara, six, and Mona, eleven, walked alongside their mother who rested her hand on Mona's shoulder and held Clara's white-gloved hand. Clara skipped with exuberance humming to herself.

"Mother, this is the most beautiful place we've ever been to," said Mona.

"That was the best dinner, wasn't it, Papa?" added Otto.

He rubbed the top of his head. "Yes, son. The absolute best."

"Mama, will we have chocolate tonight?" asked Clara.

"It is a bit late, dear. Perhaps tomorrow."

Clara returned to her humming. "Will father's friend be joining us?"

Mother looked at her husband with an understanding smile. "Oh, we met a Lieutenant in the lobby today."

"Someone I know?"

"I don't believe so."

He nodded.

"He seemed troubled. Just...not...I don't know...troubled."

The General stopped just outside their door. "We are all troubled, my dear."

She gently placed her hand on his forearm. "Troubled?"

He gave her a reassuring smile. He wished he could tell her about his concerns. The meeting with the Fuhrer could send him far from his family. Things had not turned out as he had hoped. All his ideas were summarily rejected. He said things that needed to be said despite friends warning him to be more discrete. He knew of The List, but he feared nothing. The Fuhrer was not only his leader but a good friend of his family. And he was here, in Germany's greatest hotel, with his family, compliments of the Fuhrer. All would be well.

He shut the door behind him. His family huddled around him and thanked him for such a spectacular dinner. "You are welcome, my dears."

"Papa, may we have chocolate tonight?" asked Clara.

He dropped to a knee and touched her little chin. "You are full of sweetness. Perhaps it is because you love chocolate so much."

She giggled. "So, is that a yes?"

He stood and nodded. "Dear, let's open the box of…"

Before he could finish his sentence Peter moved out from the curtain. He held his gun at his side, fixing it at the General.

The General knew instantly that his life was about to end. His hand instinctively slid to the butt of his handgun looped to his waist.

"No, General. Keep your hand steady."

He complied and lifted his hands. He stepped in front of his son who had already tightly wrapped his arms around his waist in fear.

His wife pulled her daughters behind her. "Lieutenant. This cannot be," she said with a quivering voice.

"That's Papa's friend, Mama," said Clara.

"Yes, my dear. This is Papa's friend," responded the General reassuringly. "My friend. We should step out into the hallway and talk there," he said trying to calm his desperation.

Mona, his eldest daughter, understood that Peter was no friend and began to scream and cry.

Mother covered her mouth pulling her face against her chest.

"There will be no discussion, General," said Peter as he moved closer.

"Honor me, Lieutenant. There's no need for the children to see this."

Otto fully understood. "No, Papa. No," he pleaded.

He turned to his son. "It's okay, son. I am a soldier. Remember? I am a soldier."

His son squeezed him tighter. The General peeled him away. "Stand with your mother and sisters."

But he would not obey. "No, Papa. I want to stand with you."

He grabbed his arm firmly and yanked him away. "Do as I say," he said forcibly.

"Please, Lieutenant, you make a memory for them that will haunt them forever."

Peter felt his hand begin to shake. He felt words exit his mouth, strong and certain, yet disconnected from his consciousness. "They will have no memory of this. Those are my orders."

The General's eyes widened in disbelief. He pleaded in a desperate tremor. "My family? My family?" He stepped toward Peter who raised his handgun at his face. The General stopped hoping he could reason with him. "He has lost his mind. The Fuhrer has lost his mind. We all know this." He looked into Peter's eyes hoping to see a spot of mercy but found nothing. His eyes fell into his wife's eyes in a sweet surrender, and he mouthed "I love you."

Peter let his eyes move from the General for a second, and he saw the little girl. She was different from her siblings who hid their eyes from him in terror. They understood the horror of what was about to happen, but she looked right at him with an innocence that wanted to see the best in him. She smiled at him, and he felt his hand loosen. The shaking in his hand suddenly stopped. He looked back at the General who had fallen to his knees.

"Please soldier, spare my family. Kill me a hundred times but spare my family."

Peter set his aim on the General's head for an instant kill. His finger tightened around the trigger. It would all be over now, he thought. But he felt an untethering in his soul and words freeing themselves undaunted by an evil that constrained them. "Father, father help me."

The first shot rang out.

DEATH FOR LIFE

The Final Assignment
One Month Later

Martin watched from the third-floor window of the Charite hospital in Berlin as people below hurried along the exposed streets, peering upward, expecting doom from above. The German propaganda machine no longer proved as effective in countering the steady flow of truth that followed each telegram quietly announcing another German soldier's death. The Allies had proven a much greater foe than expected. The Fuhrer's military acumen had dulled and left more and more of his leaders anxious. Germany was now on the brink of desperation, from the front lines to the halls of leadership, to the common man that fell into Martin's view below. The Wehrmacht, always on the attack, was now being pressed backward to the homeland. Supplies were draining quickly, but more importantly, the morale of Germany's fighting men and of its people was in rapid decline. Germany was in desperate need of renewed hope.

He released his last smoky breath out the window, tossed the butt into a tray, and shut the window. He tugged on his collar and entered the hospital room.

★ ★ ★

Peter's eyes were red and glassy. He felt a touch on his shoulder. "My brother. I'm here," whispered Martin.

Peter lay still, staring at the ceiling, his eyes empty, unwilling to acknowledge him.

"They say you're not human. More lead has passed through you than a train through Berlin," chuckled Martin. He tightened his lips and exhaled. He squeezed Peter's shoulder. "You're alive, my brother. That's all that matters now." He watched a solitary tear fall from Peter's eye. Martin removed his hand and sat back in his chair in silence. He gulped away his helplessness. "It's good that you didn't complete the mission. You have a soul my brother. The Fuhrer asked for too much." He examined his friend closely, hoping to read something. Seeing nothing, deciding it was not the time to discuss what he was anxious to say. He stood. "I'll visit tomorrow. Get some rest." He turned to walk out.

"I don't understand," said Peter weakly.

Martin stopped and turned to face him.

"My hands are drenched in the blood of so many, and now I kill innocent, good people in front of their children." His chin shook and then the tears fell strongly covering his face. "I deserve death. I want it, Martin. I want it badly, more than anything else." His lip quivered hard. "It cheats me again. Why, Martin?"

"Death…it has no ears, my friend."

"Possessed," whispered Peter. "Since that day on my farm, something possesses me. Is it the devil, Martin? Am I possessed?" He gripped his blanket and covered his face. "Something possesses me, Martin. Help me. Please, help me."

Martin stepped closer, his hands at his side not knowing what to do.

Peter's eyes slipped over his blanket looking at the light above him. "I let that little boy shoot me. He climbed over his father's body. He pulled out his father's gun. And I stood there waiting for what I wanted most. But it didn't come. I've been its faithful companion. I've done all that death has asked." He released his sheets and clenched his fists against his chest. He looked over at his friend and spoke with a desperation Martin had never seen. "Martin, I beg you, please put an end to me. Please. I beg you." He reached for Martin's hand, but Martin pulled away.

"Peter, you don't know what you're saying." He stepped closer. "Nothing possesses you but the greatest courage and strength I've ever seen in a man."

Peter took in a deep, trembling breath, glowering at Martin shaking his head.

"Courage? You mistake insanity for courage." He stilled his head and closed his eyes. "I am the devil's son…his insane son."

Martin stepped closer and grabbed his hand. "You are the greatest man Germany has ever known, my brother. Too much was asked."

Peter wanted death more than anything else. He eyed Martin's holstered revolver but knew he was too weak to execute his burning desire. "If you won't put a bullet in my head, you're useless to me."

Martin hated Peter's rejection. It was true. Peter didn't need him because Peter didn't need anyone. He felt his fists ball up in anger. He stepped away from his bed ready to leave.

Peter sighed heavily and rolled away in his bed giving Martin his back.

Martin remembered the day he visited Peter after the attack on his farm. He considered all he had lost, and his desperate cries for death. He knew he had to tell him.

"Your father is alive."

★ ★ ★

A few weeks later, Peter stood next to Martin on a bluff overlooking his farm. It had been years since Peter stood on the land

202

that had formed him. He imagined better days there: his mother exiting the barn carrying a bucket of warm milk; his father, hands on his hips, watching her as she walked toward him removing his hat with a bow, then delivering a gentle kiss and whisper that made her giggle in embarrassment.

"There was no other way to confirm. I'm sorry," said Martin compassionately.

Peter responded without any hint of emotion. "Let's get this over with."

A truck pulled onto the farm. Two guards jumped out and pulled him out. Max stood in the afternoon sunlight next to the barn's charred foundation. His fresh, clean clothes belied his bony frame, pale face, and sunken eye. He straightened his curved spine and took in all that he had left behind. He turned to face his once peaceful house seeing only its scorched remains. Gone were the cattle, the horses, all that once made this his heaven on earth. His shoulders slumped and he bowed his head. He wiped tears from his face and then stood as erect as he could, his hands raised at his sides, palms out, and his face directed to the sky. He breathed in deeply as if stealing away lost, precious memories. When he was done, he lowered his hands and peered over his left shoulder toward the bluff where Peter stood.

Martin watched his friend hidden behind binoculars seeing his lower lip quiver. "I didn't know Peter. I'm sorry."

Peter lowered the binoculars, fabricated a smile, his eyes glossed over by the vision of his father. "You're too late, Martin…too late."

Martin nodded and returned his gaze at Max. "I understand." His words stuck in his narrowing throat. "He's alive," he said, shaking his head bitterly. "But…"

Peter shook the vision from his mind and forced a hard stare against Martin. "He's alive…that's all I have to know."

Martin placed his hand on his shoulder, and he exhaled his tension. "I arranged this before…before he's hanged tomorrow."

The guards grabbed Max and threw him back into the truck.

Martin watched Peter's eyes fill with tears as the truck drove off. He spoke cautiously, watching Peter's every reaction. "There's a way to stop the execution."

Peter returned the binoculars to Martin, his eyes on him, hopeful and confused. "Save my father?"

Martin nodded. "A last impossible mission. One I wanted, Peter. It's been planned since the beginning of the war." He looked back at the sad remains of their past. "It won't be mine. I begged the Fuhrer, Peter. I begged him." He met Peter's stare. "It will take you to America, and will end the war, once and for all."

"And you will spare my father."

Martin nodded. "But…"

Peter interrupted. "But I must…"

Martin nodded slowly, compassionately. "You can't be captured."

Peter's face went surprisingly soft, a smile that seemed out of place.

Martin handed him a box the size that commonly contains a ring.

Peter took it and caressed it in his hand. "Well, I know you're not proposing." He put the box in his pocket. "I take the pill when I'm done, all our secrets taken to my grave."

Martin chewed on his trembling lip. "I'm sorry. There's no other way."

Peter grabbed his shoulder. "Let's go to the pond."

Martin nodded away his tears, and they returned to their childhood for one last time.

BILLY THE KID TO THE RESCUE

Little Heinz lit a candle and sat on the orphanage floor eager to read Ralph's letter. He read it three times, now dizzy with excitement. Ralph had been captured by the Americans. They were nothing like he was trained to believe. They were not crude animals or unsophisticated mongrels, mixed of multiple races, impure and weak. They treated him with respect and compassion.

Dear Heinz,

We were in a prisoner camp. So many of us lay dead. I stopped counting after a thousand. I wish I could tell you I was brave, Heinz. I was not. Every soldier to my left and right was dead. I saw what happens to our bodies when death comes. I never want to see it again, but I'm scared it's just begun. Please ask Fraulein Emma to pray that I never see it again. It's so hard to breathe here. It's so hot and all the bodies are rotten now. It's a smell I can't stand. It hurts your chest after a while. I'm not blaming you, Heinz. I'm grateful for what you did for me. And

I'm sorry I treated you so badly. I'm done for today. I buried nearly a hundred of our soldiers. After the first ten, I couldn't go on. I fell to the ground and covered my face with my hands and just cried. At first, an American soldier hit me and yelled at me, but I couldn't hear him. I just prayed out loud to God that he would take me home. Then, another one, a young one spoke kindly in German:

"What's your name?" he asked me.

"Ralph, sir," I told him.

Then he nodded and said, "Mine's Noah. Now listen to me. It's gonna be alright. God's gonna answer your prayer. You'll get home soon."

He reminded me of you, Heinz. He didn't have to care about me. I was his enemy, but I don't think he really had an enemy, like you. He stood me to my feet and put his hand on my shoulder. "Do your work. That's all. Just do your work. I promise, you'll be okay," he said.

I did my work. I buried our brothers all day and night. And I had hope that someday I'd be home again. And when I come back, I promise, I'm going to be good to you. I promise.

Later that evening I saw that soldier again:

"Hey, you. Come here. How old are ya, boy?" he asked me.

"Fifteen. I'm not supposed to be a soldier."

"Yeah, figured. You don't belong."

"Thank you for your kind words. But everyone says you're going to kill us anyway," I told him.

"No. Ain't gonna do that. Ain't our way." He looked over his shoulder into the darkness that

surrounded the dimly lit prisoner compound and said, "Look. I knew ya was a kid. I'm the one that found you hiding under all that hay scared out of your britches. I'm on guard duty tonight." He looked over his shoulder again, and then opened the corral door and asked me, "You promise me you'll go home and never pick up another gun?"

I told him, "Yes, sir. I just want to go home."

He said, "Then you tell me Hitler deserves to die, that he's, he's the devil."

I said, "Yes, yes, he is. I will kill him myself. I promise."

He told me to get going, Heinz, and I ran just as fast as I could off into the darkness.

I hope to write again soon.
Your friend,
Ralph

Heinz folded the letter and returned to his bed. The Americans are good, he thought to himself. He pulled out his prized possession from under his pillow. He returned to the light and thumbed through his comic book. Billy the Kid was his hero. He dreamed of the wild frontier, the Indians, coyotes, and Billy the Kid who wasn't much older than he was. It was a gift from his mother and all that he had to remember a better time. The stories and the colorful characters gave him hope that there was a better place and time still left for him. But not here, not in this orphanage, not in Germany. He had to get to America. They were good people, just like Ralph said. Just a few more things and he would be free.

He packed his knapsack with the little he had, then he looked at the other orphans fast asleep in their beds and smiled. He looked at Fraulein Emma's closed door and paused. She was a good woman, and the only good thing in his life. He took his mom's lock of hair, kissed it once, and pushed it under Fraulein Emma's door. He mouthed a goodbye and walked out the front door.

★ ★ ★

Two days later he was in Luxembourg. The German soldiers there prepared for another advance by the American forces. They were tired and hungry and many wanted to retreat. As he had planned, Heinz fixed a white pillowcase to a long stick and headed for the American front. At first he walked past the German line ignoring the soldiers' calls. Then he heard shots from behind and bullets hitting the ground near him. He ran as fast he could, the flag waving overhead in one hand, his comic book in the other. He could see the American line ahead at 100 meters with their guns set on him. He closed his eyes and continued forward undeterred. "America, America," he yelled. "I want America, I want America."

The shots continued from behind, one cutting his stick in half. He fell flat onto his face. His eyes widened as he caught a glimpse of the American soldiers waving him on. He could feel the air separate near his ear as German bullets narrowly missed their mark. He crawled as fast as he could, the broken stick still in his hand.

A G.I. with a row of stripes on his sleeves broke from his line in a full sprint, bullets now trained on the better prize. He grabbed Heinz like a loaf of bread and sprinted back to safety. He tossed him onto the ground, safe now behind the American line. "You crazy kid. What the hell ya doin'?"

"American, American!" screamed Heinz, holding the G.I's thick leg. He shoved his comic book into the air. "Billy the Kid, Billy the Kid, please, please."

"Okay, little feller. Okay. You okay now. You okay now."

FREE TO BE A PRISONER

Peter opened his final orders and read them with an unusual interest. When he was done his eyes darted up at Martin. "This is it?"

"You have half your instructions. The rest will be given when you get there."

"And getting there is impossible. This is foolish."

Martin gave him an apologetic smile. "I understand. All I can tell you is that this has been planned since the beginning. We've got everything in place…just been waiting for the right time… the right soldier. I'll get you there. I promise you. The rest is up to you."

"The rest? To do what, Martin? What is my mission?" he demanded.

"Nothing can be compromised. Even I don't have all the details. I'm sorry. It's just the way it must be."

Peter stood and exhaled a slow, defeated sigh. "The way it must be?"

Martin walked over to his window. Dark heavy rain clouds encircled, and he felt like the day had been called off by an eager foreboding. "You don't have to do this. I can tell the Fuhrer we couldn't make the proper arrangements. So many things must fall into place. He would accept my words."

Peter stepped close and forced a bleak smile against the heaviness of the hundred questions in his head. He slapped his friend's back. "Just take good care of my father." His hand slid away. "Be a son to him. For me. Please, Martin."

Martin felt his face twist with resolve and doubt. How could he be the pastor's son when he was to blame for all the calamity present and to come? He spoke through a throat tight with shame. "I give you my word."

Peter's jaw flexed the sorrow from his face. He looked deeply into his friend's eyes and found a tinge of their childhood innocence. He smiled contentedly. "Take care of yourself, my brother."

Martin forced himself to watch Peter leave. When gone, he sat in his chair and thought about how all this would end. There would be no glory for Germany, just a final blow to America that would give her a lifetime of sadness. But Peter, he would be memorialized; German children would sing songs about him. He was always destined to be Germany's greatest. And he would not.

★ ★ ★

Two weeks later

Peter and twelve tired, hungry German soldiers marched with their hands up above their heads carefully following the shouted orders of the Americans who walked alongside them, some disinterested, most with their fingers pressed firmly on their triggers looking for any reason to kill another Kraut.

Peter followed the plan precisely, fasting and losing twenty pounds. His face was thin, dirty, and unshaven. His uniform fit loosely as he moved with the others, no longer a standout specimen, but a simple private—just another defeated and de-moralized captive with hopeless, hollow eyes.

They corralled into a temporary camp until they could be processed. Sitting nearby was a little boy, his head laying weakly against his knees under the thin covering of the skinniest of arms. A sliver of his big eyes peeked through the narrow gap between his forearms watching Peter.

Peter felt his cheeks lift with an appreciation of the boy's innocence. Then his face dropped as he considered how that innocence must have been destroyed. He nodded a friendly hello to the boy.

Heinz opened his eyes fully and smiled. He stood and walked over, tapping down an excited skip. "Hello, my name is Heinz. What is your name, sir?"

Peter took the little hand into his and shook it gently. "Peter. My name is Peter. I'm pleased to meet you, Heinz."

Heinz's eyes stayed comfortably on Peter's. "I know where we are going," he said with a whisper.

"Top secret information?" asked Peter.

"I don't think so." He pointed at a nearby G.I. "He told me. Didn't say it was a secret."

Peter winked. "And you're going?"

"Yes, of course."

"You're a prisoner of war?" he asked with an exaggerated, playful frown.

Heinz rubbed the back of his neck, a cautious smile hiding his thoughts. "Please don't tell anyone. I'm much too young to fight. And to be honest, I'm not a fighter."

Peter tilted his head, his lips corkscrew. "I don't know about that. You look like you could be dangerous."

Heinz chuckled, stuck his hands in his pockets, and kicked the dirt with his boot. "I'm not dangerous…I assure you, sir."

"Don't you want to go home? They'll let you go home."

Heinz's chin lifted slowly, and his gaze looked past the barricade at nothing. "I have no one." His eyes fell back onto his new friend. "And you, Peter. Who do you have waiting?"

Peter felt the corners of his mouth begin to rise in a soft smile, but then he pushed his lips tight. "I guess we are destined to be friends, little Heinz. I have no one either."

Heinz's oversized front teeth jetted out from his lips and he nodded gleefully. He extended his hand again. "Let's shake on it."

Peter looked down at his filthy, strong hand and followed it as it slowly met Heinz's eager grip.

"There we have it. We are friends," he said as his free hand lay on his chest in an oath. "We are friends going to America," added Heinz gleefully.

As Peter shook his hand, he felt something in Heinz that war had not yet destroyed. He felt like an old miner on the precipice of giving up but finally finding a rare and brilliant vein of gold in the darkest mine. He held Heinz's hand feeling the same lightness and joy he had when he was child. He wanted to take the boy into his arms, but then he remembered his mission. What good was this boy? What good was his purity, his hope? All these things were no longer his to possess. Heinz was like a poisonous stream to a man dying of thirst. He let go of his hand and walked away.

* * *

From sea to land, Peter was amazed at the precision with which the American military moved their human cargo. He was surprised by the respect and kindness they received as captives. He kept to himself hoping his past notoriety would not be discovered.

They traveled by train from the East across the Midwest and then South. He had a sense of the vastness of this country, but it was far greater than he ever imagined. At the end of each day of travel, he assumed they had reached their end. But after days of travel, the majesty and diversity of a seemingly never-ending landscape eclipsed the glory of Germany a million times.

The prisoners were silenced by this expanse and good treatment. For most, the war was certainly over. No one could defeat this giant. Yet Peter watched the few SS officers that passed his view throughout the trip. He knew these men. They only saw what they wanted to see. They saw weakness. The country was too big, too disconnected, incapable of organization. And he saw their disgust with the courteous porters, all black men who said only the barest niceties, but with a dignity and intelligence that burned through the harsh, cold stares of captured men who still believed in their own superiority. Peter didn't care about a man's color. He simply appreciated their kindness. He watched the other POWs as all the lies about Americans, and Black Americans, slowly unraveled.

★ ★ ★

Peter tried to separate himself from Heinz, but Heinz would not have it. He spent every minute he could with Peter. They ate together, slept next to each other, and read and reread Billy the Kid. Peter helped Heinz with his English and Heinz touched his heart in ways that simultaneously inspired and damned him. Heinz told his story, free of any hint of sadness. And Peter saw that for Heinz, all his sufferings were mere knots along a long rope held by him as he swung joyfully through life. And he remembered what that was like. He desperately wanted to be that boy again. But he was on a train to do what no innocent boy could ever do.

Heinz was fast asleep, his face pressed snugly against Peter's side. Peter lifted his arm and softly placed it around his little shoulder tucking him close.

★ ★ ★

It was two o'clock in the morning when the train's sudden stop woke Peter. He looked out the window and saw nothing but a dim, solitary light casting shadows against a scant platform and faded wood sidings at a ticket office, just like all the other stations. But this was his stop. Days of travel across this vast country and now he reached his destination, wherever that was. He wasn't given a name, not even the state was known to him. He knew Shumannsville, and at times his heart raced when he saw land that reminded him of it. But it all began to look the same to him. He shook Heinz awake. "Heinz, Heinz. It's my time."

"What? No, Peter." He stood and threw his arms around his friend's waist. "Please don't go."

Peter's hands lay still at his side, purposeless and uncertain. He felt the boy's tight squeeze and all that it meant. He lifted his hands and placed them gingerly on his head, then pulled him close. He squeezed his eyes shut and quickly muffled the rumblings of his saddened heart. He pictured Julia standing at the station, her face beaming with hope that their love could not be disturbed by time or space, by war or tragedy. It was a strong hope set on invading his life. But that was impossible now. He blinked his eyes and sent the vision away.

Heinz pushed his face from Peter's stomach and peered up at him. "I will never forget you, Peter. Never." He let go, stepped back and saluted with a trembling hand.

The guards barked their orders in German. "150, 150. If you're in group 150, get off now. Let's go. Let's go."

Peter dropped to a knee so that he might see him directly. "Heinz. It's going to be okay. You must be strong, strong like a man."

"I know how to be strong, Peter," he said with a small, confident whisper.

Peter looked at him measuredly and smiled. "Yes. Yes, you do." He returned to his feet. "Pray that I will be as strong as you." He stepped away and turned for his exit.

"Peter," called Heinz.

Peter stopped and turned around.

"I will pray for you."

Peter returned a blank, courteous smile. He stepped off the train and saw a small sign that read, "Welcome to Mexia, Texas."

★ ★ ★

Mexia was a small Texas town named after General Jose Antonio Mexia, a Hispanic hero for the Republic of Texas Army during the Texas Revolution. It had been a prosperous town with the discovery of natural gas, but when the depression hit, the industry failed, and a majority of the population left for work elsewhere. The economy was now supported by local farming, and like all other farming communities across the United States, farm hands were in short supply. The POWs were brought to pick cotton that would otherwise be left to rot.

Peter and six others were transported to their camp. A few hours later they stood in an early morning rigid and exacting formation under the sharp orders of their *unterfeldwebels*, sergeants.

Rittmeister, Colonel Ludwig von Kliest stood before them in his displaced regality, still allowed to wear his uniform. He looked down at the discoloration on his shirt that once held a proud row of medals. They had been stripped away by his captors and their absence continued to feed his hatred. He inspected his men from afar, never too close, never speaking with them privately. He despised their gray, faded shirts, inscribed on their backs in large block letters 'POW'. He cared little about their fate. They had surrendered. He had volunteered for a still unknown mission that was certain to change the course of the war. He believed in his heart that victory was still within Germany's grasp. And now he had the news he had been waiting for. He shot a cold look at one of his sergeants who dismissed the men to their farming assignments. The sergeant grabbed Peter's forearm. "The Colonel will see you."

Von Kliest poured himself a cup of coffee from a nickel-plated coffee set provided by the Americans. His quarters were furnished with a large desk made of a wood he was not familiar with. It looked to be fairly new. His chair was thickly padded and covered in a green leather that still smelled of dye. On the planked floor was a long carpet painted in red and black blocks that formed an eagle's outline.

"I am sure you would love a good cup of coffee, Engle?" he said in his characteristic lofty tone. "It is from home. The Americans think we can be bought. Give us a few comforts and we will be good little boys," he added smugly. He smiled and began to pour.

"I already had a cup."

Von Kliest stopped his pour and glanced up at Peter taking in his lack of formality and respect. He felt his hand shaking in anger as he lifted his cup for his first sip. "So, we finally meet. I have been in this despicable place for over a year waiting for you."

Peter inspected these unwarranted, genteel quarters. His left brow rose slightly. "I'm sure Germany appreciates your great sacrifice."

Von Kliest looked him over with disdain, fighting his simultaneous admiration against the decorum his rank required. He knew all about him—all that was necessary. "The information came to me this morning. No need to know how. Only I know who you are. It will stay that way. You will be assigned a farm, to get you out and mobile." He lifted his cup of coffee in a toast. "To the Fuhrer."

Peter sat up stiffly, hearing little, caring less. "You have my assignment?"

Von Kliest took his time sipping his coffee, his brows bridged over his annoyed eyes.

Peter caught the slight tremble in the Colonel's hand. "Do you have my assignment?" he repeated absently looking out the window behind the Colonel.

He put his cup down and turned it slightly to fit his orderly desk. "As I said. I just found out this morning that you are the one I have been waiting for."

Peter glanced his way expelling his frustration through his flared nostrils.

"I expect we will know soon." He lifted his cup in a gesture. "Are you sure you don't want a cup?"

Peter nodded as his tense lips loosened and parted slightly. "Sure."

He poured another cup and offered it kindly. "I have other refreshments, those of an amber color," he said with a chuckle that met Peter's hard stare. "Not a drinking man? Should I trust a soldier that does not imbibe?"

Peter's eyes inspected him with an annoyance that wanted to slap him across his skinny face.

Von Kliest rubbed his chin. "You think you know who I am, some weak prisoner simply passing on information." He shook his head in judgment. "I have served the Fuhrer faithfully. I have lost a great deal, while others get all the glory," he added as he inhaled his pride. "None of that matters to me. Despite what you may think." He paused, placing his cup down, staring at it, again turning it rightly. He stood, his chest puffed out, one hand in a fist on his desk. "Germany will prevail. And you, Lieutenant, will always be remembered as its greatest hero," he proclaimed with an enthusiasm that could not fully veil his disdain. He lifted his cup again in an imperious toast. "To our greatest hero."

Peter took his last sip and carefully placed his cup onto von Kliest's desk and shot him a smile verging on insult.

Von Kliest extended his hand above his shoulder in enthusiastic praise. "Hail Hitler."

Peter returned a weak nod.

Von Kliest snapped his hand down at his side angered by Peter's apathy. His eyes made a last desperate search for a hint of affinity, finding nothing but Peter's blank stare. "We will talk soon, Engle. Perhaps in the evening. I will bring out my best brandy. Get to know each other."

Peter released his frustration in a long sigh that made his words unnecessary. He forced a respectful salute and walked out.

★ ★ ★

Days later, Heinz and the remaining POWs were quietly detained and put on two military transport trucks. They entered Pleasant Acres family camp, now their POW camp. There was already a presence at the camp. One month earlier, ten men, including an officer, had been secretly dispatched similarly. No one knew of their presence. The military knew how Americans were responding in other towns. It would be no different here, where many sons were gone forever. At daylight the town would never be the same. Shumannsville would never be the same.

★ ★ ★

The next morning, Julia stopped her wagon at Grey's Mill. As was always the case, the men at the mill unloaded her stock with great eagerness. She did nothing to provoke their attention. She was kind and respectful and always proper. She couldn't sabotage her beauty even when dressed in her old coveralls, her hair in a ponytail, not a touch of make-up, which she wore only on Sunday, and then only sparingly. No one garnered such attention and no one could. She smiled and thanked the men.

One mustered up his courage. "Julia, have you heard the rumors?"

She brushed off the last of corn silks and dust from her pants. "I don't pay attention to rumors, Hank."

"I know. But seems they're true. Read it in the paper. All across America, them prisoners helping with the harvest. Everywhere. Seems a good idea. Sure need some extra hands here."

"Ya think so?," she said with an agitation he understood.

"Well, the Muellers ain't gonna make it. That's for sure. And I'm helping at the Miller's but still not enough." He paused and felt his courage waning. "Maybe they can help ya out?"

She lifted her chin and spoke coldly. "Haven't heard from Noah in months. Don't know if he's dead or alive or rotting away in some prisoner camp." Her eyes filled with tears. "No, Hank… won't be needing their help." She jumped onto her cart, slapped the reins hard, and left in a huff.

★ ★ ★

Soon the word was out. Everyone knew the prisoners occupied Pleasant Acres, but no one was allowed within two miles of the camp. Julia burned with anger. Pleasant Acres was one of Noah's favorite places. It was nestled between the Tivy Mountain Range and the Guadalupe River. It was the most beautiful spot in all of Guadalupe County. Noah loved to fish there in the quiet, cool pools and inlets that were fertile breeding grounds for local trout. And now evil men, who may have had a hand in Noah's demise, took advantage of the very best he could no longer enjoy.

She had cried herself to sleep a hundred times. She was too tired and heavy laden to continue the same old prayer. She didn't

219

know if he was already dead, but his prolonged silence meant he probably was. That had been the pattern in Shumannsville. A few letters in the beginning, a silence, and then the awful final letter written by some military official who never knew the fallen soldier. It was coming; she could feel it in her bones.

★ ★ ★

Julia sat in church next to her mother and father thinking about her rifle. She knew the land and could slip through the guarded perimeter; within an hour she could kill a handful of prisoners. Her mind had entered strange territory. No matter how devastated her heart was, she knew she could never kill another human being. She took the thought and tied it up.

Pastor Bob finished his sermon. "Let me close with this." His voice cracked as he tried to get his words together. "I've tried to lead this congregation through these perilous times, and for some, I have failed. I'm very sorry 'bout that. I find I don't have the words. We've lost our sons and many 'bout to lose their source of livin'. These prisoners, just them being near, makes our pain so hard to handle. We lost our two boys…" His tears broke free, and he coughed to try to compose himself. "Our pain is…all I know, as a follower of Jesus, I can't live my life in hate. I can't…I won't."

Julia felt the ties loosen. She wanted to jump to her feet. *I can. I will. To hell with this.* Mother felt her uneasiness, so she squeezed her hand.

"Jesus said, as they tortured him on the cross, 'Father forgive them…'"

Julia leapt to her feet, interrupting him. "They know not what they do?" She looked down at her mother and father absorbing their pain, but not their restraint. "I'm sorry, Pastor. You've suffered more than I can imagine, but I can't do whatcha ask."

Mother tugged at her daughter's hand. "Julia, please."

"No one forced them to follow this evil. They chose this. We didn't." She pointed her finger toward the camp, her eyes streaming with tears. "Those men killed our brothers, our sons." She lowered her head and shook it slowly. "Please forgive me, Pastor. I just can't do it. Can't." She broke from her mother and stormed out of church.

Mother buried her face into her hands and sobbed. Father touched her back tenderly, stood and excused himself.

TO MATTER

oah sat on a tree stump looking at the maple trees that surrounded his camp. He still felt like an outsider. He had no one to talk to. He knew no one wanted to hear his story. He looked up at a pair of wood pigeons nestled comfortably above him cooing to each other. He had his limits, but he was always good at noticing things no one saw. His Lieutenant was constantly smoking his pipe when he wasn't sipping a cup full of whisky-diluted coffee, and his Sergeant stole away writing countless letters.

He hopped off the stump and approached him. "Howdy, Sarge."

"Tex." He put his pencil in his pocket, stood and forced a smile. "How are you?"

"Fine, Sarge. Ah, was wondering if you knew anything. Everybody's talkin', speculatin'."

He put his hand on Noah's shoulder. "Go join the rest. We'll know soon enough."

He returned to the stump and sat, loosened his bootstraps, and considered taking them off. Most of the men were laying on the ground, some asleep.

"Eyes up here," shouted the Sergeant.

They snapped to as the Lieutenant walked to the front of the assembly. He removed his pipe and nodded approvingly, gesturing with his hands for them to sit. "Men, you've shown yourself brave. I've never been prouder to lead anyone. You've had a few days of rest." He nodded and shot them an approving smile. "You deserved it." He cleaned out his pipe with the tip of his finger then tapped the bowl against his palm. "Boys, we got 'em on the run. The Krauts are in full retreat."

The men cheered and slapped each other on their backs.

"But we'll not be chasing them."

The cheers fell suddenly. The murmurs began.

He held his hands out, shushing them immediately. "Nothing would give me more pleasure than to hang Hitler myself."

"Waste of a rope. Put a bullet in his head," yelled one of the privates.

The Lieutenant nodded in agreement. "I don't know if you'll be able to appreciate what I'm about to say. But our new mission is greater than getting Hitler himself." He pulled a picture from a file and showed it to his platoon. He gave it to the Sergeant. "Pass it around. Get a good look at him. Let that face burn in your memory, never forget it… because he's the reason for our new mission. He's a prisoner, not one of our boys. I wish I could tell you more. All I can say is…well, he's got something we need, something the world needs. The rest is top secret information."

He slipped his pipe into his mouth and chewed on its tip for a while. He pulled it out and drew a big breath. "I've seen the recon photos. There's only one way in, no cover, and it's straight at a machine gunner. Boys…we're gonna take a significant loss. No way around it."

A soldier raised his hand.

"Not now, soldier," corrected the Sergeant.

"No. No. It's alright. I know what you're all thinking. Many of us die for one man?" He paused and struggled for words. He looked at the Sergeant as if in need of help.

He looked upon his men, boys, all young enough to be his youngest brother, some his son, and spoke with a gut-wrenching sadness that he fought with a strongly held fist secreted in his jacket pocket. He looked down at his empty pipe and nervously ran his finger into the empty bowl. His eyes painted over them again as he considered how many would die never knowing how important they were. "Some of you will never get the answers you deserve. I'm sorry about that. I wish it were different. But, if there's one thing I can promise you…what I know about this mission…when it's all over they'll say of you, each one of you… you changed the world. You mattered. Your life mattered."

Noah eyed the soldier next to him and recognized what he knew was true for all the rest. Everyone wanted to matter. And it was all he ever wanted, whether in life or death. He felt his heart begin to beat faster. He stood at attention unable to contain himself. "Ready, sir. Ready for whatever ya got."

The others followed with the same enthusiasm.

The Lieutenant swallowed hard trying to resist his tearful pride. He forced a commanding look at his Sergeant. "Let's move out."

★ ★ ★

They hiked in loose formation through empty fields and farmland long abandoned by Germans who believed that Berlin was their final defense against the evil Allies. They were twenty miles from their destination. Noah rested his arms over his M1 rifle as it lay across his shoulders. His helmet fit loose, bouncing on his head with every step. He chewed nervously on his chin strap spitting it out when he had a thought.

Next to him marched his Sergeant who carried his helmet in his hand. He was older, perhaps twenty-five, his face covered in beard stubble that hustled to catch his well-formed mustache. He took in the sunlight pulled over the horizon by the eagerness kicked by the marching boots of a hundred soldiers. "Morning glory has a way of painting a pretty picture."

Noah looked at him and his mouth tilted to the left. "Sure does. Nothin' like the mornin'. Crime to be asleep when the good Lord's doin' his best paintin'."

"You a painter, Tex?"

"Couldn't paint my way out of a can of beans."

"My little girl's already showing promise."

"You got a daughter?"

He reached into his front pocket and showed him her picture. "She's beautiful."

"Thank you." He kissed her and put her away.

Noah chewed on his strap again until his words forced their way through. "Hey, ya gonna make it back, Sarge," he said with cheerful confidence.

He nodded in agreement and smiled. "Gotta. She's all I got. But if I don't, she'll know her daddy was a good man." He looked past Noah at the glow that burned through a few lingering clouds and surrendered a smile. "A good man," he whispered to himself hoping his words would someday find his daughter's ears.

Noah looked off into the distance and then back at his Sergeant. "Great man," he said, with a grin that captured the hopefulness of the morning light.

★ ★ ★

The structure was bound on three sides by old brick buildings, primarily abandoned warehouses still untouched by mortar fire. To enter they would have to cross a large, empty field approximately

225

five acres wide, spotted with bunches of tender dandelions and no significant cover.

"Damn. Well, I do like dandelions," said the Lieutenant. He spotted a long ridge just high enough for their cover, about one hundred meters from their entrance point. At the foot of the entrance was a machine gunner set behind a sturdy bunker of sandbags and timber. The other walls were unguarded as the building was solid brick, three stories and windowless. Their package was inside, somewhere inside.

The original plan was to wait for nightfall, but now there was word that the package would be moved any moment. Waiting wasn't an option.

The Lieutenant shot Sarge a nod. Sarge peered to his left and right at his men lined and at the ready. He motioned with his hand, and they ran toward the ridge.

The machinegun fire erupted immediately and several were cut down before they could fire their weapons. The rest lay behind the ridge pinned down by the gunner fire that would soon rip the ridge to pieces.

Noah prayed quickly and kissed his rifle. "I'm ready, Lord. If it be your will, I'd like to take out a few of them bad boys before you call me home."

The Lieutenant prepared to give orders to charge. His hope, now shakier than before, was that the Germans would have fewer rounds than he had men. He looked down the row of faces pushed into the dirt ridge, all skinny, scared boys, yet all were ready to give their lives for a glory most would never see. He shot up a silent prayer.

Noah rolled to his Sergeant. "Sarge, I can lob a grenade at 'em from here."

"Too far. Can't be reached from here. Get ready. We're gonna charge."

Noah grabbed Sarge's arm. "Sir, wait. Let me do this. I ain't much, but I gotta arm like a catapult."

"They're one hundred meters out. It's impossible," he said impatiently.

"I can do it, Sarge. I know I can do it," he said with uncharacteristic confidence.

Sarge rolled to his left until he got to the Lieutenant. "Sir. Private Fischer says he's gotta rifle of an arm. Says he can land a grenade in the nest."

"That's impossible. And the second he stands they'll mow him down. No. Stick to the plan."

"Yes, sir. At your ready." He rolled back toward Noah. "No go, Tex. Hope you said your prayers. Gonna charge." He eyed his men one last time in an unspoken farewell.

Noah grabbed his shoulder in desperation. "But they're gonna mow us all down. You gotta give me a try."

Sarge's eyes shot a dagger into Noah's objection. "Get your damn hand off me, Private. You'll obey my order."

His hand fell limp onto the soil. He grabbed a fist full of it and squeezed it tightly. He released it and felt his hand move instinctively to his side. He freed a grenade from his belt and pushed the Sergeant away.

"Sorry, sir." He pulled a second grenade and stood to his feet.

The machine gunner pulled the heavy barrel of his MG42 toward his new target and squeezed his trigger, expelling a hot line of destruction in Noah's direction, missing by inches. A quick adjustment and he re-aimed, but the strap of ammunition had run its course. "Give me another strap," he ordered the boy that lay beneath him curled in a ball of fear.

"I can't. I can't. Please, I promised," shouted the boy.

The gunner reached down and pulled the boy up by his curly red hair screaming in his face.

"Then you're just like your worthless father." He tossed him aside and reloaded himself.

The boy shot to his knees trembling wildly. "He was a good man. A brave man," he said to himself.

★ ★ ★

Sarge grabbed Noah by the waist and tugged as hard as he could, but he couldn't bring him down. "Tex, no, no," he shouted.

The others looked on in shock waiting to see Noah's head blown off.

Noah broke from Sarge's grip and ran straight toward the machinegun nest, his arm pulled back snapping it forward with a heavy grunt that gave Sarge a shot of confidence. He snapped the pin off the other and took two quick steps and let it go too.

The machinegun fire blazed all about him.

He ran like a crazed animal zig-zagging in a full sprint in and out of the line of fire. The first grenade sailed through the air like a bird in flight followed closely by the other.

Sarge watched in disbelief as it sailed beyond the range of what was possible, carried by some force that was outside of the long, skinny arm of this awkward kid. The first hit the center of the nest followed immediately by the second.

The machine gunner's face slumped and singed against his hot, steamy gun.

The Lieutenant gave the order to stay behind the ridge and fire with all they had at the guns located above the gunner on the roof.

Beneath the dead machine gunner lay the boy, wounded and curled up in pain, bleeding profusely. "I'm sorry," he said quietly. He climbed to the nest and pulled the remains of the gunner from the machine gun. He held the trigger tightly and screamed with all that was left in him. "I am Ralph Becker, son of the great Lieutenant Becker. I am Ralph Becker. Son of the great

Lieutenant Becker." He pulled the trigger, shooting wildly into Noah's path.

Noah pulled out another grenade, removed the pin while still in his sprint and launched it; his accuracy no longer in question by all that watched. It spun smoothly, beautifully, its hard ridges lost in a mesmerizing blur.

Ralph felt the life leaving his body. He tried to shout again, but all that came was a weak whisper. "I am Ralph Becker, son of the great Lieutenant Ralph Becker." He pushed the big gun toward the target that came closer and closer.

Ralph aimed, fighting the final shutting of his eyes. "I am Ralph Becker…"

The final grenade fell in the center of the nest sending Ralph's body into the air, and his soul to the kingdom where boy soldiers go.

Sarge shook his head so hard his helmet flew off. He shouted orders as the battle raged on with the soldiers that pinned them from the roof.

Noah entered the building. He held his rifle stiffly at his side, his finger tight around the trigger. He found a set of stairs and climbed them. At the top of the staircase, he was met by a soldier who swung an empty rifle at him striking him across his face, shattering his thick glasses. He quickly wiped the glass from his eyes and the blood that gushed from his brow. He was blind and helpless now. The soldier dropped his rifle and removed an eight-inch knife from its sheath and stepped in for the kill.

Noah wobbled on his knees, his hands on his face, blood seeping through his fingers. He was ready. He had been ready from the day of his landing. He lifted his chin at his executioner and smiled with a peaceful resignation.

The guard lifted his knife above his head and shouted, "For Germany."

And then a crack, so loud Noah's hands shook against his face. The soldier hit the ground, limp onto the bloody cement floor.

Noah struggled to stand up, wiping more blood from his eyes. He felt a tender hand beneath his arm that raised him to his feet.

"Can you walk?" asked a kind voice in German.

He nodded, straining to see his face. "Wait." He reached out, his bloody fingers gently touching the stranger's face until he reached his eye-patch. He smiled with a childlike glee. "Is it you? Are you Max Engle?"

"Yes, yes. We must go."

Max wrapped Noah's arm around his shoulder as they ran down the stairs. Behind them came gunfire that ricocheted off the walls, several cutting through Max's legs. He fell, dropping Noah to the ground.

Noah spun on his seat throwing his last grenade toward the sound of the gunfire. He picked up Max. "Are you okay?"

Max grunted a painful yes.

"You be my eyes and I'll be your legs." Noah felt a door handle and stepped outside. They cleared the front entrance, passed the machine gunner's nest taking in the distant calls of his platoon, when several deadly shots rang out from behind striking Noah.

They fell onto their backs, neither one able to move or speak. In seconds, a hundred shots erupted above him, but Noah heard nothing but the faint beating of his slowing heart. And then, he sensed a peace, a joyous peace as if he were home at the dinner table in the presence of those he loved. He felt his spirit drifting, its knotted grip untying gently. He saw his body lying next to Max, both still, as if in a tender, eternal sleep hedged about by thousands of dandelions. He heard a voice beckoning him. "You matter, my son. You have always mattered. Close your eyes and receive…"

Shumannsville, Texas, at the edge of reality.

Noah stood in the batter's box, his hands gripping the bat as tightly as he could. He eyed the pitcher with a hard squint. A fast ball came at the outside corner, and he felt a sudden power that came from beneath the ground he stood on. It traveled up his leg, through his hips, to his upper back, down his arms, snapping his wrists with an explosive swing that cracked the bat against a hapless ball that absorbed Noah's most impossible dreams. Peter's words returned: "Make it back to Shumannsville. That's where the answer is." The ball sailed out of the park, beyond the clouds where Noah's prayers and dreams found their haven. The umpire removed his mask, the catcher stood, the pitcher dropped his head in humiliation. It was the biggest whoop ever seen in Shumannsville's baseball history. Noah dropped his bat and tipped his hat to the umpire, who watched in amazement. Noah rounded the bases in big, hysterical leaps yelling, "I did it, I did it…I finally did it!"

A LITTLE LOVE IS GREATER THAN AN ARMY OF HATE

Two weeks passed since the POWs arrived in Shumannsville. Though most in town despised their presence, a few chose to bring them on as farm hands. Out of respect for her parents and her pastor, Julia kept her distance and remained silent when she saw the Millers and Muellers at church. They were the first ones. But now the number was growing.

Julia finished her cup of coffee and headed out to the fields. It was ten in the evening. She watched Father's slow movements and grimacing face as he shucked the corn in the moonlight. She took in his smile when their eyes locked and she knew it was forced, tangled with anxiousness and pain. They had been at work since five that morning. Father still held out hope that the Mexicans would arrive soon. With their help the crop would be saved. But they were two weeks late. He made a phone call at Grey's Mercantile employing his best Spanish. He understood they were gone, but where they'd gone was unclear.

★ ★ ★

The prisoners were loaded onto a military truck to be transported to ten farms in Shumannsville. The hostilities had waned, and now the men were received with restrained jubilance. It appeared they would save the Miller and Mueller farms. Several POWs tried to offer Julia their help, some selfishly, purely to be near her beauty. No one could get within a hundred yards before the first shot rang out. Julia's aim was always precise, just inches from death.

It was six in the morning, and like all other days, Julia stood with rifle in hand waiting for the POW transport truck to drive by.

The truck made its way down the highway. The driver shifted to a higher gear as he approached her farm. He waved, as he always did, and Julia stood with her rifle, as she always did, next to the fence post like a soldier on guard. She tipped her head slightly, shooting him a thin, courteous smile.

Heinz sat next to the driver careening his neck past him to see Julia again, always sensing her pain as they passed her way. Today it was too much for him. He began to cry. "Stop. Please stop," he insisted.

"Are you crazy? She'll put a hole in my truck."

Heinz pulled on the passenger-side door and cracked it open.

"Hey boy, stop that." He slowed to a stop. "Now shut that door. You hear me?" ordered the driver.

Heinz smiled, reassuring him, and stepped outside. "Don't worry. It's all going to be just fine," he said with a confidence that calmed the driver.

He shook his head disapprovingly. "Boy, you're as crazy as she is. Go ahead, but if things don't go well hightail it back to the camp. You understand?"

"Yes, sir." He shut the truck door and waved goodbye.

★ ★ ★

Heinz waited until the truck disappeared at the bend in the road. He looked at the endless rows of corn that lined the gravel highway fighting the urge to run up and down every row—exploring, pretending to be a cowboy in search of Indians. He took his first steps down the highway toward the farm with his hands at his side snapping them forward, his index fingers pointed and thumbs up.

"Raise your hands, partner," he said in his best English. He mimicked the sound of gunfire with each bend of his thumbs. He was two hundred meters from Julia.

Julia saw him in the distance, too far to notice his age. She squeezed her rifle in her hands ready to take aim. She drew a calming breath and held it as long as she could. She watched the little boy's walk, which was closer to a skip. She released her finger from the trigger and took in another deep breath slowly easing the rifle to her side. She felt a confluence of anger and happiness that made her head spin. *How dare they try this. They think I'll bend to this?* She closed her eyes tightly shut and rolled her lips inward. When she opened her eyes, he was standing before her with his big blue eyes, an advance guard that always announced his joyful presence.

"Hello, Miss. I'm Heinz," he said with a smile barely contained by his face. He offered his hand.

Her eyes darted from his hand back to his eyes, where she felt her resolve sinking like water swirling down a drain. She let the butt of her rifle lazily hit the ground next to her using it to steady herself. She neither rejected, nor accepted his handshake. She could do neither. Her eyes were overwhelmed with tears cascading down her cheeks. He was a little Noah—same eyes, same cheeks, same perfect innocence.

Heinz watched her tears slowly rolling down her rosy cheeks. He let his hand drop to his side and stepped closer to her until he was close enough to give what he was made to give, and what she needed most. He wrapped his arms around her waist, feeling the depths of her pain, and cried with her.

Julia stood there in the middle of the highway. In her mind, she was back at the train station saying her goodbyes to Noah, walking with him on the road after his games, holding him as a baby. She pictured herself standing at his gravesite, a thought that was too painful to bear.

She let go of her rifle and let it fall to the ground. She looked at her aimless hands as they shook uncontrollably until they found their place on Heinz's little shoulders, then on his head as she pulled him into her embrace, into her heart. And healing began, whether she wanted it or not, from a little mysterious boy deeply acquainted with suffering, whose small act of love was greater than the army of hate she could no longer command.

★ ★ ★

Julia watched as Mother hurriedly cleaned up the morning dishes. Mother slowed her pace sensing Julia's stare. She dried her hands and turned around, bracing for another tearful morning between them fashioning on a fragile smile, nodding a readiness to embrace, to comfort. But Julia's eyes were different, wide and overwhelmed with tears, like adjacent ponds filled with sparkling koi so exuberant they could jump to and fro.

"Mother."

"Yes, dear. What is it?"

"Something's happenin' to me." A sliver of early morning sunlight shone through the kitchen window, briefly illuminating Julia's face before leaving her in a somber shadow.

Mother felt an ache in her heart and prepared for the worst. "Did the letter arrive? Are they here to tell us?" she asked with trembling lips.

Julia motioned with her hand.

Heinz walked in; his face still covered in tears. He looked at Mother and then back at Julia.

Julia placed her hand on his shoulder and then on the back of his frail neck. "This is Heinz," she whispered. "He's here to help us."

Mother took off her apron and extended her arms in front of her. She tried to hold back her tears, but it was impossible. He was so much like Noah. Was he gone? His reincarnation? "I can't take him without accepting Noah is gone," thought Mother. She closed her eyes against the thought as he stepped closer until he cautiously fell against her chest releasing a flood of love into her heart.

Her hesitation crumbled. Her embrace symbiotic and Heinz knew this love, for it was for him, as natural as breathing, but unfamiliar too, like an ocean breeze that, against all odds, had journeyed past towering mountains to refresh a valley kept low by haunting memories.

He peeled his face back and looked up at Mother. "Thank you for accepting me. I will work hard for you, I promise."

Mother leaned in, gently lifting his small chin to meet her gaze. Then she looked at Julia. Their eyes meeting and conspiring in a hope that had been crushed since the dream of Noah's death, and since the farm seemed a total loss. Little Heinz certainly couldn't do enough to save the farm, but what was already done had done far more.

★ ★ ★

Hours later Heinz hurried back to the camp. If he arrived after sunset, he would be punished. He waved at Sergeant Wensley who pulled open the gate.

"Thirty more seconds and the Colonel would have your hide."

"Thank you, sir. Much to tell you. But it will wait."

"You know where to find me." He shut the gate and rested his hands on his hips. "Strange little boy," he said to himself.

★ ★ ★

Heinz sat on his bunk and took off his boots. He was tired. The mine was dangerous, but the picking was draining. It was the hardest day, and the best day of his life. He talked so much, making every effort to mimic his new family's sayings. He whispered to himself in practice. *"Get on up here now. More than you can shake a stick at. Might could."* He smiled as he rehearsed the last one in his best Julia imitation. *"No place better than Texas."* He wished he could stay and help into the night, but the rules were the rules. He wished he could talk with Peter. He wished he could tell him that everything was right now. All his dreams about America were coming true. It was the greatest country. The people were the greatest people. Peter needed to know. He lay back on his bunk. "Just a little nap until…"

★ ★ ★

Two weeks later, Heinz stopped for a moment to feel the sun against his face. It was another warm Texas day, but the temperature had dropped to a mild eighty degrees. The farm was a far cry from the cold, suffocating work in the mines.

Father stopped his husking, captured by the joy on the boy's face. "Beautiful, ain't it?"

Heinz snapped out of his trance, his eyes quick and wide. "Yes, sir. Sorry, sir." He grabbed another stock and made his way with his hook.

"Heinz."

"Yes, sir. I won't lose my concentration again. I'm sorry."

"Heinz," he said more forcibly.

Heinz stopped and shot him a nervous glance.

"There ain't nothin' to be sorry for, son."

"Yes, sir. Just don't want to let you down."

Father removed his gloves and laid his burlap sack down. He crossed into Heinz's row.

"Heinz," he said compassionately. "Don't know what happened to you, with the war. I imagine it was something terrible. But you're here now. And you can stay here with us as long as you wish."

He nodded nervously in appreciation. "Thank you, sir. It's just," he hesitated. "It all feels like a dream," he said with a protective smile. "And dreams always end."

"This ain't a dream, son. You're part of the family now."

Son. Part of the family. They were the most beautiful words he had ever heard. He shut his eyes and saw his mother, smiling and her head nodding an exuberant *yes*. And he knew what he had to do—what he desperately wanted to do. "Sir, ah…"

"Yes, son."

"Can I give you a hug?"

Father nodded and opened his arms. The truth was he had wanted to do this early on, but felt a guilt over it, as if it were a betrayal of Noah. He let his eyes close softly and he saw Noah laughing, goofing off in the husking singing a silly song. He looked down at Heinz and their eyes locked.

"Thank you, sir."

Father released him and slapped his ball cap against his hand fighting the emotion that made work impossible. "Well, we got a few hours before sunset. Let's see if you can beat the Texas corn husker champ."

Heinz worked tirelessly at Father's side, never saying a word, glancing from the corner of his eye at the man who called him son. And everything was right.

I AM HERE

*You have made known to me the path of life; you
fill me with joy in your presence, with eternal
pleasures at your right hand. –Psalm 16:11*

Back at the Mexia prison camp, Peter stood near the perimeter, at the northeast corner where he could see miles of peach trees leading to Highway 14. It was the only way in and out of Mexia, and he knew someday soon he'd be traveling it toward his final assignment. He was tired of studying the highway, planning his route, every step concise, every eventuality considered as he did in the field of battle. But now it was a waiting game, and he hated that because there was too much time for other things to enter his mind.

It was happening more often now—when he opened his eyes in the morning, when he lay down for sleep. His father was alive and so were his words: "Thou shall not kill. To take a life that God created, is to be God. And to be God is to deny God." His father's words were no longer vague, whispered fragments, but were clear, resounding shouts forbidding what he knew he had to do.

So he forced himself to think of Julia. He wished he had not burned her letters. Every word she penned was stronger than a hundred memories he wanted to forget. He wondered if she had married or had children. It had been years now. There was no reason to believe she waited for him, or that she kept the ring he made her. It didn't really matter since he was no longer the innocent boy she fell in love with. He thought about what she would think of who he was and what he was about to do. Soon she would know; the whole world would know. Peter tried to reason with himself. *What difference does it make? I'll never feel her pain and disappointment. Nothing...I'll know nothing. It'll all be over.* But despite his best counsel, he felt a heaviness crushing down on his soul. *I'm sorry, Julia. My sweet, Julia.* Down at the first row of peach trees he saw a lone, white butterfly swirling from tree to tree until an updraft carried it high into the clouds out of view. *Though it is a mystery, I know what I'm about to do is unforgiveable. What it will do to your country, to you...my only consolation is that I will never know your suffering. I'm sorry, my sweet Julia.*

★ ★ ★

Peter entered von Kliest's quarters unannounced. The other prisoners had no reason to see him personally and if any did, they always knocked respectfully. Peter stood in front of his desk and spoke aggressively without any regard for decorum. "I need to know what my orders are. I'm not waiting any longer."

Von Kliest slowly patted his desktop with the palms of his hands counting silently to himself. "But for the mission, I'd have you hung. I don't care who you are," he said as he balled his fist and hammered down on his desk. He stood suddenly, challengingly.

Peter forced a challenging smile, empty of any respect. "I've always obeyed my superiors without question. But you..." he said with piercing eyes that could cut a hole in his chest, "... you're just a messenger."

Von Kliest could feel the heat of his stare and knew Peter was a dangerous man that could not be intimidated. His eyes searched the ground for courage. "I have no information at this time." He lifted his head and raised his chin in an awkward defiance. "As long as I am the ranking officer here, you will follow decorum, or I will…"

"You will what?" Peter answered defiantly.

Von Kliest's lips tightened then fell loose in defeat. He sighed heavily. "It is all I have, Engle."

Peter looked away not wanting to show his pity. He snapped his heels together and saluted formally, abruptly leaving without another word.

★ ★ ★

Julia worked until the oil in the lanterns burned dry. It was one o'clock in the morning. She blinked at the sputtering light.

Father noticed and gave her a nod. They both pulled their corn sacks off their shoulders and stepped toward the wagon. She emptied hers first. Father tossed his into the wagon and climbed into the bed to make room for tomorrow's crop. He touched Mother's shoulder as she sat with the reins in her hand and jumped off the wagon.

That was all he remembered.

★ ★ ★

Father had a ruptured intervertebral disc. The pain was so bad he lost consciousness. He lay in a hospital bed, the slightest movement shooting daggers up his spine. He needed surgery and only a few doctors in Texas had any experience in the matter. He stared at the ceiling, sweat beading on his forehead. His eyelids swelled with tears. It was over. It was all over. The little hope they had to not lose the farm was gone.

Mother gently dabbed his forehead with a damp cloth and kissed him on his cheek, her lips meeting a tear that broke his resistance. "You need to make arrangements, dear," he said with a pained voice.

"I'll go to the church…our friends…they could spare one, maybe two."

"No, dear. They can't. They help us, at their peril. I won't have that. Sell what we got and save it for a move."

"To where? This is all we know."

Julia stood outside their door. She slid her body down the wall as her legs gave way to a weight she could no longer carry.

* * *

The next morning Julia sat on the porch sipping a glass of lemonade with Heinz.

"This is the best drink I've ever had," said Heinz with sincere glee.

Julia grinned. She was tired. She had worked alone until three in the morning and was up at five. She appreciated Heinz's enthusiasm, knowing it was much more than that. But today she felt his words were more trouble than help. She was tired of trying. She knew it was all impossible now. The hardships were changing her. Her faith was a heavy anchor she was tired of dragging across an arid land. She had already left all her hopes and dreams with a paper cup of tepid water in her father's hospital room next to a receptacle of dirty linen.

She looked at Heinz scratching his ear. He felt her stare and looked back at her, painting her with his enormous smile. She knew he would never be enough. Like Mother's hands clasped around Father's—a kindness that changes nothing.

Her eyes rejected him as she looked down the highway and saw a foreboding dust swirling in the air. She shot to a full sprint toward the highway.

"Julia. Julia. Where are you going?'" yelled Heinz.

Mother opened the screen door and saw the same dust in the air and her legs weakened. She fell to her knees.

★ ★ ★

Julia waited at her property line. The dust pushed a hundred feet in front of the car. She could see it was painted an army green with a large white star on its side. Two military personnel sat in the front seat.

Since her dream, she had tried to prepare herself for this day. But now as the car came to a stop, she wanted to run away to Guadalupe River and throw herself into her deep currents to be taken away forever to a place where she couldn't feel anymore.

She prayed, "Our Father, who art in heaven, holy be thy name. Thy kingdom come, thy will be done on earth as it is in heaven…"

The men stepped out of the car, both dressed in formal military uniform. They approached and removed their caps. The first spoke. "Ma'am, I am Sergeant Smith. This is Sergeant Ramsey."

She heard nothing else. She swayed in her anguish ready to fall as her grip on the post weakened. Then a few words broke into her consciousness here and there.

"Hero. A great American hero."

Sergeant Perkins removed an envelope from his jacket and handed it to her. His hand lay suspended in the dusty air without a response.

"…hero…will change the course of history…"

Then she saw what she never expected…a smile. They were both smiling. She had never felt so confused in her life. *Why were they smiling? What kind of cruelty is this?* And then her bewilderment gave way to a familiar anger. "Why are you smiling?" she demanded, cutting off their words.

They looked at each other in equal confusion. "Ma'am, your brother is alive. And he's a hero, ma'am."

Julia felt faint falling into Sergeant Perkins's arms. He carried her to the farmhouse.

Mother and Heinz had already made their way halfway up the road when they were met by the men.

Julia's eyes were glazed over in confusion. She was in and out of consciousness when she whispered to the sergeant. "What did you say?"

"Ma'am, your brother is alive, ma'am. He's alive and well and he's coming home. He's coming home a war hero," he said proudly.

"My little brother's alive?"

"Yes, ma'am."

He sat her on the porch. Heinz held her hand and Mother stroked her head. The sergeants spoke with Mother, and then said their goodbyes.

Julia looked at the acres and acres of unpicked corn. She thought of her father in his bed, and she fell deep inside herself at the very core of her soul where God's presence sits undisturbed, pure, immovable by all the calamity that runs afoul in the earth. She heard His voice enraptured by His very Spirit, echoing what always was…"I am here. I am always here."

THE LETTERS

Julia sat next to Father's bedside as she read Noah's letter.

> *"My family, it's so hard to explain what happened.*
> *One day I lost everything, everyone I cared for, my*
> *best friend and to be real honest, I begged God to*
> *take me too. But he kept me alive, and I couldn't see*
> *why. And then somethin' happened that changed my*
> *life forever… did somethin' that changed the war*
> *forever. Little, ol' me changed the war forever…"*

St. Louis Hospital, near the battlefields of France.

Noah sat up in his hospital bed. Bandages covered both eyes and his chest. A light blood stain spotted the area near his right ribs. The morphine still ran through his veins. He smiled and did all he could to pay close attention.

Colonel Richards removed a medal from a small wooden case and held it up in presentation. "Private Noah Fischer, it gives me great honor to present to you, for your display of extreme gallantry and risk of life in actual combat with an enemy force, that which was above and beyond what was required in the battlefield, this

Distinguished Service Cross, and as you were wounded in battle this Purple Heart. I will lay them both here in their receptacles and have them pinned to your uniform when you are better."

"Wish I could see 'em, sir," he said with a droopy smile. "Just doin' my duty, sir."

The Colonel shook his hand. "Son, you have no idea what you've done for your country. You're an American hero."

"Thank you, sir. Thank you," he said in a slurred and thick tongue.

The Colonel stepped back and saluted him. He looked at the attendant doctor and whispered, "Take care of that boy. He's going home."

The doctor saluted in agreement.

Julia finished the letter…

> *And that's what happened. I'm coming home.*
> *I love you all,*
> *Noah Fischer, Pvt., United States Army*

Julia pressed the letter against her chest and sobbed with an unction that healed the most stubborn pain and anger that still held onto her once joyous soul. She looked at her father who smiled with a peace that belied his great pain. "Nothin' to worry 'bout now. Nothin' can take away our hope now father. Nothin'."

★ ★ ★

On the other side of St. Louis Hospital, a group of American leaders, including two generals, crowded into a small hospital room. Outside the room, six heavily armed soldiers had thoroughly screened the room's occupants, most of whom were brilliant American physicists and mathematicians. Max's hand raced across another page, transcribing every letter and symbol etched in his heart and mind. He handed each page to the scientist closest to his bedside, who held it as if it were the Holy Grail. Max continued until he had shared all of Professor Greenberg's inscriptions. He observed the men examining the information, their eyes widening in awe. They congratulated each other with pats on the back, hugs, and tears. The admiration and almost religious reverence for the information on those sheets of paper felt disconnected from the immense suffering that had preceded it. He couldn't help but wonder what these men would do with the knowledge if they failed to recognize the humanity and death embedded in every detail. His head grew heavy, reclined in his bed, closing his eyes.

★ ★ ★

The following morning Lieutenant General Leslie Groves entered Max's room and sat quietly next to his bed looking over his notes. He felt his stare.

"Good morning," he said with a kind smile. "Pastor Engle, I am Lieutenant General Groves," he extended his hand and they shook. "Good to see you again, Pastor. It's been quite a whirlwind for you. Sorry we couldn't let you rest. Couldn't take any chances." He stood and handed him an envelope. "It's a letter from Professor Greenberg. As I understand it, he wrote it before he was imprisoned. He was a friend. I wish I could have saved him. Anyway, I'll let you rest. We'll talk soon about your future. America, and the free world is at your bidding, sir. If you need anything until then, don't hesitate to have me contacted." He shot him a kind wink and left.

Max read the letter:

To the one who reads this letter, I will call you friend, as it is my expectation that by the time you get this we will have passed through an agony that forever binds us. And further we will be bound forever by the decisions we've made. By now you know they are decisions that will change the world forever. I am sorry that you must carry this weight on your shoulders. But with all the hope that is in me, perhaps it is of some consolation that I believe you are chosen. Though this mystery may not grant you peace at the present, I ask you to try to think on that which we are certain of. For we know evil abounds in the hearts of men like Adolf Hitler and his minions, and they should never receive this knowledge. History shall confirm this belief. As for the future, who can know what we have set in motion? In some ways this knowledge is fruit from the tree of good and evil. It should never have been eaten, but alas it has. Perhaps we will be banished from Eden, from His presence. That is up to God. We have done our best to do what is right. May God have mercy on us.

He folded the letter and placed it back in its envelope to never read it again.

★ ★ ★

Back in Shumannsville, the town rolled out the red carpet for its local hero. The train came to a hissing stop, enveloping the platform in thick steam.

Noah stepped out onto the platform and the steam fell in a grand announcement revealing his formal army uniform, his chest decorated with two large medals that caught the morning sunlight and the dark glasses that slowly pulled down on the mayor's smile. Next to him, a nurse from the Red Cross held his arm closely and directed his steps toward his family.

The welcome music weakened prematurely. No one was told that Noah was permanently blind. He felt their stares, pulled away from the nurse, and held out his arms waiting for all the homecoming hugs he had dreamed about. "Hey, everybody!" he shouted.

Julia ran into his arms followed by her mother and as many of the townsfolk as could get close to him. Noah squeezed Julia and kissed her on the cheek. He felt the tugs of love from all those who knew him, he heard their cries of appreciation. He breathed in the familiar smell of the cornfields, of Guadalupe River, of his mother's faint perfume. He was home...and although he was blind, he had never seen so clearly the boundless beauty that surrounded him.

With the formalities complete, he returned home tired but too filled with excitement to sleep. He visited with father who was still confined to his bed.

At dusk they sat at the Guadalupe's edge; Julia held his arm tightly with no intention of ever letting go. "Ya know, there's so much I'd like to hear 'bout what happened, but right now I just wanna sit with you and listen to the river."

"Me too." Noah said nothing for a bit, then reached for Julia's hand. "They say it's permanent this time. Ain't gonna see again. But don't really matter to me." His other hand found a stone and he tossed it into the river. He shook his head. "I've seen enough," he said with a raspy voice.

Julia stroked his back and then pulled him close with both arms and kissed the top of his head. She watched the river float lazily by.

"Don't let me fall asleep...don't wanna miss a second."

She tucked him closer.

His eyes fell heavily and locked.

"Sleep, Noah...you're home now...you're home."

CONTACT

With every passing day Peter grew more anxious. He wanted his mission defined; his end known. It was 5:30 in the evening. He was a mile from his farm assignment walking back to the POW camp when he heard the rumble of a truck approaching from behind. The truck stopped and the driver rolled down the passenger side window. "Hey there. I'm making a delivery to the camp, jump in."

"No thanks."

The driver laughed. "Come on, it's hot, and you still got another three miles. I insist." He swung the door open.

"That's kind of you, but it's against the rules." Peter forced a smile and began to step away.

The man's eyes tightened, and his voice went stern as he spoke in perfect German. "Get in the car. Now, Engle."

Peter looked instinctively over his shoulder then inspected the man closer. He jumped in and slammed the door shut.

The driver kept a steady eye on the road, tossing an occasional stern glance Peter's way saying not a word for the first two miles. He was a tall, thin man, wearing wire-rimmed glasses over a thick reddish nose. He spoke again in German, staccato, angry. "There are one hundred of us here. We came just before the war started.

Even then, we were told America would join the war. We've been waiting for years under assumed American identities waiting for this time, waiting to strike America. We always assumed it would be one of us. But you're the chosen one, Engle. I wish it were me." He shook his head slowly. "You are the chosen one," he said with disdain. He broke his stare and looked over at Peter, his eyes steady over his glasses. He watched Peter's listless reaction. "My name is Wagner. I am your contact."

"Von Kliest?"

He chuckled to himself. "He's nothing more than a diversion. You are known, a hero, they say," he said with compunction. "Too much attention drawn to you. We assume you're being watched." He pulled over and opened Peter's door. "Get out."

Peter hesitated. "I won't wait anymore. Give me my orders."

"You'll get them when it's time. No sooner."

Peter grabbed his hand and twisted. His bones began to crack as his body lifted up out of his seat.

"I don't have them yet," he grunted.

Peter released him and shoved him back onto his seat.

He held his wrist tightly against his chest. "Damnit, Engle. It's not that complicated. I get the assignment and I give it to you. That's it."

Peter leaned toward the injured spy and spoke through gritting teeth. "Get me those orders, or I'm gone." He jumped out of the truck and slammed the door shut.

Wagner watched him walk away, eyes set thin and hard with the hate he already had for Peter. He opened his glove compartment, pulled out a flask and took a long drink.

* * *

Two days later, again at dusk, the truck slowed behind Peter as he walked back to the camp. It stopped and Peter jumped in.

Wagner handed Peter an envelope. "I was supposed to wait for another two weeks."

Peter opened the envelope and read the assignment to himself.

"You must follow the instructions strictly. One compromise and the whole operation will fail." He looked over at Peter. "You understand, Engle?"

Peter continued reading the instructions. He folded the paper when he was done. The assignment was the most grandiose scheme he had ever seen. For his part, it was not complicated. He placed the letter back into the envelope and returned it to Wagner.

Wagner waved it away. "I'm not to know. I've given my whole life to Germany, but I cannot be trusted," he said with a bitter sarcasm.

Peter accepted the letter and slipped it into his jacket pocket. "Stop here."

Wagner stopped the truck, grabbing Peter's arm before he could exit. "Tell me one thing. Now that you know, is there hope?"

Peter pulled away and exited. He turned around and poked his head back in. "I will do what is ordered without fail. Germany will deliver a great blow. The tide will turn in her favor." He began to step away, clutching the door firmly, and spoke with a dispassionate, weary tone. "But there's no hope. There never was."

Wagner's eyes searched desperately for clarity, finding nothing in Peter's empty eyes. He forced his truck in gear and sped away.

★ ★ ★

Later that evening, Wagner made a call from a pay phone. He looked over his shoulder, speaking discreetly in German. "I delivered the assignment. But I have my concerns." He waited for a response. It came. "Yes sir, of course. I don't doubt the Fuhrer, but this Engle…something is not right." He dropped his head in submission as his superior berated him. "Yes, sir. No. There's

252

nothing he said that raises my suspicion. He just seems to do things his own way. Yes, sir. I will. I will watch him closely. Heil Hitler."

★ ★ ★

Noah felt his way through the cornfields with his left hand skimming the stocks that abutted the narrow road between the north and south parcels, toward the distant chatter of his family hard at work. It was hot and he could feel sweat on his forehead slipping down his face.

Julia emptied another sack of corn into the wagon. She brushed her hair from her face and turned around. Her eyes widened but she hatched down her concern. "Noah, you should be inside."

He lifted his head toward the hot sun. "It's a hot one today. Father's asleep, rather be outside with ya'll."

Mother dropped her sack and trotted over to him. "Doctor said you need your rest, son. Please. I'll take you back in." She grabbed his hand.

He pulled away gently. "I wanna be here."

Heinz jumped off the cart. "Hello, Noah. It would be great to have you stay with us."

Julia could tell that Noah had been crying. "What's wrong, Noah?"

He took in a deep breath of the thick corn scented air and let out a slow breath of peace.

"Just been thinking. Was sittin' on the porch, and I see somethin' now, never saw before."

Julia stepped closer, her eyes filled with concern.

"I know I was supposed to be gone a long time ago. Heard the doctor tell you, Mother, when I was six. You thought I didn't know. Didn't bother me much. But there was just one thing. I wanted to know why I was even born. I was sittin' on the porch.

I remembered all my friends, my brothers, my best bud Franco, and I was remembering how much I wanted to die. And now I got these medals, I did somethin' that changed the world, they say." His tears found their passage onto his flushed cheeks. He fought them back with a sternness in his voice that fell quickly. "I know now why I was created, why the Lord kept me alive." He searched the sky he couldn't see, struggling against the emotions that pointed his way. "Guess there ain't nothin' left now," he said with a forced half-smile that turned his head in a nod.

"Noah," answered Mother with tacit disapproval.

"It's all done, Mother. Nothin' left." He shook his head disapprovingly. "I won't settle into… just being a burden now…little blind Noah. No…can't have it."

Julia grabbed his hand. "I'll tell ya." She pulled him toward the wagon. "You get up there and take this load to the barn. No more foolish talk. You get up there and help us all live. Okay?"

Mother smiled and nodded.

Noah reluctantly found his way up onto the wagon and grabbed the reins. He forced a smile. "Okay, Julia. Whatever ya say."

DES STERBEN

Peter leaned against a tree, concealing himself from Wagner who would soon drive by with another camp delivery. It was three in the afternoon, two miles from the camp.

Wagner gripped his steering wheel tightly still feeling a residual pain in his wrist from Peter's strength. He had new instructions to deliver.

Peter stepped out from behind the tree into the road causing Wagner to skid to a halt. Wagner's breath caught in his throat before he turned his startled eyes on Peter. "Damnit, Engle."

Peter jumped in.

"I have new instructions," said Wagner.

"I have all the information I need."

"No, you don't. There are details."

"I need your truck."

Wagner chuckled nervously. "That's not the plan."

"And a map."

"You're not listening. You're not ready."

Peter opened the glove compartment and found what he was looking for. He folded the map and put it in his jacket pocket. His chin lifted and shifted left. "Get out."

"You are not following orders. This has all been planned. You must follow the plan exactly."

"I make the plans. That's how I operate. Now get out or you'll need someone to take you to the hospital."

Wagner reached for a gun under his seat.

Peter's fist delivered a jaw breaking punch that dropped Wagner against the horn. Peter pushed him out the door and dragged him to the side of the road. He emptied Wagner's pockets and put on his clothes.

He had two weeks…

★ ★ ★

Peter drove south from Highway 14 until he connected to Highway 35 following the advance of the setting sun. He pulled into a gas station in Austin.

An old man got up from his stool next to a blaring radio. He labored his way out to attend to him. "Fill 'er up?"

He pulled out Wagner's wallet and leafed through it. He nodded.

"Heard the latest?" asked the old man.

"No, sir."

"Krauts on the run. It'll all be over soon."

Peter gazed past the man with far away eyes.

The old man forced a grin, casting a sideways glance confused by Peter's lack of interest. He topped off the gas. "What's the matter with ya? Damn Krauts finally gettin' theirs." He straightened his posture and his eyes tightened in awareness. He tightened the gas cap back on and bent over to see him straight. "Oh. You must've come back from the war." He gently patted the top of the truck. "First war got a piece of me too. You'll be alright." He examined him closer. "You'll be alright," he said compassionately.

Peter slapped a twenty into the old man's hand. "Keep the change."

The old man smiled a toothless grin. "Well, that's mighty kind." He grabbed Peter's hand and shook it. "Mighty kind. Thank ya." His eyes dropped as he spoke with a deflated enthusiasm. "You're gonna be alright, son. Been through hell, but it'll all be behind ya soon. All gonna work out in the end."

Peter shot him a smile and tipped his hat goodbye.

Shumannsville was an hour away.

★ ★ ★

Wagner awoke finding himself in Peter's POW uniform. He ran to the nearest pay phone. "He has the assignment and he's broken away. He stole my truck and…"

He was interrupted by his superior's shouts. He bit his lip, angry at the accusations of incompetence and disloyalty. "Yes, of course. I don't know. But we must implement operation Des Sterben immediately. We cannot take a chance. He's reckless. He's compromised the mission. Our backup plan must be implemented now, sir," he said with too much insistence. He listened anxiously. "I'm sorry, sir. Of course. Yes, sir. You're in charge." His superior's voice cut through as if he were present. "You have, sir? That's excellent, sir. When will the second agent be dispatched?" He shook his head approvingly. "And what shall we do about Engle?" He smiled widely, then grimaced at the pain his jaw gave him. He nodded approvingly. "Yes, sir. That would make me very happy."

★ ★ ★

A few days later…

In the Gulf of Mexico, a hundred feet below the surface waters, a German U-boat set for its rendezvous.

Two hundred kilometers from the Galveston, Texas shore a small fishing boat waited in the calm waters.

It was 2:30 a.m.

Fifty feet south of the boat a sudden rumbling shot up a powerful percolation that split the ocean water in half. Five-foot waves emanating from the uprising rocked the little boat to-and-fro. The captain, an old man who wore a black skull cap, held strongly to his helm. He watched in amusement, as if seeing a mighty sea creature rise for air.

The hatch cracked open, and a man climbed out dressed in a black scuba suit. He tightened a long pack around his shoulder and dove into the water. He boarded the old man's boat without a word.

The next morning the old sea captain slapped a set of keys into the man's hands. "Our time has finally come. Restore Germany to its glory," he said passionately. He reached into his jacket pocket and pulled out a letter. "You are instructed to read this letter." His eyes sharpened as he looked in his eyes. "It is directly from the Fuhrer."

The man nodded in agreement and walked out without a word to sit in the truck and read the letter.

> *You have been a faithful servant, my son. I have done many things right, but I know I have failed in some respects. I should have seen that you were the chosen one from the beginning. From this day forward, for all eternity, you shall be known as Germany's greatest hero. Go now and do your duty.*

He folded the letter and tucked it into his pocket, slipped on a black fedora, the last of his disguise, and glanced into the rearview mirror, nodding at his reflection. This was the day that everything would finally be made right, he thought. He shoved the gears in reverse and left to fulfill his duty.

ARE YOU A GHOST?

*Miracles often come in pairs—the first to knock us off
our feet, the second to stand us upright and capable.*

Julia quietly left her father's room at Brackenridge Hospital in
Austin where he was heavily sedated and sleeping. His condition had worsened and there would be no miraculous recovery.
The doctor said he needed surgery and, even if it was successful,
he would never be able to work the crops like before.

Her hands gripped the steering wheel tightly on her drive
home, trying to hold onto the little hope that was slipping
through her fingers. Her head and shoulders fell defeatedly,
and her fingers spilled from the wheel. She cried openly for her
father. He had worked so hard and long for the farm, and now
it was only a matter of months before the bank would call on
the note. And it was her fault. She was a stubborn woman. She
let her anger and pride hurt the ones she loved most. She could
go to the camp and beg for help, but the prisoners were already
assigned elsewhere.

She fought her tears and forced herself to think about Noah.
He was alive. And if he was alive then there was a reason to keep
going. She regrouped, gripping the steering wheel as hard as she

could. An hour later she pulled into her driveway off the highway too tired to notice a truck parked nearby.

★ ★ ★

Peter sat in the dark, his head set to his left watching the lights go off inside the farmhouse. It was one of the darkest nights ever. The moon was smothered in thick, black clouds that threatened rain. The front door swung open, and he saw someone step off the porch headed toward the river. It was midnight.

★ ★ ★

Julia stood against a cypress tree with her arm wrapped around its trunk. She heard the river jetting into the two large boulders at its belly that split the river in half, slowing the current on one side, quickening the other. Like the river, life had been slowed with Noah's arrival, and now it had been quickened with the extant end of the family farm.

The river had always been a single calm, harmonious voice. But now she heard the boulders split the waters into two distinct sounds she had never noticed before. On one side, the sound of a lazy, lullaby-like flow, on the other side, the noisy haste of impatient waters trying to escape. Everything was changing. Even the steadfastness of Guadalupe River could no longer be counted on.

She wiped her tears and closed her eyes waiting to hear. The river swept its way in the darkness whispering with every splash and turn words that seemed to say, "I am still here, Julia, in this river, in all I created, in all that is beautiful, all that is peace, all that is love… and in your deepest fears. I am here." She nodded her head softly and took a step away from the tree when she heard a man's voice.

"Everyone should have a special place."

Startled, she jumped behind the tree and balled her fists. "You better get away from here. I swear I'll hurt you. I have a knife," she lied.

"I'm sorry. I'm not a danger."

"Get away from here, I said. Now," she ordered.

"Well I wouldn't want to disturb the sacredness of this place."

She felt her defenses weaken. "Who are you? Are you a ghost?"

"If I told you, you wouldn't believe me. I can come closer, but I can barely see my hand in front of my face."

"What do you want?"

"I'm sorry. I should have waited for the morning. But I couldn't."

Her eyes darted in the darkness in a desperate search to know. She peeked from behind the tree seeing only a large dark figure. "I asked you. Who are you?"

"Julia, my Julia."

Her breath left her throat in a gasp. "No. Can't be. It can't be."

"Julia. It's me…Peter."

Oh God, what is this? I'm dreaming? What are ya doin' to me? What is this?

"Julia, can I come closer?"

A dream can't answer me. "Tell me what happened here, many years ago. Tell me."

"As much as a boy can, I fell in love with you."

She put her trembling hand over her lips and shook her head in continued disbelief.

Peter turned his head, straining to see her. "I thought my memories were all destroyed. But they're not. They kept me alive. As much as I tried to deny it, my heart still has a place for love. I'm here, Julia. I can't explain it. It makes no sense. But I knew I had to see you before…"

She stepped away from the tree and strained her eyes to see the dark outline of her dream.

"Is it you? Is it really you, Peter?"

He took a step closer, his arms weakly at his side burning with a desire to embrace her and never let her go.

Then shouts came from over the hill. "Julia, Julia!" shouted mother. "Julia, come home now. There's a dangerous prisoner on the loose. Julia!"

Julia turned from her mother to the voice in the dark but there was nothing.

And she knew it was all just a dream.

★ ★ ★

The next morning, Julia and Mother sat at the breakfast table, sipping their coffee in a silence that demanded to be fed.

"Mother, I don't know if I'm losing my mind."

Mother inched over and touched her hand. "What is it, dear?"

"I don't wanna say. Not yet." She sipped her coffee and looked toward the front porch. "God gave us a miracle, Mother. You think I can have another?"

Mother placed her cup down slowly, gingerly giving herself time to respond. "If I was God, I'd give you a million." She tapped her hand gently and smiled. "God's heart got enough room. Ask, dear. Just ask." She stood and removed her apron. "Gonna go see your father."

Julia waved goodbye as Mother pulled onto the highway.

She returned to the kitchen and turned up the radio.

"The prisoner is tall, blond haired, blue eyed. He is armed and dangerous and is driving a stolen red truck."

Julia shut off the radio. She opened the screen door and sat down on an old rocker quietly asking for another miracle.

★ ★ ★

Peter hid the truck in a ravine a mile from the farm. In minutes, he was there, his hand on the post that separated the long gravel driveway from the highway. He watched her on the porch. *Why am I doing this? I'll only hurt her more.*

262

He wanted to run back to his truck, but it was too late, his legs carrying him with a purpose greater than his reluctance. And there she was, more beautiful than he had ever known or imagined. He held his hat in his trembling hand and forked his fingers through his hair. He couldn't look directly at her for fear of melting into a complete fool, or worse, a crying child. He lifted his eyes and set them on her. He wanted to say something…that she was beautiful, that he was sorry, that he still loved her, but nothing came.

Julia's eyes had locked on him from fifty yards out. He was a boy when they last saw each other and now she was taking him in as a grown man. Taller now, stronger, if that were possible, his face a chiseled display of artistry and mystery. And his eyes were a blue that pulled at every ounce of resistance she could muster. She followed his muscular arm down to his hand that held a single yellow rose. She felt the edges of her eyes stretching in her fascination. The few words she could think of were inept, out of place for all that stirred in her heart. She felt her legs unfold and she stood wobbly to her feet, one set in the ground like a fence post marking the line between what could be and what couldn't, the other nimble, electrified by what had to be.

The screen door slammed shut and Heinz gasped. "Peter. Peter," he exclaimed. He ran to him and fell into his arms.

Peter held him and cupped his little head in his hands. Despite the delightful intrusion, his eyes never released from Julia's face. And for a moment, Peter felt as if he had finally found himself again—a devoted pastor's son, a kind boy to his mother, a young man desperately in love, a friend of God. His smile widened to places on his face not touched in years.

Heinz delivered a barrage of excited questions. Peter dropped to one knee and looked him in the eye. "I need to talk with Julia. I'll answer all your questions later, okay?"

Heinz tilted his head in question. "How do you know Julia?"

"I promise. I'll answer all that later."

Heinz looked at Julia who gave him a reassuring nod.

★ ★ ★

They sat on the porch gazing into each other's eyes restraining their passions with a back and forth about what had happened since their parting. Julia cried over Peter's losses and felt ashamed about her concern for her circumstances. He withheld all that he knew would trouble her, never speaking about his heroics, never mentioning his interaction with Noah, and giving no hint about his final assignment.

"I can't believe this. I still can't believe this." She reached over and gently slid her index finger along his chin. "I just gotta make sure this is real…that you're real."

He caught her hand before it could fall to her side and caressed it. His finger touched the ring he had made for her long ago. He lifted her hand and kissed it. "You kept the ring?"

She fell into his eyes nodding weakly. "Of course. We made a promise."

"Yes, we did. But it seems life didn't want it."

She squeezed his fingers. "Life's a liar, Peter. I don't wanna listen to it anymore. The fact that you're here tells me that life's a liar."

His head dropped and he spoke hoarsely. "I wish I could believe that. But there's something…"

"I know," she interrupted. "They're looking for you." She lifted his head with a gentle tug of her fingertips. "Whatever time we got, we're just not gonna listen to it. Gonna rise above it."

They heard hurried footsteps finding their way to the front door. Mother opened the screen door and screamed. "Peter! I just couldn't believe it. Peter." She ran to embrace him.

"I told you. I told you. He's my friend too," cheered Heinz. Heinz yelled back into the house. "Noah, Noah. I'll get him." He ran back inside.

Peter looked at Julia wide-eyed with surprise. "He's home. He made it back?"

"Yes. And he's a hero. A genuine war hero," she added with pride.

Heinz held Noah's arm as he walked him onto the porch.

Peter felt his muscles flex impulsively. He was suddenly sober, no longer intoxicated by the love he had for Julia. Did Noah know? Had he figured it out?

Noah stood in front of Peter; his eyes set beyond him.

Peter stretched out his hand, and Heinz connected it with Noah's. "Noah. I'm glad you made it home."

Noah heard his voice, and it was suddenly, painfully familiar. The voice was all he had to find his retribution. He had studied it—its tone, every infliction, the accent. He could never forget it. He snatched his hand away and charged toward the front door searching for the doorknob.

Heinz hurried before him to open the door.

Noah pushed him onto his rear. "Get away dammit. I don't need your damn help!" he shouted. He opened the door and stomped off.

"I'm so sorry," said Julia.

"You have nothing to be sorry about. He's a soldier. He's lost his friends. And I am the enemy," answered Peter.

"How could you know, Peter?" asked Mother innocently. "He lost his whole platoon. He was the only survivor."

Peter wanted everything to be known. He was tired of living as a ghost—neither of this world, nor of eternity. And now standing before Julia his heart was beating with a newness that unchained all he had known and believed. He had to speak the truth. He cleared his throat and his stomach tensed. He would confess his awful deeds, one-by-one, until he was free to live and to fully love Julia. That was the end he wanted.

Noah burst through the screen door pointing Julia's rifle in all directions. "You'll pay, you son of a…"

In a split-second Peter had disarmed him and set him on the floor before Noah knew what had happened. Peter handed the rifle to Julia. "I'm sorry, Noah. I'm sorry. Please. Please, you could have hurt your family."

"Let me go. I'll kill you. I promise, I'll kill you," he hollered, frustrated under Peter's enormous strength. He gave into his despair and a painful cry broke from his heart as he sobbed over the loss of Franco and his platoon.

Julia and Mother rushed to his side and held him.

Julia saw the look on Peter's pale, expressionless face and knew.

His eyes filled with tears. He mouthed, "I'm sorry." He stepped off the porch and walked away.

Mother looked at her and then at Peter. "I'll take care of Noah." She lifted him off the floor and he struggled to walk into the house.

Julia ran to Peter's side. "Don't go."

He continued to walk, each step a battle against his heart. "It was a mistake to come here, Julia. What can be of us? I bring pain wherever I go. I can't do that to you or to your family."

She grabbed his arm and turned him to face her. "Look at me, Peter."

But he resisted. *Oh God help me…why did I come?*

"Peter, please look at me."

He weakened, as he knew he would, and his heart melted at the sight of her face. "Please, Julia, you don't know. You don't know what I've done."

She reached up with her hand and let it fall onto his cheek. "I know the boy who saved my life. I know the young man that held me every summer. I know God called for the impossible and it happened. You're here, Peter. I know God called all this into being." Her hand slipped down to his wide shoulder and rested there. "I'm not scared of the rest I don't know."

He reached for her hand and gently moved it from his shoulder. "I'm sorry, Julia. I love you too much." He bent down and kissed her sweetly on the cheek. "I'm sorry. Should've never come."

Tears spilled down his cheeks. He touched her face tenderly with the tip of his shaking finger. Neither his greatest losses, nor the ripping of life and limb under cannon had brought him to such despair. She was his last hope to find sanity, to find the hope he needed to continue living. But as he looked into the depths of her kind, beautiful eyes, he decided that what he wanted most could never be. The die was cast. He had but one duty left. One greater than any other before. A sacred duty—his life for the life of the greatest man he knew.

Julia watched him walk up the driveway and cross onto the highway until he was out of view.

★ ★ ★

An hour away, the old gas attendant turned down his radio as he studied two military jeeps come to a screeching halt. Four military police jumped out and approached, a tall one leading. "Howdy, sir."

He nodded a hello.

"We're looking for a feller that escaped a prison camp in Mexia. May have come this way."

"Ain't no prisoners come this way. Just ordinary folk. Ordinary."

"Well, sir, he had on regular clothes, driving a red truck. May have had a bunch of supplies in it."

"Oh, there was a strange feller come through here yesterday. Had supplies."

"Remember what he looked like?"

"Well not really. Big feller. That's 'bout it. I'm a veteran of the first Great War. Got the feelin' he was too."

"Yup. He is. German war veteran."

"Don't say."

He nodded. "Say where he was goin'?"

"Nope."

"Thank you. Been helpful." They shot him a polite salute and turned to leave.

"Hey!" shouted the old man. "Where's the feller gonna go? War's 'bout over. Seems like a waste of time."

The leader turned around and took two steps back toward the old man. "Well, the war ain't over…ain't over for him."

The old man cocked his eyebrow in disagreement. He turned his radio back on and forgot about them.

★ ★ ★

Peter drove down a gravel road that led to his grandparent's farm. The windows were boarded up and the front door hung precariously by a single hinge. He shook his head sadly. It had been nearly six years since he'd visited.

He touched the front door and pushed it gingerly. He would wait here until it was time.

★ ★ ★

Julia could hardly lift her hands to pick another ear of corn. Mother left her side an hour ago with Noah who had not said a word since Peter's visit. And as much as Julia wanted to help him heal, her broken heart was incapable of easing anyone else's suffering.

It was midnight and the generator was running on fumes. She tried to pray throughout the day, but it was impossible. Seeing

Peter, touching him, had resuscitated her love and now every beat reminded her of how much she needed him. She dropped her sack and stumbled to her bed.

The next morning she awoke to screams in the cornfields. She jumped from her bed and looked out the window. "Julia, Julia!" shouted Heinz. He ran up and down, row after row of picked corn piled as high as a barn wall. "How did you do it?"

She rubbed the sleepiness from her eyes and stuck her head out the open window. "Oh my God," she said to herself. She ran outside in her nightgown. She looked down the rows of picked corn, more than she and the whole family could do in a week. "Heinz, go wake Mother."

"Who did this, Julia? At this rate the farm will be saved, Julia. It will be saved." He hugged her and ran into the house.

Julia looked over her shoulder, then in all directions trying to find him. And her lips caught her tears as she whispered, "Peter. My Peter."

★ ★ ★

Peter watched from the top of the hills that surround Guadalupe River. He turned and walked along its banks listening to hundreds of trout smacking their lips as they broke from the water to take in a hearty breakfast.

Nothing had changed here. The river never stopped giving. It was its nature. It never took, never asked to be given, because it was eternal and beautiful, void of need. And for a moment he saw his father—preaching with tearful pleas, giving the last of their food to an elderly woman, in the barn before the sun rose on his knees pleading for broken people and for his demoralized country—his life a gift to others, his message eternal and beautiful, like the river, void of need. The world could not exist in peace without him and his beautiful message.

But God's work would have to be built on the devil's scaly back; there was no other way.

Someday the world would understand.

Someday Julia would understand.

★ ★ ★

Two days later, Heinz and Julia loaded the piles of stacked corn into the wagon. "Can you tell me now, Julia?"

She smiled at him but said nothing.

Noah reached out and touched Heinz's shoulder. "It's Peter."

Heinz's eyes widened. "But he's only one man. It would take five, at least, don't you think?"

"It was Peter," answered Julia.

"But who else?"

"Just Peter," she answered, looking away toward the river.

Noah could feel love in her words, and it sickened him. He stepped closer to the wagon and felt his way to the reins. "You don't know what he's done. You don't know who he really is, Julia." He snapped the reins.

But Julia held back her horse. "I don't. I don't know much anymore. You were dead. I was sure of it. The farm was lost. I was sure of it. My love for Peter was impossible, but here he is. And here you are, and a war hero. None of that makes any sense." She pulled tight on the reins to still her restless horse. "There's a thousand reasons why I shouldn't love him, but I do." She reached over and touched his hand. "I'm sorry that hurts you."

He pulled his hand away and pinned his eyes on her in a way she had never seen. "I guess I can't stop you. And you can't stop me." He turned and stumbled away.

★ ★ ★

Noah stayed awake all night until a few hours before sunrise when he heard what seemed like several men picking corn with a frenzy. He waited until all was quiet, then followed the sound of someone cutting through the fields toward the old Engle farm. It was a familiar path, one he'd taken all his life to school. He waited outside the Engle house for an hour and then stepped onto the porch as quietly as he could. He touched the door and felt for the knob.

Peter sat in a chair waiting, watching Noah moving in the darkness. He turned on a lamp and the click stopped Noah in his tracks. "Hello Noah," he said with a cold, assassin's tone that made Noah freeze.

Noah turned toward his voice, his head low and submitted. "Came to talk to ya."

Peter got up and guided Noah to an old easy chair.

Noah lifted his chin mustering up courage. "I know it was you," he said with tight lips. His chest raised and then dropped with a deep sigh. "You called me Noah…and your voice. It was you."

Peter sat silently, his hands gripping the chair arms.

Noah sat back in the chair with his eyes drilled to the wall in front of him, as if finding a picture to admire. "I know. I know why you didn't kill me."

Peter's fingers loosened and he inched closer and nodded approvingly. "That's good, Noah. I guess I didn't understand at the time. But I know too. I love Julia…always will. I couldn't take your life. Couldn't do that to her."

Noah cocked his head and smiled cynically. "Love? That ain't got nothin' to do with it." He rubbed the cynicism from his face and let a big smile loose. "No, somethin' bigger than love. Bigger than you and Julia."

Peter sat back in his chair in exhaustion. "I'm tired, Noah. Gotta sleep."

He shook his head impatiently. "I was supposed to live to save a man's life, a stranger, a damn German. And you, whether you knew it or not…you were part of the plan…whether you believe it or not." He took in a deep, shaky breath and exhaled to calm. "Don't like it though. Just looks like evil's a bridge angels gotta cross."

Peter's eyes clenched impatiently, temporarily setting his fatigue at bay. His mind scanned his darkest days—his men that died in Belgium, Elise, Franco, his mother's horrific death, the death he would soon bring that would destroy the heart of a nation. And there was no order to it all, no master plan, though he wanted it all put together, sensible and meaningful. He wanted to see as clearly as Noah. He looked out the window resisting sunlight's call to wake. "Gotta sleep, Noah."

Noah's lips tightened fighting against the impulse to find Peter's nose and punch it as hard as he could. He turned to walk away, then stopped. "I just came to tell ya. That's all."

Peter nodded a slow, insincere thanks and his eyes sewed tightly like they'd never open again.

GOODBYE FOREVER

Love is like the wind; it follows no course
except what fate has set forth ages before.

Peter and Noah continued to meet every morning. They talked about their childhood, about family, and about the war. But Peter concealed what needed to be concealed. They sat on Peter's porch drinking coffee.

"And what about Julia?" asked Noah.

Peter took a short sip and set his cup down. His eyes offered kindness, but in a way that said this topic was off limits. "Noah, it's been great talking, but I gotta get some sleep."

"You still love her. And ain't no doubt she still loves you. Always known that. When this war's all over, come back." He nodded to himself. "Start a new life here."

He took another sip of his coffee then tossed the remains on the ground shaking his head despondently. "That would take a miracle." He stood, his towering frame over Noah, making his words more of an edict. "Men like you get miracles." He shook his head to propel his words. "Not men like me."

Noah looked straight at him, like he could see again, but sharper, the fuzziness of adolescence gone. "You don't get it."

Peter shut his eyes dismissively.

"Okay…I'll let ya sleep." He stood and brushed the dust from his pants.

Peter let out a long sigh and opened his eyes softly. "You're a good man, Noah. Take good care of Julia."

He stood and entered the house, slamming the door behind him with a thud that told Noah he'd never see him again.

* * *

The next morning Julia dawdled carefully through a row of corn, stopping and starting like a hungry field mouse wary of barn cats in the field. Her eyes widened as she tried to follow his fleeting hands. The pace was impossible to keep up with. The stack of corn that reached her shoulder told her she was in the presence of a power that must have delivered terrible damage in battle. She stepped back in awe simultaneously fighting an urge to embrace him. She took in a deep breath of composure.

"Peter. Peter," she repeated with a weak command.

Peter stopped, his back to her. He tore off his gloves and slapped them together, sticking them in his back pocket. He hesitated to turn around, hoping she'd leave him alone, but her tender voice twisted his resolve forcing him around to face her.

The sunrise set on her face giving her a glow that made her look like the angel he knew she already was. She smiled at him, and he felt like he should run, but his feet were tied by corn stalks. It was like he was seeing her for the first time again.

She stepped closer and lifted a shaky pail of fresh water.

He took the pail from her and pressed it against his lips, never taking his eyes off her face.

Julia's eyes traveled up his body as water trickled down his chest, absorbing his muscular arms as he lifted the pail. His knowing gaze met hers, causing her to blush and shield her face from the sunlight.

He handed her the empty pail. "Thank you."

"You did so much. I still can't believe it. You must be tired."

"No. I'm not. Not at all. I could never grow tired doing something for you," he said as his head turned away having said too much.

Julia stuffed her hands in her back pockets and tried to recite the words she'd practiced, but they tripped in her throat. "Peter… ah, ah, please stay for breakfast?"

"I can't. I can't do that to you."

"No one knows you're here."

Peter pinched his lips together and inhaled strongly. "I can't do that to you. I'm sorry."

He turned to walk away uprooting his heavy legs but moving nowhere.

"Peter, wait."

He spoke over his shoulder. "Please, Julia. I'll be gone tomorrow."

"Where ya goin'?" she asked, catching the desperation in her voice. She looked down and spoke calmly. "I can arrange to have our pastor take ya to the camp, here. He has influence. It'll be alright. Then you can—"

He interrupted her. "No, it's not."

She stepped closer and felt her desperation again but didn't care. "Yes, it will. This war will be over. And I'll wait. Got no problem waiting."

Peter felt his chest heaving up and down both with a passion that wanted to take her in his arms and with an agony that tied them to his side. *Oh Julia, my beautiful Julia. I can't deny life like you. It has a stronghold on me. It commands. And I must obey. I love you, Julia. I love you. But I will obey.*

"I'm not coming back. Ever." He turned and walked away.

"Peter!" she shouted. "Do you love me? I need to know."

He stopped. *I love you so desperately. I love you with all that is in me. My Julia. It's because I love you, that I won't let my heart speak. Goodbye, my love. Goodbye forever.*

He ran off, never looking back.

* * *

He stumbled into his grandparents' house and fell onto the chair. His face dropped into his hands, and he muttered a prayer. When he finished, he sat upright, and his eyes shot at an old desk in front of him. He grabbed a pen and began to write. He poured out his heart and said everything he wanted to say. He ended it with this.

> *So, my love, by now you have discovered, along with your entire country what I've done. I'm sorry. I don't understand it. I don't understand God in it. But He is here, somewhere in it. I don't expect forgiveness from you, or from your country. Somehow it seems a twisted fate that I was made for this final purpose. I love you with all that is in me, but in the end, even love must submit to fate.*
>
> *Goodbye, my love.*
> *Peter*

He pressed the letter to his chest, then gave it a final look before crumpling it in his large hands and tossing it into the fireplace. It symbolized the purification he sought and everything that could never be. Striking a match, he ignited the letter. This was the day he would strike terror across the world.

As he left the house, never to return, the front door closed behind him. Suddenly, a gust of wind descended down the fireplace, smothering the letter and extinguishing the flame.

DREAMS ARE FOR BOYS

Julia sat at the breakfast table in silence. Mother placed a cup of coffee in front of her knowing she wouldn't touch it.

"Sweetheart. I wish I could say something to help. I know I can't. I'm here when you're ready." She reached out and touched Julia's hand. "I'm leaving soon to see your father. Lots of commotion for the big visit. Don't know if I'll be able to get through." Mother hoisted her body from her chair with a sigh under the heavy weight of Julia's sadness and smiled hoping to cheer her up.

Julia seemed to not hear a word.

★ ★ ★

Peter crouched under the red truck. His hands searched about the gas tank until he felt it. He tugged and it snapped away. He released it from its leather case and assembled it with quick, certain snaps. He examined it, wiped away any dust, and then broke it down again so that it fit neatly back into the case. As he turned the key in the ignition, he heard a rap on the driver's side window.

"Where are you going, Peter?" asked Heinz.

Peter looked away, out the windshield at nothing.

"You haven't explained anything to me. You said you would. How do you know Julia and Noah? Can you tell me? Maybe when you come back?"

Peter gripped the steering wheel with his right hand and then let it slide down to the ignition. He shut the truck off and turned his head to face him again. "I'm not coming back." He shook his head. "I wish I could explain everything."

Heinz gripped the door frame and inched his face closer to Peter. He spoke with a soft rasp. "You can't go. That's not part of my dream, Peter."

Peter inhaled deeply wanting to crush his despair, and then he spoke with short, deliberate words. "You're a special boy, Heinz. I hope your dreams come true."

Heinz reached out and placed his little hand onto his shoulder. "But I've seen it, Peter. I've seen it all." His desperation fastened to his lips, his eyes glimmering a dream that blackened Peter's view. "I don't dream of my mother anymore. She kept me alive. She kept me happy. Now all I dream of is us. Julia, you, Noah and me. I dream of all of us together."

Peter looked down at the ignition and turned the key trying to fight the anguish that overwhelmed him. He opened the door and stepped out. He grabbed Heinz and hugged him tightly.

"I dreamed of a good life…I have it now. Please, Peter…don't take my dream away," he cried.

"You keep your dreams as long as you can. That's what good boys do." Peter caressed the top of his head, his tears choking his words. "Take care of Julia." He peeled him away and climbed into the truck.

"I will Peter. I will."

Peter sped away leaving Heinz in a cloud of dust waving his forever goodbye.

★ ★ ★

Julia sat by the Guadalupe River, her eyes swollen and tired, tearless now. Her heart was changed forever here, when their tender lips met, when he saved her. Their souls had been set in a perpetual spin melting away the time and space that separated them. But she knew he was gone. She scrutinized the river's flow sensing it hurried like a disinterested stranger speaking in a foreign language, or in unsolvable riddles. Either way, what had brought her peace, what ordered the chaos of the world, her very own eternal spring of hope, was gone. *This is not holy ground. There is no such thing anymore. No such thing.*

She hated that life was a giant hand that could not be prayed against. She could no longer will herself to be above it, nor around it. Her strongest faith whimpered at its cruel command.

She heard a voice from behind.

"Julia," called Heinz with hesitation. "I don't want to bother you, but I found this. It was in Peter's fireplace. It's a letter to you. I think you…"

She snatched it from his hand before he could finish. She read it and then read it again. "Oh my God!"

★ ★ ★

Heinz followed closely behind Julia as she rushed through the house. She opened a hallway door and pulled out her rifle.

"Where are you going, Julia?" he asked.

She turned and bent down so her eyes met his. "Heinz, I want you to run to Pastor Ramsey at the church. You tell him the escaped prisoner was here and that he's headed to Austin. You understand? He'll know what to do."

"But, Julia, you're talking about Peter. And why are you taking your rifle?"

She squeezed his shoulders. "Go to Pastor Ramsey. You understand? I gotta go. Hurry now," she ordered, pushing him along.

THE FINAL ASSIGNMENT

*A true hero is compelled not by the screams
of others, but by a whisper within.*

Peter drove until he hit Highway 35 just outside of Austin. He was running on fumes. He stopped for gas and saw the same old man sitting there on his stool, his radio filling the station with crackles and distorted music.

He lumbered over and lifted the front bill of his crinkled, ten-gallon hat. His bushy, white eyebrows lifted high above his brow as he peered into the cab. "You again?"

"Yes, sir."

The old man surveyed what he knew was his empty lot, and then glanced down Highway 35. *Oh, hell. Ain't nobody here when I need 'em.*

Peter stepped out of the truck and took note of the old man's nervousness.

"Whatcha up to, boy?"

"I just need some gas. That's all. I'd like to get on my way."

"Where ya headed, boy? Why the hell ya out here? Ain't nothin' ya can do. War's 'bout over."

"Wanted to see someone."

The old man smiled. "A girl?"

Peter nodded.

"Well, can't blame ya. But them military boys…" he shook his head, "…don't appreciate ya being on the loose. Seems they think you're up to no good."

Peter chuckled. "What can one man do?"

"Well, that's what I said." He slapped the truck's roof. "How much?"

"Just need to get to Austin."

The old man's brow lifted again then dipped with a heaviness. "Austin…" He stepped around the truck and loosened the gas cap.

Peter looked down the highway at the early morning sunlight that strained toward downtown Austin.

"You ain't goin' nowhere, boy." The old man pointed his gun with a shaky hand. "No funny business. I put my share of lead in you Krauts in the first war."

Peter's eyes caught his skinny finger daringly around the trigger. "No, sir. You're right. I'll stay right here. You got me."

He cut the air with a flick of his gun. "Get them hands up."

Peter complied and smiled wryly.

"If I were a young man, I'd smack that smile off your face. You up to no good. I can smell it."

"Sir I don't want anyone hurt…especially you."

The man laughed so hard he choked on his spit. He cleared his throat. "Might be best to just shoot ya. Ain't no one gonna care." He stepped a little closer and around the truck. "Should I?"

"That's your business. But I get the sense you're not that kind of man."

The old man's shoulders dropped, and his grip weakened around his gun. "Somethin' 'bout ya. Just can't believe you're a Kraut."

"Sir, I'm gonna get into my truck and leave. It's what I have to do. That's all I can do. I'm sorry that I disturbed your day. But I'm leaving, sir." He slowly lowered his hands.

The old man squeezed his gun and waved it around. "No, you ain't. Get them hands up. Get 'em up damnit. I ain't playin'. Get 'em up," he ordered.

Peter stepped toward the truck door, his hands at his side. "I'm sorry, sir. I don't want to bring you any pain."

"No boy, don't you do that. Get away from that truck," he yelled. He stepped closer and took his best aim. "No, boy, no."

Peter opened the door and climbed in.

The old man pulled the trigger and his hand snapped back hard. "Damnit boy. I told ya. I told ya."

Peter slumped against the steering wheel, blood flowing from his left bicep. He winced in pain and tried to slow his breathing. He turned the key and drove off.

The old man dropped his head in despair. He watched Peter drive away and ran to a phone booth.

★ ★ ★

Peter parked the truck a mile from the crowds that filled the corner of 5th and Main Streets. There were thousands of Texans, mostly from Austin, huddled about a temporary stage set on the corner. A small band of Austin's best musicians played "Deep in the Heart of Texas." Men in their cowboy hats, women in their colorful summer dresses, and children of all ages sang along with great pride.

Carlton Lee Cook, mayor of Austin, stood on the stage with a smile as long as the space between a Texas longhorn's crown. He had every photographer in town primed for the perfect re-election photo. He sang with the crowd and waved his arms in the air like a conductor. He glanced at his watch.

Peter tore the sleeve from his shirt and tied it around his arm. The flow had been intense, and his bicep had been so damaged that he could not lift his arm. He was weak and knew he would soon lose consciousness.

282

★ ★ ★

Julia jumped from her truck and ran toward the crowds. She searched for Peter and eyed a tall blond-haired man facing the stage. He waved a cowboy hat over his head and shifted his weight right to left with the song. She ran to him and grabbed him by the shoulder. "Peter, you …"

The man looked at her with wide eyes. "Hey, what ya doin', lady?"

Her eyes said she was sorry, and she turned around to continue her search. It was impossible. There were too many people. She thought of going to the police, but they were all stationed around the stage, separated from the crowds a hundred feet away behind temporary barriers.

She ran to her truck and pulled out her rifle.

★ ★ ★

A tall man in a greasy mechanic's uniform cut through the crowd carrying a large box. He entered the Bank of Austin located across the street from the stage.

A guard smiled at him as he entered. "We're closing. Ain't no one here. Aren't ya gonna hear the speech?"

"I have a work order for the elevator."

"Ain't nothin' wrong with the elevator."

He showed him a work order.

"Okay, go ahead, but you'll miss the speech."

He stepped out and left the man alone.

The man removed his black fedora and raked his hand through his thick, dark hair. He punched the elevator button headed for the top.

★ ★ ★

Peter clutched the steering wheel with a firm grip. In that moment, a flood of memories washed over him, a swirling mix of joy and sorrow, camaraderie and loss. He remembered the faces of the men he had fought beside, the haunting final gazes of those he had taken from this world, and the enduring love of his mother and the kindness of his father. Thoughts of Julia, her radiant beauty and unwavering strength, overwhelmed him, along with the pure, untainted love he held for her. The memories surged through his mind, demanding one last farewell. He wanted to sit in quite reflection until he could say goodbye to every memory, but his body told him to hurry.

Then, out of nowhere, came the memory of the devasted church in France, where he stood before the bullet-ridden crucifix, abandoned and defeated. He looked into the eyes of Christ and saw tears spilling down the statue's broken face. He tried desperately to shake the vision from his mind, but it whispered a tearful plea, "Be true to thyself." He slammed his hands against his face and shook his head against it. "Be true to thyself." Blood pooled at his lap. He steeled himself, gathered his courage, and grabbed the pouch that held his rifle.

* * *

The wind blew briskly on the roof of the Bank of Austin. The man tugged his black fedora down tight around his head and walked over to the north ledge. He had a clear shot at the stage. He smiled with contentment. This would be the greatest day for Germany. He dropped to one knee and opened his box. In seconds he had assembled the rifle. He wiped the scope and looked through it. He attached it to the rifle and made adjustments. He removed his fedora and took aim.

* * *

Julia climbed the stairs to the Austin courthouse next to the Bank of Austin. The courthouse was empty, along with all the other buildings downtown. She sprinted to the rooftop entrance. The door read NO ACCESS. She hesitated and then pushed the door open. She hurried to the south ledge and examined the crowd below still searching for Peter.

"Oh, my Peter, my love. Please don't do this," she cried. Wiping her tears, she looked up at the sky for a moment. "Lord, I need a miracle. I can't let him do this, but I can't kill the one I love. Give me strength. Please help me. Please." She breathed deeply, calming her shaking body. She dropped to a knee holding her rifle tightly in her hands. "Dear God, help me."

★ ★ ★

Peter kicked in the rear door to the Bank of Austin and ran for the stairs as planned. He looked at his watch. He had five minutes. At the top, just before the roof entrance he stopped and tried to gain his focus. He had lost too much blood. He felt his body spinning out of control. He dropped his rifle and fell against the wall. He struggled to stand steadying his weight against the roof door until it opened.

★ ★ ★

His replacement for the mission turned to face Peter, holding his rifle across his chest. "There's no time for explanation. You've been replaced."

Peter shook his head in disbelief. "My brother. My dear brother. Has this been the plan from the beginning?"

"Peter, you've been replaced. Step away."

"And what will you do with me, Martin?"

Martin's eyes fell into a memory that could never leave him. "You taught me well with Elise, brother, Duty…duty before all

285

else. Today you die. Today I die. I will join Elise, you, your family. It is meant to be. Alea iacta est."

"No, Martin."

Martin's fingers rippled across his rifle. His eyes wide, crazed with an empty glory that he believed was his salvation. "I'll be remembered forever. The Fuhrer will be proud…my father will be proud." He tried to fight the tears that blurred his resolve. "And you, my brother…you'll get what you've wanted. No more orders…no more killing."

Peter stepped closer then stopped suddenly, eyeing Martin's finger gripped around his trigger.

He spoke with calm command. "Please, brother, listen to me."

Martin shook his head and raised his rifle in aim. "The die is cast."

Peter raised his hands and stepped closer. "No, Martin. It is not. It never has been. God…"

Martin interrupted with a lift of his rifle, a deadly aim and a chuckle. "God's will? Who decides that? You, me, men like your father?" He shook his head defiantly. "Look what you've done. You could have saved him. But today you chose not to. That is God's will?"

And for a moment Peter couldn't speak, his protestations all tied up in his throat. He saw the noose tightening around his father's neck. He saw his eyes, sad and vapid, with all hope of a glorious eternity gone.

My father, Lord…I can't let him die. Forgive me one last time. Let me fulfill the mission.

"I will see you in the afterlife, my brother. Wherever our choices take us."

Peter leaped forward, his hands out like deadly clamps ready for death.

Martin pulled his trigger.

***

Bone crushing, desperate blows too vigorous and animal-like to comprehend entangled them until another shot rang out breaking the chaos. Then stillness, and tired, pained moans. Hurried footsteps followed toward the ledge.

He picked up the rifle, his shaking hands holding it tightly. He aimed through the scope and released a calming breath as the presidential motorcade pulled up to the stage. And as he had done hundreds of times with his brothers of The Knifepoint, he prayed, "Our Father who art in heaven, hallowed be thy name. Thy kingdom come, thy will be done, on earth as it is in heaven. Forgive us our trespasses…"

***

Julia saw the bright reflection of the sun in the rifle scope coming from the roof of the bank. She pleaded one last time. "Oh God, I beg you…one last miracle."

She heard a cold demanding silence. She fell to her knees and took aim. Her body convulsed in tears making it impossible to set her aim properly. "My Peter, my only love. I will always love you." She took deep breaths fighting her sobs until her hand steadied. She drilled down on the scope's reflection atop the bank knowing she would not miss. "I will never stop loving you."

***

President Roosevelt stood on the stage waiting for his introduction. He looked into the bright Austin sky and considered his thoughts. He folded his speech and shoved it into his assistant's hands.

A little girl in a bright pink dress was given the honor to present him with a bouquet of yellow roses.

Mayor Cook spoke his final words, "My fellow Texans, I give to you the President of the United States of America…President Franklin Delano Roosevelt."

The crowd cheered and the President stood at the podium. He waved his hand in the air. "Texas, you couldn't have given me a better day."

★ ★ ★

His duty set before him, his past soon a crushed earthen vessel, his future a golden chalice generations would drink from, he took a final calming breath, his eye tight against his scope. He fought to steady his trembling finger as he fixed it on the trigger. "…and deliver us from evil. For thine is the kingdom, and the power, and the glory, forever. Amen."

A shot rang out…

★ ★ ★

Julia dropped her rifle and fell to the floor sobbing. "My love, my love. I'm sorry. I'm so sorry." She sat in her agony for several minutes praying mournfully, her words broken with sobs that neither she nor the angels could understand. Then she stood and moved toward the ledge looking over it at the scurrying crowds below.

If there was any justice in God's heart, perhaps she could be with Peter in the afterlife. That was all she wanted now. "Have mercy, Lord. Please have mercy for what I'm about to do." And she looked down again seeing where her body would soon fall. She nodded in acceptance. "Please have mercy, Lord…"

★ ★ ★

At the roof of the Bank of Austin, his body lay still and lifeless against the rifle. The scope shattered by a precise bullet that entered his skull.

* * *

The wind picked up, blowing the black fedora over the ledge. It tumbled down, then up again, with a strong updraft, as if riding the wind like a black crow not wanting to ever find its resting place. The draft ceased and the hat toppled down very slowly ten stories until it landed next to a scattered bunch of yellow roses.

* * *

Julia could not bear to live another second. She prayed for mercy one last time. "Into your hands I commit my soul." And she let her body go, one foot stepping off the ledge into her eternity, the other losing its touch of the present she could never accept.

Her limp body teetered over, then was suddenly pulled back and carried away from the ledge. "Peter? My Peter?" She felt the hot Austin sun on her face. She heard the commotion in the street below, and she saw the blood spilling from his side where a second bullet had entered him. "We're in heaven, Peter? But you're bleeding."

And Peter smiled with a wild freedom that he had not known since childhood. "No, my dear. You're here with me."

"But I…I…killed you."

"My dear, you shot the man that I came to stop. It's over. It's all over."

* * *

A few months later Berlin fell. Hitler was dead and the dream of a great and indomitable Deutschland was over. Germany was in ruins and would soon be separated into a provisional division of four zones under the control of the United States, Britain, France, and the Soviet Union.

Of the more than 425,000 POWs in the U.S. none were officially allowed to stay. Unofficially, exceptions were made.

EPILOGUE

1950, Shumannsville
Five years after the German surrender

Heinz sat on the bluff that overlooked the Guadalupe River, fifty feet from the eminent cypress tree where Peter first kissed Julia. From this precipice he watched the long gravel road waiting for the first sign of his arrival. His eyes sparked at a distant movement he hoped brought him. He shot to his feet and cupped his hand over his brow shielding the intense morning brightness. He turned back toward the others who stood below the bluff in the shade of the cypress.

"He's coming," he yelled.

Peter's heart pounded in his chest. He wanted to run to meet him, to take him in his arms, but she lay asleep in his hands, swaddled in a pink blanket.

Julia touched his hand, and with the other, she caressed her child's face and kissed her forehead gently. "Emily. Sweet Emily."

Peter was allowed to return after the war. His efforts to stop the assassination were quietly recognized. No one knew of Julia's part in it. That's how she wanted it. Peter understood. He fought to forget all the killing and wanted to shield Julia from the horrific memory of taking Martin's life.

He married Julia, lived on the farm, and when Emily was born, he looked into her beautiful eyes and began to comprehend a truth he had only known in words. Emily was more than his child; she was God's expression of His love and total forgiveness. No one explained this to him. No one needed to. God saved him from a certain death, and from his terrible life. But even more than that, God had given him what he never knew he needed. He cried for days after her birth. He cried whenever he held her. He cried whenever he thought of her.

He pulled Julia in closer, and she saw his eagerness. She took Emily from him. "Go. I'll wait here."

Julia's father ambled over with his cane and put his hand on his shoulder. "Our family's complete now. Bring the great Pastor here."

Mother wiped a tear from her check and nodded.

Two years had passed since Lieutenant General Groves, who had overseen Max's recovery, had arranged a visit to Texas to visit Noah. He wanted to reunite them. When he arrived in Texas he gave the family the information, and Peter, who had already returned, couldn't believe it. The Lieutenant laid out a picture of the man Noah saved, the black eye-patch, his tired, yet hopeful smile.

Noah slapped Peter on the back. "Ya see! Out of all the Germans I could've saved…"

Peter's hand hovered over the picture shaking like a dragonfly's wings over the depths of the Guadalupe. He dared not pick it up, his mind telling him his defiled touch would extinguish the miracle.

Noah squeezed his shoulder and spoke calmly, soothingly. "Miracle's got nothin' to do with you, what good you did or even all the bad. Just somethin' we gotta breathe in, now and again."

Peter never forgot that day. He took the deepest breath his lungs could muster and felt what miracles do—the piercing of life's cruel lie—that we are all enveloped by its commands, some damned, some blessed, that all is set, and all one can do is follow its course. Alea Iacta Est. Every vestige of his resistance was obliterated—first by Julia's ceaseless love and commitment when all hope was lost, then with his daughter's birth, and now this final miracle of an impossible reconciliation. His heart was completely God's to do with whatever He pleased, to willingly follow His course wherever it may lead.

Peter hugged Julia and left in a hurried jaunt up the hill.

✳ ✳ ✳

The truck stopped in a plume of dust. He stepped out of the passenger door wearing a dark suit that had been given to him by a Japanese official of the Provisional Japanese government. For the last five years he had taken care of the injured and disabled survivors of the Hiroshima bombing. Though he could not escape the reality that the formula he memorized had brought their suffering, he was at peace with what he had done. For he now understood that the enormity of his failures, and of his decisions, could never be balanced by a million years of good works. He saw his soul for what it truly was…dead, dark, condemned, yet fully salvaged, redeemed by a love that would never leave him, that was never dependent on him, or his goodness.

The Japanese called him *Tamashi o miri day,* "the eye that sees the soul." Max saw their innermost pain, he felt it, he understood it, and he responded with a love that came from an endless well of love not his own, but from the hand of God that plunged beyond the depths of the burial ground of his past wrongs—all the darkness he had finally learned to keep in its rightful place… forgiven…forgotten.

But now his time had come to rest forever. The doctor's had given him a year to live. So he wanted more than anything to finally see Peter and his new family. He shut the truck door and trudged toward the river.

★ ★ ★

Peter stood next to Heinz, his powerful hand resting on the teen's shoulder.

"That's him?" asked Heinz.

Peter nodded. "That's my father," he said with tears. He saw the tattered, and frayed patch set where it had always been like torrid skin over his eye. He was frail, shorter than he remembered, his chin low as he gathered strength to scale the hill.

Peter ran down the hill with long strides until he reached him. He stopped just before him, trying to gather his words.

Max lifted his head to look into his son's eyes. "Peter. My son. My son." He fell into Peter's arms and both men wailed on each other's shoulders.

★ ★ ★

Peter led his father down the bluff's soft end toward the river. Max met the family, shaking hands with Father and Mother, and then pausing at the sight of Julia. "I didn't think it was possible, but you are even more beautiful than Peter described in his letters." He stepped forward to hug her, pausing as she gave Emily to Peter. He held her tightly and whispered. "Thank you for never giving up." He released her, stepped back with a bright smile formed by a deep inner peace that already connected with the sacredness of this place. He touched the mighty cypress tree and smiled. "This is the tree where you two first met?" he asked softly.

Julia nodded and smiled as her cheeks met the first of her tears. She wrapped her arm around Peter's waist.

"This is where it all started."

His hand slid carefully down the tree's scaly gray bark understanding her sublimity. He took in the green, smooth slope that fell into the muddy riverbanks, and then into the river's rippling from the near bank to the north shore, each independent wave reverently colored in an amber by the sun that venerated at this holy moment. "I've imagined this a hundred times." Then his eye squinted and his finger tugged his eye patch as was his habit when thinking. "The young man, the one that saved me, is he here?"

Heinz had already returned with Noah at his side.

"I'm sorry sir. I was fishing. Been looking forward to this day," said Noah past the dark glasses that hid his searching eyes.

Max nodded and his smile stiffened with prideful joy. He bowed as in Japan, a deep bend at the waist, and rose speaking with a weak raspiness abiding in tears. "I honor you, young man...you gave me this day...the best day of my life. Thank you." He stepped close and took him in his embrace. "I have reached my end, and it is more glorious than any lifetime I could have imagined." He lifted his arms to heaven in praise, said a silent prayer, then extended his arms calling for their approach.

Peter fell into his father's embrace. Julia followed, laying Emily between them. Father, Mother and Noah rested into Julia's back, and Heinz wrapped his arms around them all.

They were all separate journeys, different stories, foreign streams merging into one mighty river. Forever bound, stronger than the forces of hate, or brokenness, or mans' empty, audacious efforts to right his wrongs. All conscriptions of the Enemy—lies upon lies upon lies—forever silenced. For Truth stood in their midst like the mighty cypress, its roots deeply set in the soil of their experiences, and in branches extending to heaven in a knowing, eternal praise.

Texas Correctional Institutions Division, Mountain View Unit
Gatesville, Texas – Summer of 1977

The guard on Peter's side sat back in a chair he had earlier positioned close enough to hear everything. "Damn…damn, damn, damn. Not what I expected. I mean, glad it didn't go the other way. But one hell of a story."

Lisa's eyes tightened shooting darts of doubt at Peter. She spoke mockingly. "Oh, such a beautiful ending. All works out in the end. What a crock of bull." She shook her head and spoke with mean sarcasm. "Maybe we should all bow our heads and thank the Lord."

"Is it really a beautiful ending? You know better than anyone else."

Lisa's eyes bounced around the room looking for a hard place to anchor feelings that wanted to lift her to a place that scared her. "Whatcha talkin' 'bout?" She stood, bent over, constrained by the length of the phone cord. "Ya know what? I really don't give a damn." Her voice shook thick and messy. "I waited twenty years…for this damn story? For what? Ya still haven't told me what ya after, Mister?"

"Not after anything. I just came to give."

"Give what?"

He stood and smiled. "You'll know." He smiled goodbye and left.

"Give what?" she yelled as he exited. "What the hell ya give me? Ya ain't give me a damn thing. Mister…Mister…what did ya give me?"

She put her sleeve against her eyes before a tear could escape. She hung up the phone and was escorted out.

★ ★ ★

Forty-eight hours later Lisa Means was strapped to an execution chair. She sat calmly, quietly. The prison warden, a doctor, and the sheriff of the county where the crimes were committed stood nearby.

On the other side of a mirrored window, unseen by Lisa, was the victims' family. The doctor had already affixed a line to her right arm and held the deadly cocktail in a syringe. It was midnight.

The warden spoke and then ended with these words. "Lisa Means, do you have any last words?"

Lisa had never denied her guilt, had laughed throughout her trial, never looked at the family of the people she brutally murdered, and never once said she was sorry, because she wasn't.

But now she looked into the mirror realizing who was on the other side and she felt her body shake, her muscles convulsing, and her breath stuck in her chest in a panic.

Something had entered her, something strung throughout Peter's story, something beneath the mud, and now it swirled in her insides at war with a fortress of granite and ice that had been her only defense. Pieces of her resistance were breaking, running through her, finding her tongue, twisting it in gags and coughs, until she clenched her teeth down hard like a steel trap. "He's here? He's here, ain't he. I feel 'em. I feel 'em…" She pushed her chin down toward her chest. "…right here…right here. I understand now."

The warden slipped a handkerchief from his pocket and wiped a line of sweat from his brow. "Your last words are on the record. Doctor you may begin." The doctor held the syringe with a shaky hand.

"Wait, wait, please let me say it. Please."

"Hold it." ordered the warden. "Go ahead. This is it, Lisa. Make it quick."

She stared into the one-way mirror and the words broke free, softly at first, then in a roar— words that were always there, fighting for freedom, words that could finally give a chance to life and healing. "I'm sorry…I'm so sorry. Sorry for killin' yo' family. If I could, I'd die a thousand times to give 'em back…what I took…I would. I'm sorry…I'm so sorry." She dropped her head in exhaustion and now muttered her words. "I'm sorry…I'm sorry."

On the other side of the one-way mirror stood a man and his adopted son, the only family of a murdered woman and her daughter. The man held one hand around his son's shoulder, the other he pressed, palm open against the glass like he was taking in her pleas, but also projecting a burning wave of forgiveness; this space between them, glass, concrete, steel, pain and suffering consumed by a cosmic force too great for this world, yet born into this world, for this world.

The warden nodded at the doctor who injected the syringe into the line and Lisa's words fell to a hush. "I'm sorry…so sorry." Her head fell limp.

The man removed his hand from the mirror and turned to embrace his son as they both stood weeping. After a few moments, the father placed his hand on his son's shoulders and ushered him toward the door.

"Come on, Heinz…let's go home, son."

A heart laid bare; truth nestled there…a
Sacred Duty fulfilled.

ACKNOWLEDGMENTS

To my wife Patricia, you are the voice and the gentle hand that set me on the path of righteousness and discovery. Before you, I had no aim, no vision of what could be. Your whispering way and quiet sacrifice have always been a hallelujah chorus in my heart, directing me onward and upward. None of my books exist without you.

To my children, Bianca, Anthony, Moriah, and Joel. You are diamonds in a crown I feel unworthy to wear. So I hold it in my hands, drawing from your brilliance, each one a unique reflection of our Father's kindness and creativity. My children, you have all inspired me and supported me on a very practical level. Your songs, pictures, and words of affirmation invade my books.

To my father, Anthony C. Peters. I wish you were around to read what you planted in me as a child. You loved to read, especially all things WWII, from which I gleaned a similar passion. I believe you would have loved this book and the others.

To my mother, Eva Peters. Your strength and perseverance to courageously care for others while under a lifelong storm are nestled in every story I've ever told.

To my siblings, Yvette, Denise, Andres, and Annette. Thank you for your support, and I promise to write our amazing story someday before our eyes grow too feeble to read it.

To my publisher, Keith Glines. Carlson Gracie, Sr. said, "If you want to be a lion, you must train with lions." You are the new lion in my life. Under your tutelage, direction, and vision, I feel strong and capable. May this trilogy of books change the world.

To my editor, Stephanie Glines. You took this book to another sphere of existence. Your questions and suggestions, especially about the ending, inspired me. Your kind and gentle manner makes it easy to attach to the flow of God that emanates from you.

To the Back Porch Publishing Team. Thank you for making this a hilltop experience.

Michael Hari, you are a genius. Your cover design is magnetic.

Leanne Perezcano, thank you for your early edits of the first handwritten drafts. How you deciphered my hieroglyphics remains a mystery to me.

To my friend, Dennis Cook. There were many times I wanted to give up on this outlandish idea. I was too old, too inexperienced, and it just all seemed a little crazy. But in your covert way, you did the impossible, and I learned there was room at God's table for the audacious.

Sacred Duty was ignited by a reading of *Bonhoeffer: Pastor, Martyr, Spy* by Eric Metaxas.

To the thousands I had the honor of knowing in my thirty years in the Los Angeles Criminal Justice System, over a decade as a criminal defense attorney, and twenty years as a member of the Superior Court Judiciary, thank you for informing the themes of redemption, hope, impossible odds, horrible suffering, and all that is the human experience, the good, the bad, and the ugly, that fill these pages.

To the many men and women of our military, the gallant, the brave, the broken, and the dismayed who never stood in the light of proper glory and recognition, may this story find a place in your heart, a tiny seed of appreciation against the enormity of your sacrifice.

To my Father, Son, and Holy Spirit. You led me to leave a certain and secure world into the swirl of bewilderment that is authorship. I have never felt closer to you—the hundreds of three-in-the-morning celestial deposits that made the best lines and ideas, the many long walks, each step solidifying your thoughts and promptings, the countless moments at my computer keyboard that felt like intimate prayer and praise—and am more aware that I'm exactly where I was called to be. May this book and the others bring your love, peace, and healing to all who turn the pages.

www.ingramcontent.com/pod-product-compliance
Lightning Source LLC
Chambersburg PA
CBHW010451310726
48979CB00013B/2155/J